Thank

"The Game say love don't get no bread.
Love is the easiest way to fall."

—Miss Rakim Moet Divine

They Call Me Miss Divine

No Heart. No Conscience.

SEXY URBAN DRAMA

BY TRI SMITH

An Original Publication of
MillerSmith Publishers
www.millersmithpublishers.com
e-mail: publishers@millersmithpublishers.com

ISBN: 0-9759511-0-6

Cover Design by Candace Cottrell www.ccwebdev.com
Photographer: Keston Duke
Type Setting and Interior Design: Jonathan Gullery
Cover Model: Jaira McDonald

"Thank You..."

This book is my baby. Now that she's on her own, I must thank all the people that made it possible.

Shawndetta Miller, my business partner and strongest supporter, thank you for the title. You've always believed in this book, your actions proved it. I value our friendship. My loving sweetheart Louis July, I couldn't have done this without you. You are my blessing, my hero, my gift. I appreciate how you accept Me. My daughter Inkimbia Parker, every mom should be so lucky, I admire you, so beautiful inside and out.

To my late, loving parents Arcelia and James Smith - Mom, thank you for my style, love of language and courage. Poppa, you gave me creativity, street sense and taught me how to think like a man. Big brother James, I'm glad you were my first role model, I hope "Dollface" has made you proud. Brian Ellick, family is made from the heart, we're brother and sister for life. Renee Foster, I love the way we share words. There's no doubt you're in my corner. Michele Calloway, you said I could do it, long ago you made me feel like a writer. Amadou Ba, I know you're glad my doubts and fears are gone. Charles "C.P." Perry, you were the first to hire me as a professional writer, thank you.

My darling Advance Readers, especially Aunt Body, December Thomas, Sharon J. Miller, Darius Costen and June Louis, your input and time were priceless and my thanks are sincere. To my editor, Red Pen, a taskmaster who climbed inside my head and pulled out my best, real thanks.

Cover designer Candace Cottrell, sister, you're all that! Cover model, Jaira McDonald, you're gorgeous and definitely "U-Neek." Page designer Jonathan Gullery, your patience is awesome. Simone Miller, thanks for a hot website. Michelle Blackwell, you're an administrative wonder, thank you.

To all the young people I've mentored, teacher also loves being student, you keep my ears and eyes tuned to present culture.

Thank you and praises to the Creator. You make me feel like I'm one of your favorites. Love you back, God.

I even want to thank the mainstream publishers scared to touch me. I might have missed the opportunity to debut with MillerSmith Publishers.

And finally, thank you to every reader. You're giving me my dream when you read the first word. Thank you for choosing my book.

Tri Smith
August 2004
New York City

210 Jefferson Avenue

Once a day began brightly and maples directed summer breezes with dark green leaves. Sidewalks were spotty with sunshine and shade, the air held odors of anticipation, smelling like weekend picnics and meeting someone new.

Landlords and supers picked up what was left by beer drinkers and people who eat on the street. They wondered what was happening to the world today. Used to be a time when Brooklyn folks didn't leave their garbage on the ground like this. Folks used to care about other folks' property.

Children hadn't yet dressed the sidewalks in a garment of twirling activity. The streets were still of shrieks taken to piercing by their summer-free exuberance.

Those who weren't already at the babysitter's or watching TV unrolled from their sheets stretched in their beds and yawned.

Those who were doodling through their breakfasts or morning body washings were cautioned that if they wanted to see tomorrow, they'd better clean their rooms sometime today.

Soon it would be time to go outside, call for their friends and begin games that used balls and bikes and water guns. Lipstick, their mama's good shoes and play-play babies.

Stoops were hosed and greetings exchanged by tenants who left every morning at the same time, hurrying to catch that "raggedy train" or that "slow-ass bus."

Somebody's mother with her nightgown stuffed into a pair of pants and feet stuck in the first shoes found, quick-stepped to the corner grocery for milk, cigarettes and something to put in her husband's lunch.

Nighthawks and barflies hadn't long slid into their beds and pulled covers over their heads. They smiled and tasted their tongues, lullabyed by the shuteye replay of goodtime kisses and curses, the conversations thick with fly phrases.

Easing into sleeps either fitful or serene, tipsy rhythms played as background music to their dreams. These people usually missed the beauty of a morning like this. These nightbirds flew highest, best, when natural light was scarce. Mornings, even lovely ones like this, were only useful reminders that it was time for them to go home.

At 210 Jefferson Avenue, Herman Drayton and his janitor's broom swept Bed-Stuy dirt from the tiny cement yard that bordered his stoop. The three steps down to his basement apartment also led up to this gray yard, that's why he kept it clean.

A bent hairpin lodged in a crack, remained unswept and caught his eye. Herman remembered to tell Susan, later on when she and Baybay came out to sit, that they had to stop fixing their hair on his stoop.

Brushing, combing, greasing, rolling, braiding, sewing, bobby pins between their teeth, they'd been sitting outside since warm weather, trying to command their hair into duplications of what they saw on TV and in the latest magazines.

Herman thought it didn't look good to have that private kind of woman-business aired for everyone to see. He'd let them get away with using his stoop as a salon and a social club for too long as it was, because yesterday, Sunday, they just went overboard.

Right here where he stood, about three in the afternoon, they had crowded their friends and themselves in his little yard. Brought out meat to barbeque on some cheap grill, served baked beans, potato salad, coleslaw, Louisiana hot sauce and sliced white bread along with the chicken and pork.

Handed out plastic cups of mixed liquor or wine to the grown people, Kool-Aid to the kids. Dragged kitchen chairs from the apartments of whoever didn't mind. Invited friends with little monsters that ran wild in and out of the building and hung off the stoop like they never been nowhere before.

And their big brothers and sisters! Fast-mouthed teenagers that funky-danced to that hip-de-hop blasting on a big portable radio that Jocelyn's son brought from his room. Some kind of bouncing and smooth jerking, they all did the same steps over and over because it was the new dance.

Acted loud like they never heard a word about home training. Right in front of their mothers and the men, they'd thrust and swayed their hips, trying to outdo each other in his yard, out on the sidewalk. People walking past could hardly get by. Herman had recognized some of the same young knuckleheads who normally didn't speak when they passed him on the street.

Yesterday, the grown folks had filled themselves with charred meat gnawed to bones, chased by warm liquor over ice, then sat back, blowing, ready to step in each other's business. "So! Gary an' Christine! Ain't nobody seen Marcus aroun' lately..." "Hey! Louise! Shamika pregnant?"....

When daylight had begun to leave and the wine in the gallon jug sloshed only two fingers deep and all the scotch and most of the beer was gone, two of them had struggled up, then reared back and took giant staggering swings at each other. Ready to break up the good time and battle over an old lie that would not matter now, even if it was the truth.

Herman was supposed to let all those folks carry on in his yard, all through the night? While he sat restless in his place, uninvited? Nuh-uh. That wasn't happening. He did what he had to do. You ain't got to leave no name when you call the police. They come quick if you complain that somebody outside drunk waving a gun with little children running around.

It would have been different if he had received an invitation, even a last minute one. That's what right-raised people would have done. After the meat was cooked and heaped in a speckled roaster pan and everyone had been served a plate.

It would have been different if somebody had noticed his head through his basement window and held up a cup to him. Shouted for him to bring his rusty, short tail on out that little room, come on have a taste of V.O. Come get some of these good ribs and slaw, then maybe the law would not have been involved....

If they knew how to act right, maybe he wouldn't mind a little more outside his building than coming and going. Maybe, some early evenings he would have let them set up a card table in the yard and play some friendly hands of whist. Everybody laughing and bidding, sitting easy, sipping cool highballs in real glasses, or sweating cans of brew enjoyed in folded-down paper bags.

But you can't teach nothing to common people. Last week he'd found a dead vodka bottle propped in the corner of one of his steps and that would never do. He wasn't going to have no hard out-of-the-bottle drinking on this here stoop and that's all there was to it. Shuh.

Herman started to steam. He decided to post a notice in the vestibule. Remind them jivers whose building they was living in. He was letting them stay in *his* house. That's right. They did-n't own nary a brick *here*, goddamn it. Not a *piece* of copper or steel.

Big ol' vodka bottle too! Next thing you know, somebody in the building be tricking, somebody else selling reefer. Shuh! Not at *210* they wasn't. None of that mess lived here. Let'm keep on. *Somebody* would be packing and getting the hell up on outta here! Shuh. They could think he was playing if they wanted to.

Posting a notice was the best idea because that Baybay had a mouth on her and usually spoke for the others. Herman didn't like saying more to her than he had to, he knew well the feeling of walking away carrying a piece of her mind piggyback on his own.

As he thought, Herman collected the debris he'd swept on a torn away piece of cardboard box, dumped it in the trash can and checked his watch: 8:15. He heard somebody opening the front door and looked up at the top of the stoop, leaning on his broom.

There she was, first time he'd seen her in about four days. "Well! Good mo'nin' Miss Divine!" he wiped his hands on his pants. "How you doin', beautiful? You sho' look good! Where you headin' so early this mo'nin'?"

"Hey, han'some, I didn't sleep too good last night...just heading to the store, need some milk for my coffee. You want something?" Rakim winked at her balding landlord as she headed to the sidewalk.

"Heh-heh. Sho' do, but it ain't at the sto'." He felt taller, younger messing with her.

"Uh-huh. Watch out now, Mister Drayton. We might get ourselfs in trouble." Rakim winked at him again and ran her tongue slowly across her top lip.

As she passed him and walked up the street, Herman watched the rhythm of her stride. Lord, he thought, look at the behind on that young gal. I could live right there and die a happy man. Herman's thumbs rubbed the insides of his fingers and his bottom lip hung down.

She always flirted with him but he knew she was just playing. She didn't want him. He was too old and didn't look like the type of man a woman like her stuck a photo of in the edge of her mirror. So she could appreciate and thank her good luck each morning.

And even though she joked with him every time they saw each other, Rakim wouldn't let him inside her apartment. He hadn't seen it since, lessee, about a year and a half ago, in January, right after he'd put her money in his account and helped the furniture store men and the moving truck men carry in her things.

Lord, that woman had looked so fine that day. Skin tight jeans that showcased her beautiful, healthy ass and round thighs and a short loose sweater that gave away teasing glimpses of her tight little waist.

Herman remembered Rakim's ample behind flexing as she ran up and down the stoop supervising the men, her generous full young breasts, braless, proud and moving loose. A long ponytail switched on the back of her head. Introducing herself to every helper, she'd asked his name and replied, "Nice to meet you. Thanks for helping me move in. They call me Miss Divine."

Young woman had some expensive stuff too. Furniture straight from the store. Long, plush black leather couch and loveseat ensemble, chrome and smoked glass wall unit, smoked glass coffee table and end tables.

Her bed was a massive brass queensize with intricate scrollwork between its head posts. It took four men some doing to struggle it inside to the bedroom where they set it up. Put on the premium new mattresses.

Her carved dark wood dresser and nighttables were heavy too. Brand new big screen TV. From the sound system to the pots and pans, everything was factory sealed in their boxes. Herman knew which ones held what from the pictures on the outsides.

Not like when most people moved, when the contents of the boxes never matched the outside illustrations. Her lamps were too new to have bulbs. He'd carried in stacks of linens and bed covers still encased in plastic. Pastel towels rested in the shopping bags from the store where they were selected, never used.

Herman never knew anybody except this new tenant, Miss Rakim Moet Divine, who'd furnished her apartment all at once without bringing anything from someplace else. Not even one box of books or a desk, a bag of knickknacks or a favorite chair.

The only things Herman figured she'd used before were the clothes in the heavy suitcases he helped bring in. One of the men had whispered behind his hand that the garment bags he toted were full of furs.

The only things Rakim carried into her new apartment were a battered, paint-stained wooden box that she immediately sat inside her bedroom and a large red quilted jewelry box that she kept tucked tightly under her arm.

When all of her possessions were inside the apartment, she gathered the men in the livingroom. She'd sat the jewelry box on top of the TV and cracked the red top open just a slit, she slid her fingers inside and eased out a flat pile of cash. Each man was thanked and handed a hundred dollar bill as a tip.

Herman knew he wasn't the only man who would have returned the money for her personal invitation to return alone at another time. But they said nothing except to reply "Thank you," "Thanks, Miss Divine" and put the money in their pockets.

All made sure she had their numbers, just in case she needed anything else, anything, before walking wistfully out her door.

It hadn't taken long to settle her and after they were through Herman had joined the men in the back of the furniture truck to drink beer and talk about how good she had to be in bed.

Stamping like stallions, adjusting the tightness in their crotches, these men had held up their cans to hail Rakim. Those strong men, all much younger than he, all not a lot older than she, had slapped Herman on his back when they were ready to leave and called him a lucky son of a bitch.

One of them said, "Maaan, I sho' couldn't live right here with all that temptation and not put my hands on that hellified woman! Damn if I wouldn't find out why they call her Miss Divine! Shit, my ass be in jail for rape!" To cap his confession, the strong young man had punched Herman in the arm who'd acted like it didn't hurt. But even under liniment, Herman's shoulder had deviled him that night and all the next day.

Since then, Miss Divine knocked on his door the first of the month and handed him money. Or slipped a sealed envelope under his door. And unlike some of his other tenants, her rent was always cash and never late, never one time. Sometimes she paid in advance.

She never came inside his place either. He couldn't persuade her across his threshold. "Come on in while I write your receipt" was answered with some variation of "Oh, I trust you poppa, just slide it under my door later."

Rakim never needed repairs, exterminating or some lifting done. Had changed her lock too, the day after she moved in. Herman knew because he saw the locksmith do it. She never said a word about it until the day he mentioned it. She'd promised to give him a copy of the key and he was still waiting.

Rakim was just so pretty and young and sexy and kept to herself so good, Herman let it float. Actually, he kept forgetting to remind her. He saw her so seldom that when he did thoughts far more lascivious than a key flagged his attention. Besides, he didn't want to get on her nerves because he didn't want her to move.

He knew she had a man. Had heard them buzzards on the stoop talking about him. Herman had seen him through his window many a night too, when everybody thought he was sleep.

He let his tenants think that he went to bed early, it made them relax, not hide what they were doing when they believed he was snoring. Then he could see what was really going on in his building under evening shade.

In his dark apartment peeping through his blinds he'd seen Rakim's man. Looked like a street man. Always parking too late to be respectable, dressed like he was too rich to work. Wore fur coats just like Rakim did. "Pretty," even men would call him, with curly hair. Came to 210 by himself or with her in a shiny, big black Mercedes.

Herman knew what that meant. Shuh. Miss Divine better watch out for them fast men, they ain't mean her no good. Not a bit.

In fact, he'd been seeing a different Mercedes, a big white one, pulling up lately, dropping her off, at about dawn most times, but this one didn't park and come inside.

He also knew Miss Divine didn't work, but he didn't like to think about that, it messed up his fantasy when he thought about how she got her money, about her and them slick men....

Herman had no problem having his own women, though. But time had taught him what he could expect to catch on Crab Night at The Fantasia Lounge.

Especially when he got sharp. His tan flare leg double knit three piece suit. With the pale green rayon shirt that looked just like silk. Watch out! Real silver cufflinks with real jade stones. Uh-huh, the brown and tan striped tie. Hit it with the real gold and diamond-chip tie clip. Go 'head! The oxblood wingtips and sheer wine silk socks. Wait a minute, the dark green stingy brim. Sharp as a tack goddamn it! Shave away the gray on his chin and slap on some English Leather. A man's smell. And the finishing touch, his keys. Then he'd stroll the few blocks to the bar.

Lots of times big women with breasts like pillows and copper-colored wigs liked a small-built man like Herman. He knew it was because he had a little extra change and they thought he was desperate or stupid enough to slip some of it into their palms.

These close-to-fifty broads could also bat him around with their bodies and their words. "You ain't much bigger than a shrimp," they'd say, chesting up to him like they wanted to belly bump, "Uh-huh, go on and don't do right and I'ma fry yo' little ass up in some grease like! a shrimp and pop! you in my mouth!"

Sitting at the kitchen table were her keen-eyed friends, all laughing, sipping scuppernong wine, asking where he thought he was going if he tried to escape the room.

Herman usually went with the kind of women who put him down around other females, her so-called "girls," whose own narrow lives held no diversions. Lounging women who couldn't, and they tried, feel superior over how this sister, with both her front teeth edged in gold, talked to her little man.

After all, they told themselves, he wasn't thaaat old, he did own a nice building and didn't have no wife or kids. Owned all his money. Collected rents too. More than one of her homegirls would eventually sneak surreptitious lips close to his ear to quickly say something nasty or needy. Letting him know that he still had a choice.

Herman was lost in reverie....

Valerie was one of those women. Met her the night he'd cashed his tax return at The Fantasia Lounge. He'd bought her and her two friends two bottles of Cold Duck and two fried jumbo shrimp plates deluxe to share.

After that, Valerie had wanted him in her house every single night and the times he went, would pick, pick at him like a pigeon at seeds, until her hooting friends departed.

Then she'd switch up. Send her teenagers out, lock the grand-kids in their room, push him into hers, turn on the radio and get naked real quick, start good-squeezing between his legs, put them big nipples in his mouth, make figure eights with her big behind....

Just when he was almost asleep, she'd lean into one of his ears and ask nicely if she could "please hold a hundred an' fifty dollars, sugar?" Gave it to her a few times too, until she got to acting like it was her salary.

Couldn't cook neither. Tough chicken pink at the bone, cheap rice sticky and wet, thin pork chops fried like leather, macaroni and cheese was mostly macaroni, didn't know nothing about gravy or serving a salad.

Yassuh, Herman mused, I might be a little man and I ain't young, but I got me a giant money brain. I work like a damn dog praying the damn dimes I scrape together grow into dollars before I die. And I was supposed to hand it out one-fifty-a-pop to a moody woman with five grandkids who don't even put no meat in her greens? Lay on her back like a big slab of meat in the bed?

"Shuh! What I look like? Be different if she was temptin' like that Miss Divine. For a chance to taste that muffin, a man like me wouldn't mind pinching off a little piece of regular change to give her...." Herman wasn't aware he was talking aloud.

Herman never had a beautiful young woman like Rakim, even when he was a young man. He'd always held his wallet too close. But even at his age now, his ring of keys and careful conversation were still enough to get him a few exceptions to what he was used to. He still had an occasional, not ugly, youngish, pretty-good-figured female waiting for him at the bar.

By the time he'd had her perched on a stool looking at the door every time it opened, he'd already bragged plenty on being his own man. Had "neither wife nor chile," and "more than one digit before the comma" in his balance at the bank.

He'd say with a sigh, perhaps rubbing his palm lightly up and down her back, all he wanted, at his mellow age, comparing himself to a fine wine, was a righteous woman to halve it to.

He'd hint about that cheap two bedroom, with the connecting french glass doors with diamond-cut glass doorknobs, just about to be vacant in his building. He'd give her fifty dollars to take a five dollar cab ride home from the bar.

He'd buy a thick porterhouse and broil it perfectly in her kitchen. Serve her the tenderest piece along with a sharp knife, wide slices of beefsteak tomato and sweet Bermuda onion, a dab of mayonnaise, a dab of spicy mustard, slices of soft white bread for sopping the juices and a cold gin and tonic highball with an olive. He wouldn't let her use a fork.

Herman was proud of how many of those sweet ripe plums that had never eaten steak with their fingers before, let him lie them on their beds.

But soon, those warm, youngish eyes would chill and fill with gravel, becoming narrow screens to reflect the apartment lie, the one-shot fifty and the steak becoming burgers she found herself buying and turning over. Then they cursed him deeply and called him an old man, a bum-ass fool.

Herman wasn't about to let no woman worry his mind, so when one dogged him, called him out his name, he stayed away. And when he was good and damn ready, pulled out his tan three piece and went back to the Fantasia.

"She Ain't Fooling Nobody!"

Susan and Baybay didn't like Miss Divine.

Never did, never would and had talked about her since the day she moved in the building going on two years ago. They said she wasn't fooling them.

Baybay said she could tell right away that Rakim thought she was hot from the way she walked.

Susan said, right, she had noticed that too. Plus, she hardly spoke to a person, like she was better than everybody, like it hurt to open her damn mouth.

They also knew for a fact how she got money. She didn't go nowhere every morning so she didn't have no real job. All you had to do was look at her man and check the clothes she wore when she left the house, especially at night. Expensive, ho-ish. Probably wore them up-the-butt thong panties and nipple-out bras.

"She sure ain't cashing no paycheck," Warming to her favorite subject, Susan held out her palm to get a pound from Baybay. They were finishing morning coffee in Jocelyn's apartment.

"Ha!" Baybay's palm met Susan's. "She ain't on no welfare neither! That bitch a ho! and that's a fact!"

Baybay and Susan fell on each other in agreement and knocked Baybay's cup off the table. They froze and looked at the linoleum because Jocelyn kept a clean house. Seeing that the cup didn't break and there was only a drop left to spill, they knew Jocelyn wouldn't get mad.

"Y'all need to quit," Jocelyn from the top floor said getting up to reach for a paper towel. "When you two gonna get tired of talking about that girl?" She picked up the cup and put it in the sink. "Damn. Y'all just don't like her because she minds her business and never invited y'all inside her house. That fine man she got also got y'all's nosy asses bent outta shape. Maybe Rakim works at night...and you got to give it to her, she is real pretty and do got a nice body." Jocelyn always spoke her mind.

"I ain't got to give her nothing! Joss, why you always take up for people you don't know? Especially when you don't know what you talking about? You don't be seeing what me and Susan see." Baybay sucked her teeth, took the paper towel from Jocelyn and bent to wipe up the little mess. "How you think she pay for all them fly clothes and shit? Huh? Bitch don't wear nothing..."

"But the best!" Susan finished the sentence, snatched the dirty paper from her friend and threw it in the trash. "And you seen her jewelry? Rakim wear that drug dealer shit. But Joss, you right. She *do* work at night, flipping in and out of cars, *ho*-tel rooms, wherever a ho get paid." Susan balled up her napkin and tossed it too.

"I still think she also a stripper," Baybay tried holding in her ample stomach as she thought about gyrating before men in less than a bikini.

"And? Even if she is tricking or dancing, unless y'all Mister Drayton, her finances ain't your business. Baybay, you and Susan get on my nerves sometimes. I'm serious. I get tired of hearing y'all talk about people all the time." Jocelyn rolled her eyes. "Want another doughnut?" she pushed the box on the table towards them.

"Hmp," Baybay rolled her eyes right back, chewing a pow-dered sugar, "hmp. You gon' see. And for your info, I only talk what I know..."

"I know that's right!" Susan butted in again, breaking a chocolate dipped in half.

"...And, I know Rakim's a straight up ho. Even though I ain't seen him around here in a while, why you think Shipell was parking here late at night? Him and Miss *Dee*vine just friends? He was here to play cards? Trust me, Shipell was picking up his money. I ain't saying that she wasn't getting paid too, but he's a goddamn *pimp*, Joss. He's like, the fucking king pimp of Brooklyn and shit!"

Baybay grabbed the other half of the chocolate doughnut Susan was holding and finished it in two eager bites. She scanned what remained in the box and selected another powdered sugar and another chocolate, in case Susan wanted one.

"Wait, and what about that white Benz that been pulling up lately, Bay? The one you said you been seeing picking her up late and dropping her off early, when you're up getting Charles ready for work." Susan turned in her chair to look in Jocelyn's face. "Whoever he is, that muthafucka ain't no goddamn bus driver Joss!" Susan wagged her head as she licked chocolate from her fingers. "I don't know who he is, but he a hustler too!"

Jocelyn waved her friends away, "Ain't no use talking sense to y'all."

She watched Baybay eat both donuts then closed the box of pastries to save the rest for her children.

"Nah, the point is, me and Bay stays up on the one! And if you don't watch her, Rakim will do your man!"

"Okaaay?" Baybay confirmed. "I can't stand that bitch Rakim. Suzy, set my hair for me when we go sit outside? I want to try that style I was telling you about in Essence but I need you to help me roll up the back...."

"I Know You Want That Bitch!"

Baybay didn't explain that her hate for Rakim had peaked early one evening a few months ago, when she'd caught her husband Charles intently watching something from their living room window, concentrating like she'd never seen him do.

From the kitchen she'd come up behind him, intending to ask if he wanted meatloaf or hamburgers to go with the mashed potatoes for dinner.

She found him shifting his weight, hands deep in the front pockets of his pants, inching closer to the pane, stretching his neck until his right cheek was nearly pressed flat and rising up the glass.

Standing less than two feet behind her man Baybay stood on her toes to look over his shoulder, to see what had his birddog attention, why he didn't feel her presence behind him.

She caught a glimpse of that damn Miss Divine disappearing out of their view.

So instead of tapping him on the shoulder like she planned, Baybay punched Charles as hard as she could in the middle of his back. He banged the side of his forehead on the pane.

Loudly, she accused him crazily about "wanting to get with that nasty bitch!" until he got fed up and stuck a strong finger in her face, yelling back that she "had a fucking problem!"

He thought he'd seen Shabar, "And you know he owes me money!" going up the street.

"You a fucking *liar*! Charles! I was just looking *right* at you! That wasn't no goddamn *Shabar*! You was breaking your neck looking after that ho Rakim! You think I'm *blind*? You was so busy watching her nasty ass you didn't even *know* I was fucking standing right behind you, you fucking bastard! I know you want to fuck her! You probably fucked her already! Damn *dog*!"

Baybay flung her dishtowel at him, stomped, cursing, into

their bedroom and cracked the door slamming it.

"You out your fucking mind! Since you talk about it all the time, you must *want* me to fuck her! Crazy ass woman! And you better not never punch me in my fucking back no *god*damn more! Arbayelle! I'm going out to find that bitch, *okay?* That's what you what to hear? Goddamn your ass!" Charles hollered as he stormed out the front door making it shake the wall behind him.

He barreled down the stairs embarrassed and angry. Guilty and caught too, because his wife was right, he sure was thinking about stroking Rakim when Baybay hit him.

After all was quiet, the boys, Devante and Delqwon, crept into the kitchen. They made peanut butter and orange marmalade sandwiches for themselves. Delqwon turned off the slowly burning potatoes. They got the bottle of pineapple soda from the refrigerator and tiptoed back into their bedroom closed the door and ate watching TV.

Charles didn't finish his hamburger at The Fantasia Lounge. He nursed a few beers until eleven o'clock. Then he called the place where he wanted to stay the night. He apologized for calling so late and explained why he needed to come over.

She hesitated only a moment, then said okay.

Charles said, "Thank you, baby" and told her he'd be there in about fifteen minutes. They hung up, but not before she cautioned, "Be careful nobody sees you come in the building."

He knocked softly on her door. When she let him in, Charles took her in his arms. When they released from a deep, searing kiss, she ran a finger over his lips and told him they were alone. The kids were gone, but he had to be out before they came back in the morning.

Charles didn't ask where she'd sent her children, but he knew it was with someone who wouldn't look at the lateness of the hour and wonder why they couldn't dream in their own beds.

"Mmm-hmm," Baybay's husband agreed, slipping down the nightgown straps of the woman he'd been sleeping with for five months.

Usually, all he could do was steal an hour or two after work to be with her. One, two times a week they mated, caressed, under the cover of his lies. Long trips to the store, the mechanic, a buddy's house.

Because he was good with his hands, especially with wood, saying he was going out to price an estimate for a handyman job was his most frequent excuse.

When all of his reasons grew thin and he couldn't think of a new excuse to get out, while his wife cooked dinner and mothered his sons, Charles yearned to be relaxed by another woman's touch. Baybay was a good wife, she just wasn't...wasn't...this woman, his "Mellow."

When he managed to swing some time, she was always willing too. That's what he dug about her most. Since their first night together, if he called and said he'd be over in ten minutes, her kids would be down the block at a friend's in five.

They were very discreet; reveling in quiet, robust lovemaking that was fulfilling for them both. But Charles was getting worried, he had never really cheated, fondling a few tramps in a bar somewhere before driving his drunk ass home didn't count. What he had gotten himself into with his lover had become more than perfect sex. They had talked about it, about what had happened between them, how they'd both wanted it and now, how they couldn't, wouldn't do without it. Charles had a wife, but he and Mellow had created a bind.

Five months ago, she and Charles were on line in the corner store, she was cradling full arms of oranges and potatoes, he was behind her with a six pack of brew.

They'd spoken, he'd made a silly joke about the store's slow cashier and her laughter had bounced most of her armload to the floor. Charles stooped with her to pick up the produce and they'd just looked at each other.

But that gaze was all the conversation they'd needed.

He'd carried her bag from the store, both acting as if he was just being chivalrous. Good thing, because in front of 210 they'd met Susan coming home from work.

She'd greeted them both and remarked, "Oh? You ain't never carried my bags, Charles!" Narrowing her eyes at him she added, "What kind of tip you getting?"

Charles' laugh was too hearty and his jovial answer of "Susan, you crazy!" was forced. He'd given the bag to its owner and said goodbye to both women, bounding up the stoop through the front door.

That night Charles couldn't stop thinking about her. Watching television with his family, he'd stood up abruptly and told Baybay that he'd almost forgotten, he'd promised to stop by Pierre's house to see about some new shelves his wife wanted put up in their kitchen.

He kept his eyes averted, Baybay could read him like a novel.

"Pierre? This time of night? It's nine thirty. Pierre who? Where he live? Charles? I never heard you talk about no Pierre." Baybay, frowning, sat up on the sofa and stopped putting cheese popcorn in her mouth.

Shrugging into his shirt taken off the sofa arm, he thought, that's because "Pierre" is the first woman I've really wanted since I met you, and I've got to put my hands on her tonight.

"Pierre Ville, honey. Over on Chauncey. Haitian brother, he was referred to me. Watch your show. I'll be back in about a hour and a half." Leaving quickly, he pretended not to hear his wife call, "It's going to take you that long?"

Charles had eased to her apartment, carrying the hammer he stopped to retrieve from his van, it was his beard, his prop in case someone he knew saw him standing before her door. Everybody knew she was a friend of his wife. He knocked.

Before he rapped a second time, her door cracked. She'd expected him, she'd willed him to come. Poking her head out, she'd whispered, "Give me twenty minutes, then come back. The kids." she'd winked at him and eased the door shut.

He'd waited two blocks away at The Fantasia, one of his usual haunts, so there would be no reason for anyone who saw him there to suspiciously mention it to BayBay. The night it all started with his outside woman it took three fast Heinekens to slake his sudden thirst.

In a half-hour he was received through a door flung open wide and closed behind him just as effusively. Impatiently, she pulled him straight to her bedroom.

She was nude under a floating, transparent pink robe that puddled on the floor as soon as they got there. She pushed his back on the bed and took her time undressing him, cooing lazily,

"I want to pop these fucking shirt buttons, baby, I want to break the zipper on your pants...but you got to wear these clothes home, don't you baby?"

She wouldn't let him touch her swaying breasts or feel her big ass as she got him out of his clothes.

When Charles was finally naked he was fully aroused, so she straddled him. Slowly she lowered, joining with him, eyes closed, wholly savoring the beginning of their fit. Her moans and full pleasure on her face made him grab her waist, pull her hips down and give her the rest of his rock right away. Her eyes opened wide but she sat right on it. Took it all looking in his eyes.

Nodding her head she said, "Uh-huh, that's right, be gentle next time," answering the question pressing his mind.

He was crazy ready to do her like he really wanted to. Charles wanted to lust, rut, be nasty. He wanted to sweat and pull her hair, grind her, maul her breasts, suck her flesh, hear their bodies slap against each other, change positions, make her quiver, watch himself disappear deeply over and over inside her, hear her gasp his name, wind up on the floor tangled in the sheets with the mattress twisted.

"I want to make you feel so good so bad," he promised, starting to thrust his hips. She caught his rhythm and made it her own. They turned on.

Starving, they devoured raw sex until they were spent. "Like ex-cons," they'd joked afterwards. And it was better, more delicious than they'd hoped.

Charles had nicknamed her that night. Roaming his eyes over her sweaty naked form while he dressed, he'd leaned over to kiss her moist thighs and said, "Baby, you're my Mellow." She'd smiled, stretched and told him to close the door tightly when he left.

When Charles got home it was close to one, Baybay was in bed pretending to be asleep. Her husband undressed silently and quickly, eased into bed and soon slumbered like a lamb.

Baybay had smelled faintly, the foreign air he still wore. And she knew. Charles had been with a woman. Another woman had fucked her husband. It was all she could do to lay still next to him. She wanted to scream, "Did you put your dick in another woman?!" But she couldn't confront him because talk would make it true.

She prayed that it was a one time thing. Her thoughts froze. What if it was that bitch Miss Divine? She couldn't compete with that young ho.

It never struck her that Charles' lover was not the woman she accused.

When she got up to help him get ready for work, neither said a word about how long it took for him to measure for Pierre's wife's shelves.

Baybay felt she had legitimate reason to hawk and dog Rakim.

Now, nearly a half year after that night, Charles used the stupid fight he had with his wife as reason enough not to go home.

He fortified his thoughts with guilty logic. Shit. When a man can't look out the window in his own home without his woman flipping, then, shit, it was time for him to remind Baybay who wore the muthafuckin' pants. It don't matter *what* the fuck he was looking at, he paid the muthafuckin' bills! Let her spend the night by herself, shake her up a little, she had a good man and he wasn't going to take her bullshit.

Since they'd been together, this would be his first whole night with his woman and Charles meant to take full advantage of it. Shit, since Baybay was accusing him of cheating, he'd show her. Mellow was always ready for him and she loved sex any way they tried it.

His wife had never sat on the edge of the bed with her legs opened so wide, turning up her essence for his mouth to pleasure. Or met his strokes bucking on her hands and knees on the floor. That's why he couldn't resist her, Mellow took his sex like she was made for him. She was vivid, she let him explore his imagination. She was greedy, made him realize that he wanted a whole lot more creative mating in his life than he was getting from his wife.

This time they had all night.

Looking at her now, naked, ardent, he growled, "Mellow," and grabbed her flush against him, feeling her body roughly, making her pant.

Charles moaned when she reared back and cupped her full bare breasts together, offering them to his mouth. He revealed his tongue to meet their thrust and his mouth welcomed them greedily, noisily sucking her nipples to stones. He slid his hands between her thighs. Mellow began unbuckling his belt...

They got frantic. It was taking too long to get it in.

Passion rushed to meet them, haste flung away caution, lust gladly popped his shirt buttons, burst his zipper.

"Hey," she whispered breathlessly, sinking to the living room floor with him, widening her knees, she didn't want to hear one word, "Not one, you hear?" about the fight he'd had with his wife....

"Who You Trying To Clown?"

Susan also kept to herself that incident one Sunday morning two months back, when she was washing dishes after serving Raymond her special downhome country breakfast of buttered scratch biscuits, smoked bacon and sage sausage, butter-yellow grits, eggs over easy, homefries, fresh orange juice and fresh coffee. Salt, black pepper, apple butter, ketchup and clover honey on the side.

They'd had some real good fun the night before. Raymond told her over and over how good it was and she'd come so strong she howled his name.

In her bathrobe Susan smiled as she cooked, gladly preparing the kind of meal a woman only makes for her feel good man. The one she may decide to enter the fray over, for the right to lay claim.

Relaxed on her couch looking up at the ceiling, Raymond, sated, had belched and sucked sausage out of his teeth. With his hands cradled behind his head he'd mentioned in a musing tone that he was surprised that Miss Divine was such a nice sister. He'd run into her in the vestibule a few days earlier, it was the first time they had ever "chatted for a few." Susan quit the dishpan to watch him from the kitchen.

"Ha! A brickhouse built like that usually be a reeeal bitch," Raymond was chortling like he was talking to one of the fellas. "She what my father call a 'bad mam-ajama', nice height, little waist, big thighs, ass like a amazon, titties like a stripper."

Susan was amazed that he had the nerve to talk like that in her house about another woman, right after swallowing her food.

"Yeeeah," he drawled, "looks like all that long, thick hair is really hers. Rakim's a pretty color too. Creamy like a caramel. Looks like a Creole. Young." He figured, "She's what, about twenty two? She's at least five, six years younger than you, right baby?" Raymond lifted his twenty-nine year old head to free one hand to rub his chest under the clean teeshirt he'd put on after his shower, taken freshly laundered from his drawer in her dresser.

Susan wondered whose titties he was really feeling and almost asked him, but said, "Uh-huh," instead. She didn't want him to stop talking. This was the first time she'd seen this side and knew it would be revealing.

"Yo, you know Jordan on my job? The one we call Big Time?" Raymond twisted on the couch to look at Susan in the kitchen, saw her nod her head.

"I had mentioned that Rakim lived in your building. He said he know her from a few spots uptown. Big Time said she only go with money." Raymond paused to think about something, "Nah, a working man can't afford no woman like Rakim. Big Time talking shit, she ain't checked him out...Baby, how long Rakim been living here?"

Nope, Susan thought, she'd figured wrong, this one wouldn't last long. She'd been going with Raymond for about three months and could see now what she had. Nothing. Uh-huh, I got to get all I can from this dog while he thinking he can fool a way to get to Rakim through me.

Who he trying to clown? Cheap, bus driving, studio renting muthafucka, laying on my fucking couch belly full in his gotdam drawers and a snow-white teeshirt that I fucking washed, asking me about that ho bitch.

He lucky he sweet between the sheets and don't mind handing over a few bucks, but, please. Fuck that bitch Rakim, but she wouldn't even let a broke ass like him smell it. And it ain't gon' be no time soon he tasting Sunday breakfast up in this damn house.

Susan put her hands back in the suds so Raymond wouldn't see them balled into fists. "Hmmm, I think she been here about a year and a half? Baby, you want some more orange juice before I clean the juicer?"

"Uh, yeah, and gimme a couple more biscuits with sausage and bacon when you bring me the juice, a big glass...thanks, baby. If any homefries left you can bring me a few of them too."

Raymond had gone back to staring at the ceiling. Then,

"Baby? Big Time asked me if I could get him Rakim's number. I told him I couldn't promise nothing, but I'd ask you...."

Susan had to hold a wet, soapy hand over her closed eyes so she wouldn't call Raymond the most ignorant, transparent shit she ever met. "I don't have it, but if I see her...Oh, honey, don't forget to give me the hundred for the phone bill. You said you'd give it to me today, remember?"

"I didn't forget, Susan, damn!" Irritated, Raymond sounded like she'd pinched him. Even though she couldn't see it, she knew his face was a frown.

She answered easily, "Oh, I know babes, I was just mentioning it."

Susan came into the living room a few minutes later carrying a tall glass of fresh juice and a plate full of breakfast seconds.

Eat hearty muthafucka, she thought, 'cause this sho' is your last. She kissed Raymond on his forehead.

He looked up at her and winked, not reading the "trifling jackass" in her sweet smile....

Call Me Bird. Word.
Cause I'm So Fly.

I want you for fast money
I'm in it for your car
Got to be gifting plat and diamonds
Get paid like a recording star
Hope you known for sweet talk
And famous on the Set
Is you cooling in the Big Time
I'm in it for what I can get
I know your shoes is baby gator
Let me see that Rolex on your arm
I know your rags is the finest made
Do you got that pimping charm?
When you gon give me a mink
Loves to go fine dining
Leave a bankroll for me playa
Where it be easy finding
Loves to sip Moet Cristal
Roll dice in Atlannic City
Got to be a real OG
To feed this greedy kitty
If you paid like my man Tyson
Then I'm your main girl Givens
Got to dress rest and impress
Just chilling for a living

Rakim Moet Divine

The first time I saw Shipell was on Valentine's Day night at the Blue Parrot in Manhatten.

I only been in Brooklyn a little over a month living on the low. Found a cute crib my second day here. Since then I been roaming incognito. Checking shit out. Looking for the spots I like to be. Juggling a few interested wallets because I don't like to use my money.

Ran into Chante a frengirl I knew from some spots back in Detroit. Went through the Heeeey girrrl! How you doing? and whatever. Told me she been in Brooklyn about six months so I figure she know what's up with the real dough.

Axed her what she know no good.

Big Girl hip me that New York is a ocean of money if a shaker know where to go. Told me to check out the Blue Parrot because real cake be in there on the weekends. Especially this weekend because of Valentine's Day.

I thanks her for the info and took her number even though I know I ain't gon call.

I remember that I don't like Chante because she's a snake.

When I got to the club that Friday night it was jammed. It was Lovers Night. Free for the ladies including a free drink and a live show.

Got this fool to give up his seat at the bar then told him I was waiting on my man.

I was mesmerizing. Cherry red strapless silk mini mini size eight. Short and tight because I'm a full ten but wasn't no rolls nowhere. Just popping titties and thighs. Booty and teeny waist. Fine in the face. The lady in Saks who sold me the dress said it was du-pee-yo-nee silk. That's how she said it. Bought matching cherry red kicks in po-da-swah. I know that means skin of silk in french.

Titanic gold and ice chain. Matching big rock ring. Long ponytail and red lips. Black ranch mink resting over the back of my barstool. Wasn't sitting at the bar ten minutes before playas wasting they money sending over splits of Moet that I wasn't accepting. Executive cats kept theyselfs in my sight.

Then he just walked by.

Looking like the rest of my life. Finally knew where my heart was. Brother was head to toe incredible in black leather. Superfine. Smooth caramel color same as mine. Mighty gold and crazy diamonds. Beautiful thick hair that texturizes just right. Black shiny curls. Went so good with his need kissing big lips.

I'm five seven he look like six feet. Bowlegs holding up a thick hard body under all that cowhide. Couldn't help but peep the toes of his bad lizzids. Looked like a superstar moving in a spotlight and ehhbody else in darkness. Looking at me so sexy. Making me look at him. Making me feel like something big gon happen. Like I was about to be a winner.

I didn't know who he was because he kept on going.

So I selected somebody else. Start dazzling this gorjus light-skin sweetie throwing my head back because my neck is nice. One big leg crossed pretty over the other high on my thigh toes pointing down.

About a hour go by then here comes that spotlight again. Walking up to me looking like too much candy. Seemed like I could smell him. Not his cologne but like how animals raise they noses when they smell a mate.

Black leather introduced hisself close in my ear. "Baby good evening. This must be your first time here. I would remember a beautiful woman like you. Since we have not had the pleasure of being aquainted I am very pleased to meet you. I'm Shipell baby. And I would like your number."

"They call me Miss Divine." There was ice chips in my voice.

He stepped back to look at me. I looked at him. Neither one of us smiling. Shipell looked away.

It was something close to two and he was about to leave because he had on a sharp black mink jacket. Shipell voice base. Deep with sugar and strength silking through it. My type. Hard sexy eyes got a look that make a woman act stupid. Rest on her just long enough to make her greedy to catch that glance again.

And I know the same way I know my name that a lot of wimmen been hipmatize by this man. I mean blasted. Left whatever spot she met him in to climb in a three hour bed she might have paid for. With Mr. Seduction. Who left her there the middle of the night. Right after all that pressure gone between his legs. Maybe a hour later. Before she have a chance to really put her arms around him good. He getting up getting dressed saying Baby I'll be back. But he really on his way to whatever he doing next.

I didn't really know that but I knew that.

Tried hesitating with my number because this other beige brother was still sitting beside me. Looking like he don't quite know what to do. Looking like he don't know if he suppose to be mad. He watching this other sharp man pushing all up on me. And lightskin couldn't hear what black leather had to say in my ear. And it's true me and lightskin had been groovin. Up until now we was enjoying ourselfs.

He was alright too. Had me considering trying something different. Somebody daytime.

His name was Craig Jenkins but said people call him Sky because he played ball in college. Twunnynine. Good hair hazel eyes. One of them good looking longtall brothers. Executive at IBM. Live in the Bronx. Jag keys on the bar. Single. One eighteen month old daughter name Cherise. But he's not with his baby mother. Ex Marine. Bad suit fit him real nice. Thin Italian shoes. Fly cologne smell like Gucci. Nice flash. Only one ring but it was heavy and had a nice piece of ice. Heavy gold bracelet. Gold and diamond watch. Didn't have to look hard to see that big sparkler stuck in his ear.

Uh huh. That ain't the kind of jewlry IBM men spend they money on. Craig might work nine to five but Sky moonlighting. Sky doing something else. No question. He a undercover baller because only steppers step to me. I look expensive.

So when he say he single that just mean that this pretty muhfucka ain't married. If I'ma tailor a plan for this man evry other kitty entertaining him must scat.

But Craig know what's up. I don't look like I work. Or wait. We was getting around to making plans to go to dinner next Saturday.

But Shipell standing there squashed all that. Deadlocked my eyes again and held out his hand to help me stand up off my stool. We was so close we should have started kissing. Looking in his eyes it felt like we was.

When I recall it now I know it was love at first sight. Shipell had me right then. I'm saying. Shipell had me open right there.

But I passed that easy test. I didn't swoon. I'm a Big Girl. Heart ain't got no face. Can't.

I'm one of the rare breed fully paid from playas fully paid.

And since Shipell didn't peep my raw desire I knew he knew that I was cold. Just like him. Also knew that Shipell was hard because I was wet.

He moved back one more step. Shifted his broad shoulders around. Eyes blinking off to the side Shipell said "Give me the number baby stop playing with me."

Craig cleared his throat excused hisself and booked. Soft muhfucka.

That's how me and Shipell first met.

Jones

You so sweet
Sugar is what swells
Your pretty lips
In a shape so nice and round
You so sweet
That Daughter be grabbing
At your collar
Wanting to get
At that sugarlick
Sweetening the base
Of your throat
Just a little bit
A tonguetip taste to wallow around
Inside her cheeks

You so persuasive
You that tippytoe
Persuasive
Invading like warm molasses
Thick suggestions
Crowding Daughter's ears and
Pushing
Up her nose
Coaxing persuasion
Must be you because it makes her
Repeat your name

You a mighty fine doctor too
Waiting
With your loaded sack of TCB
For that Daughter sick

From no kissing
Waiting
To fix her up
Ease every dull ache
By pumping her full of another need
Introduce a jones for your
Prescription
Catch her wiping at her
Shoulders
In case you left some teeny specks
Of your touch behind

Me and Shipell

We was quick. Took it off the street to my place after about three weeks.

I was truly caught after we started steady flowing. Sprung for real. For the first time in my life. Please. Looking in the mirror Shipell face looking back.

Had to shake my head hard sometimes to ignore thoughts suggesting what I could do to keep his attention. Wash his feet and drink the water tried to crawl inside my mind.

Kept thinking what's up? Beause real love emotion was new to me. Shocked because I realized I would cuss a bitch for even looking at my man sideways trying to like him. I don't mean the ones giving him money. I'm on guard for barracudas with true Game.

Confess. Yes. Shipell made me jump and rush. Spun me all out my style. Before this unique muhfucka came along my feet ain't never been no higher than on my toes when I'm yawning. Now my feet leaving the ground. Jumping up happy when I know it's him at my door.

Before Shipell flipped me I never stepped no faster than a stroll. Now I'm going for the gold. Doing the Carl Lewis at any request.

Got me doing e.s.p. responding to what he thinking. Got me caught up being his perfect dame. Daddy the first the only one to bust open my virgin love. Stroke my cherry heart. Blow my mind.

A few weeks later I got a parttime job at this boujee nightclub name Genesis. Downtown Manhatten near the Empire State Building. Being a charming hostess walking around smiling at folks axing if they alright.

Genesis attract men from the U.N. Plus entertainers lawyers athaletes money men like that. So you know Big Girls was in there too. I took the job out of curiosity. Wasn't looking to really gig because I truly don't nine to five.

Just happened to pass Genesis one afternoon out spending Shipell money. Noticed it because of the type of men I saw going in. Decided to check it out. Went in and was offered a job three feet on the other side of the door.

I said "What?" because I didn't really hear what the white man smiling at me had said. He repeat if I'm "here for the hostess job" I'm hired. We talk.

He was the manager. Fine Italian from Conetticut. Mr. Gianolo. Kept calling me beautiful. Started running weak Game. Told me he gon start me at a hunnit over what the last hostess got. Because I'm so fine. Laughing all in between his talking. He trying to see if I'm a ho or just slow.

Reaching out trying to stroke my arm but I turn my shoulder out of range. I'm chuckling too. Inside. He don't need to know how I flow. I just look at him and axe when I start. What the hell. Took the gig as a joke to meet and simmer some backburner resource. Wasn't nothing wrong with me and Shipell in fact we a perfect pair. But my nature say stay in the Game.

Told Shipell the job was just something to pass time until he got ready to go out. I get off at midnight.

He didn't like it at first. "I know Genesis." Then he said no.

So I said "Baby what's eight to twelve? Just four hours. Just three nights a week. You know I ain't trying to gig for no money. It's something to do. I just get itchy and bored waiting for you. Shipell this is just something to do until you ready for me. Let me just see if I even like it baby."

Axed him to hold my money. *My* money. When I get it. I remember Shipell laughing and grabbing me up.

But this is what Shipell did. It was a Friday night. My second night on the job. I'm in the back putting my things away greeting my coworkers getting ready to do my thing and they call me to the phone. Like twunnyfive to nine.

"Yeah." Shipell deep tone was mad. "I just lost money. Be with me before nine. See me at 44." Shipell hung up. All I had a chance to say was hello.

Lucky me. I had twunnyfive whole minutes to get where he was. 44 was this la la restaurant midtown not too far from my new job. Shipell liked to go there. Sit spend money rest impress and wind down.

I'ma just say this. I got there eightfiftynine rushing through the door axing for his table.

Can't say what I told my boss but I think I quit. Anyway I never went back. Can say I got there quick cause I jumped in a cab this lady was about to get in. Can say that I was gone.

I was so nervous maybe he said quarter to nine. Then like ninefifteen he walked up to the table. I didn't see him until he sat down.

Shipell didn't say a word. Sat back looking around with his leg crossed glimpsing a wine silk sock. Wine gator. Diamond face Rolex on his wrist draped over his knee. Shipell still didn't look at me. Look ehhwhere else to say "I saw you come in pretty baby. I was across the street with a associate of mine. My baby can run!" He was happy because he seen me hurry.

Shipell ordered what we ate. While we was dining his face set like stone. Complaining how much money he lost throwing dice. I'm sipping white wine saying nothing. Shipell cut his eyes at me push his plate away suck his teeth.

This me "Baby I ain't got nothing to say and I'm sorry you upset. I'm just glad to see you sugar. Money can't stay away from you baby. Honey you just gave the next man one night to count cash the way you do evry day. Forget that change moneymaker."

I show Shipell the tip of my tongue and the bottom of my eyes. He looked at me almost smile pull his plate back to him and eat. When we close like this Shipell tells me how he really feel about things so I understand when he act different.

Shipell made me sit close beside him in that pretty black Benz smell like cherrys inside. Ride us to The Royale through all the bright lights shining looking exciting. Got us a nice room and we expressed ourselfs. In silk boxers Shipell hard legs look pretty as mine. Yes. That night we gave another meaning to sex.

Some of the nastiest words I ever heard was base whispers in my ears. I lick his sweat like syrup. Shipell lick me clean places his tongue never been. Shipell be thick so well it feel like two. Lost my mind like evrytime.

Mating Shipell always feels like we inventing something. He fills up my cup. Takes more than I got. Never lets me rest. Makes me surrender. Holds me in a hot spot when I try to arch away from him lengthening the end of my road. Shipell don't stop until I ain't got nothing left. When my breath all gone that's when baby get his. Grab me up set my hips gather me up wrap me in his body head to heel and get that fit. Seed me like a spring garden. And Shipell the first man in years and years I let know me skin to skin.

But God must didn't want us to make babies. My mind was crossed up about it too. My feelings pulling opposite. Evry month when I saw my fren my mind say "lucky" but my heart sigh "dam."

I be anywhere anyway anywhy with Shipell whenever he call. Shipell call all the time. When we not together in the street he comes to my place when he finish his bizness. But even if he go to sleep in my beautiful bed Shipell always leave a minute before it start to get light.

Must be some deep rule of the Game that say except in a hotel Shipell can't break day with me in my bed.

He always bringing arms full of fly rags but never say they mine. Just hang them in my closet. Ehhthang sharp and perfect fit. One time Shipell bring three floorsweeper minks all my size but different. Let me pick. I selected the blond stunner.

Shipell trusted me. Like to stand in the middle of my bedroom to take off his jewlry. Walk over to lay that heavy pile on my dresser. Take off his jacket and shirt or sweater and give it to me. Reach in his back and slip something something under his side of the bed. Take off his pants. Go in his pocket and take out his money. Peel that knot before he put it back where it came from. Give his pants to me to hang up neat while he arrange bills on my dresser like a fan. That's mine. Never less than what I need. And I Need. Sho you right. My man know.

It got so that Shipell was with me in my little place as early as he can. Be here sometimes by eleven. We together five out of seven. I'm his relax.

Shipell like the pretty way I paint my apartment. I'm grocery shopping and he discovering favorites. Looove my cuban black beans with smoked pigtails and onions. Over my fluffy butter white rice. My baked barbeque turkey wings. Or my west indian whole red snapper steamed with shred carrots and escallions. Fried sweet plantins. Steamed kale with garlic. Scratch cornbread. He axe for my yams baked with brown sugar nutmeg yellow raisins and pineapple chunks. And my coconut cake. I served Shipell too. Right down to the gold toothpick I bought for him with his money.

Went out of my way to keep special body oils. Always kept one warm and ready sitting in a small pot of hot water. Know just what his feet look like because I rubbed them often enough. Along with the rest of his gorjus body.

Evrything Shipell touch was clean. Had two of his own white double thick oversize turkish terry robes. They so thick that when he step out the shower and put one on he be dry right away. Seven silk lounging robes in seven colors. Always good music. Big color remote tv vcr dvd.

We wasn't big drinkers but I kept one of evrything waiting for his request. Perfume candles and incense. Whatever kind of convasation he want.

My big comfy queensize with my big comfy ass like hot clay ready to play.

Went around with him. Shipell took me around. One night in Manhatten down some stairs on West Fortyseventh and Sixth Avenue. Through a alley to a backroom where he did some bizness over some diamonds with a Arab looking man. They discussed a bunch of diamonds sparkling by theyselfs under a bright light. Perfect ice spitting colors in a black velvet tray.

Shipell held up a few rocks dealing with this man like they familiar with each other. Convasating in code.

Shipell end the meeting when he say "Amsterdam Monday seven. These six. Double back and I got sixteen. Hit me at Cooly for two five."

Shipell had told me not to open my mouth. I acted like I didn't speak or understand english.

Shipell took me to Heartbeat birthday party at the Martinique deep somewhere in the Bronx. Shipell told me

Heartbeat throw this party evry year and it was a playas ball.

Baby dressed me like I make money dates. Axed me if I can handle it. Shit. I told my muhfuckin man if he ice me right I ain't got to wear no muhfuckin clothes what. Shipell laughed and laughed. So here we go.

Pulled up in front of Martinique and there was a crowd of people outside waiting on line to get in. Shipell made me get out the car first.

Miss Divine poured out of that Benz. The first thing the crowd peeped was the silver hooker heel on my white suede boot that go half way up my big thigh. Then my big ass showing in tight white leather booty shorts riding my hips. Showing a lot of my tight belly.

Shipell had closed a diamond chain tight around my teeny waist. My titties spilling out the matching weeny white leather bikini halter. My pure white mink bolero jacket didn't hardly cover nothing but my arms. Silver lips eyelids and claws. My hair flat dead straight and stop the middle of my back. I shook my head. So muhfuckas know it's thick and mine.

Posed like a runway model waiting for my Bad Poppadaddyman. Eyeballs burned holes in me. Whispering and crowding closer. Females wishing they was me. Secondary moneymen wishing they had me.

Baby froze me solid. I didn't wear none of my own jewlry. Evry stone set in plat. Shipell claim me with his name running across my chest in big sweeping diamond script on a plat chain. Samson piece. Shipell owned the diamond bricks igniting my ears. His six carit icecube pinky ring fit my longest left finger. My wrist had frostbite from the chunks of hot ice screaming rainbows.

See. This the kind of jewlry Shipell know I want. Don't get me wrong. I wouldn't dare refuse his gifts but after being flooded in plat? I really don't want my diamonds set in gold no more. Time to step up. Plat even felt cooler next to my skin.

When Shipell got out his Benz muhfuckas act fanatic. Like my baby a movie star coming to his premiere. Lying to each other that they know my man. Calling my baby. Calling my muhfuckin sharp ass spotlight.

Boss baller nod his head at people and speak to a few but ain't none of these fans nowhere near his level. His people already toasting at the bar. Shipell like to come last.

Shipell freaked hisself like a king straight up. No wonder he won the trophy that night. Snow white silk suit with a long jacket and a single diamond button. Pure white silk shirt with square ice buttons. White raw silk tie with a glitter ice tie pin. Virgin white baby gators. White silk socks so thin he can't wear them but once.

White floorsweeper mack mink with diamond cluster buttons was riding on his shoulders. A white mink gansta fedora with a diamond band was Shipell muhfuckin crown. Pharoah stones in plat was cussing on his wrists and fingers just cutting ehhbody up. Shipell iceberg almighty.

After my spotlight came around to where I was standing he made a few unnecessary adjustments to his perfection then grabbed me around my waist. Posed with me to give the photographers a chance to take our picture.

Me and Shipell always took a lot of pictures together. Almost evry time we went out. Photographers always be where playas go. But he always kept them all.

Shipell head toward the door of Martinique never looking back at me. But you know his pretty drug was his shadow. I walked behind his left shoulder. When we entered the club the crowd opened like the Red Sea. Other playas started talking short to they wimmen.

One bitch jumped from her man to get up in my face. Wanted to fight me just because she ain't me. She's another one evil because I'm number one. Shipell had that bum put out.

And she got what she deserved too. Her man caught up with her outside on the street and knocked her ass to the ground for getting out of pocket. Calling attention without permission. Bitch was all out of line.

Baller made that tramp come back inside the club with her face swelling up and apologize to Mr. Love and me. I tried to backhand her in the mouth but Shipell caught my wrist and ran his other hand across my shoulder saying "Baby. Stop."

Shipell put me in a spotlight seat at the bar then went to

enjoy hisself. Ignored me and all the moneymakers throwing sly looks my way. I understand. Bossbaby needed to see how I really act. See if I'm greedy in a deep green spot like this. I was in a forest of money trees. All gleam was legit. No imposters at this event.

Made no eye contact. Sent back evry drink. Stopped evry convasation before it got started. Enjoyed myself by myself because I knew a test when I was taking one. Especially in a room wall to wall with fully paid lip licking true Game muhfuckas. All Steak. But I wasn't about to risk my fil-lay min-yon for no chuck. Never even considered interviewing something for my backburner. I proved a point.

So Shipell proved one too. Standing across the dance floor with his partnas he just looked at me and was the center of my full attention. I got up right away and moved through the party crowd slow and cold sexy like he wanted me to.

Got close enough for Shipell to pull me hard against his chest by my ass. Rubbed his thumbs across my nipples so his associates could see my eyes close and my lips part. See me push up on him licking my bottom lip trying to keep his fingers right where they was.

Shipell laugh that playa laugh and called me his hot box. Told me to say hello to his people and go and sit back down. We be leaving soon. I know he wanted them to see my ass. So I walked away with the stroll that made it roll.

I heard one of them pythons say "Bossman I see why you accepted that bitch." Shipell let them think that I'm the main reason why he so well paid. They think I'm his platinum magnet. A private number call. That's why I'm not on the track.

They don't know I don't work.

Another snake started laughing pulling air through his teeth and said "You breaking Game too. I know you hitting that ass for free." Evrybody chuckle. Soon Shipell came and got me and we left. We spent the night at The Bristol Hotel.

Dam. I hated giving Shipell back that jewlry the next morning after the ball. He didn't let me keep none of that plat. Not one piece. And you know I axed real pretty more than one time. More than one way. Almost turned myself inside out but it didn't do no good. Shipell wasn't moved.

One time he convinced me to enter a leg contest at Club Papillon. The grand prize was a G. After I won Shipell told me to give him my first place money. Wrong. Shipell insist. I resist. Since the legs mine the money mine.

Later in our room at The Royale he gave me a thick gold chain. But in the morning after he dropped me off home I got in my apartment and discovered my prize money was gone out my bag. Shipell proved another point.

He stayed away for a whole week. I didn't try to know no other man. I'm caught tight.

Shipell showed up on day eight like my lonely wasn't nothing and not his bizness. Didn't want to hear one word about my feelings. We was back together like we was never apart until one night he got mad.

Yes he did. After we been together about three months. One night right behind my london broil with onion gravy. Herb butter noodles with cucumber salad on the side. Peach and apple cobbler. Peach ice tea.

Started pacing in my place looking at me like I could use a slap. Cussing. Fierce. Beefing about cash and my lazy ass. Stressing that I never gave him "One! fucking dollar." I'm the laziest most brickhead woman he ever had.

Slapped his hand on his forehead. "What the fuck am I doing?" Talking to hisself about keeping a bitch who ain't Never made him a dime. Keeping her ass! That ain't how his shit work. "Let me find out you got some of that west indian shit on me. That's what I'm thinking Rakim. Because this shit ain't me."

Shipell flick nothing off his pant leg and look in my face. "You ain't gon do what you want to do." Remind me who come first and it ain't me. Say this shit stopping right now. Told me to get ready for my new life.

Told me my ass ain't that sweet to a muhfuckin Man keeping plenty honey dripping money. In fact I'm starting next week. Investing in my future with boss muhfuckin Shipell. He gon give me a choice things I can do. On and on like that.

I acted quick. Had to step in with something grand before Shipell stepped out thinking our thing was really gon be different.

I showed him my. And before he can say what? my baby

hush. I wasn't about to start paying him but he want a ho? I got one right between my thighs. And another one between my lips.

Zipped down Shipell pants in the kitchen and my mouth with no words soothed him slow showed devotion.

But he didn't want placating. Shoved me hard to the floor and jammed my hoochie poo. Baby know I'm his Vanessa del Rio. Anything go. But right after I heard that long growl Shipell zipped up and left.

Left slamming the door. Didn't leave my money. First time that ever happened. My rent was due the next day and I hated to think my cash was gon pay it. But my rent is never one day late.

Shipell didn't call me for another long two weeks. But some of his wimmen did because they had my number.

They rang my phone axing for Love. Axing for my man. Telling me to tell him to meet them such and such a time at such and such a place. Got something for him.

I took whatever information they gave but never said "He ain't here." Said he was in the shower. Sleep. Shipell don't want to talk right now. If they axed "Whodis?" sometimes I said "I'm his sister."

Most of the time I sucked my teeth and hung the fuck up.

Shipell Spank Me

Shipell said he'd kick my ass if midnight ever catch me in the street without permission if I wasn't with him.

One time I wound up staying overnight at my girl Lighteyes place because she was all fucked up over some man who quit her.

She a lightskin girl with green eyes and they real. Got good hair long like mine. Look mixed but she all black. Frengirl tall all titties little waist and big country ass. Twunnytwo. Stay iced and pressed. Choice. So she don't know why he gone.

I wasn't over there listening all night because Lighteyes was emotional from love. I was with her because she was buggin over her expenses. He was her main moneyman. I was there to help Big Girl plan a plan. Rent must be paid.

She tried to get strong calling me sister and saying we just alike. Even though she claimed to be just like me with "No real gaps between her money" I know she my opposite.

Lighteyes was broke with a clear horizon and I stash cash for the what if.

Got home about one the next afternoon and didn't hear from Shipell all that day or all night. He didn't answer none of my pages. I finally went to bed. So I wasn't expecting him to ring my bell about three in the morning.

I don't sleep in nothing and I didn't see them four oversize brothers standing behind Shipell until I fully opened the door. Ehhbody was looking at me.

Shipell said "Close the gotdamn door and put something on. Hurry up."

When I opened it again Shipell walked in with them robo dudes in his footsteps. I'm just standing there in my waterblue silk robe watching from the livingroom near the front door. Because I don't know what's going on. Big Girl like me might need to lam.

Shipell come back into the living room fling me on the couch say "Your ass was out all night last night so give me my money."

When my eyebrows went up Shipell walked back in my bedroom over to my closet. He opened one of the sliding doors and started pulling out what he gave me and what he didn't.

Snatched evry single one of my gotdamn minks off the rod. Robbed my top custom leather pieces. Flung damn near all my designer silks and linens off the hangers. Ripped my best sequence dress pulling it out with the other sparklers. Piled mountains in the arms of them concrete thugs who was leaning back on they redwood thighs so they didn't drop nothing.

Next Shipell over in my jewlry chest on the dresser. Plucking out all my big shit. A lot ain't his gifts. He stuffed my biggest and best in a small black leather bag and gave the overflow to one of them buildings. Gigantor had to cup his ham hock paws to hold it all. Ice and midas was waterfalling all over that fool hands.

He left all my kicks. Shipell slick. Where I'm going in just shoes? I'm looking cool and being dummy but my blood was turning to steam.

Then Shipell and the four muhfuckas who got all my real shit passed by me going out the door. Not one of those goons said a word I heard yet. Left my front door wide open.

In the foyer Shipell looked back at me said "Stay home until I call you." They left. The whole situation took about ten minutes.

I was hipmatized. Shipell had hit me hard. Couldn't hardly think. My man came in my house and walked out with my style and my jems. Wasn't no punch Shipell could have given me more violent than taking away my image.

I just closed my front door and went and layed across the bed.

It ain't no thing. Refused to trip and wasn't even mad no more. I knew there had to be some regulations with the riches he was giving. But Shipell didn't have to refrigerate and cold interrupt me like this.

So wasn't nothing to do but chill. What happened happened. I had to believe that he would bring back my stuff.

Midnight the night after he robbed me I answered the

phone. Shipell tone was so blizzid my ear got chapped. "That's right. You better answer the gotdamn phone." Hung up.

Tested me a few times over the next week and a half. But since he took my closet and jewls I was forced to stay home anyway. Always kept plenty of food in my kitchen and my nest is very comfortable. I cooked watched tv played music got drunk.

It was a Thursday night about two in the morning when my baby came back with the same four apes. Brought back all my visuals. Along with a new set of Louie. Garment bag two suitcases. Carryon bag. And a shoulder bag with the matching wallet and makeup case. My rent plus my allowance was waiting in the wallet.

See how Shipell wreck me? What's up? Me and him going to the Bahamas? Or are these parting gifts because he considering moving me up from the bottom? Which sure ain't what I want.

There got to be a word for what I'm trying to say. A word that means giving somebody a deep roundabout clue hoping they figure out what you really mean.

Shipell tossed his car keys to one of his mandingos and told them all to wait down in the car. I know he ready for me to do Thank You and I'm Sorry.

So I gave my baby what he came to get. My pleasure. I wanted Shipell so bad he could have let them muhfuckas stay to watch and learn.

I already had six Louie pieces and now I got thirteen. But I decided to tighten my Game.

Paying Shipell

I put hazel contacts in my eyes.

Poured nude into a itsy spandex tube same color as my skin. Pretty smooth bare legs looked like they like to climb. Four diamond Perreti bangles. Gold and diamond Rolex watch. French manicure and only one meteorite diamond ring. My long diamond earrings looked like glittering exclamation marks.

Feet almost nekked. My kicks was just soles with tall copper snakeskin heels and two strips a real Swarofski crystals across my copper toes. I showed off my face. Natural eyes and glossy lips. Combed my hair straight back to the middle of my back ending in a lot of big soft curls on the bottom.

I had heard more than one Big Girl convasating about this joint I went to. Had heard about the money raining in this la la jazz bar in a hotel near the U.N.

I picked Independence Day to star. I arrived about eight.

O baby. Lots of men was in there but O Damn. I saw that the stars was really out this Fourth of July. Real fireworks. Big Bad Girls was ehhwhere.

Looked like a buffet. Pick a color. You got it. Pick a flava. Here it is. What age you want? Illegal babies to old ladies.

All captains of the C. Which mean Convasation. Confirmation. Cash.

So it all came down to profile. I'm Rakim Moet Divine. Took my time. Whatever I want is mine. I felt good because it had been a while since I worked my skills. Flexed. Threw out a few hooks. Showed the contenders a champion. Caught and threw back three men because don't nothing get heard past the first few words but the right money.

Number four who axed to sit down was the one with the proper introduction. He introduced hisself as Mr. Bone Green. Then axed if I would allow him a hour of my time to buy me a two thousand dollar drink upstairs in his room.

I replied. We agreed. We got up from my table to exchange our transaction as soon as we got in the elevator.

A hour later I was back in the bar on my cell leaving messages on Shipell cell for nearly a half hour before he answered.

Before he could start talking I told him where to meet me and hung up.

Shipell met me on the corner at Fortysecond and Park. Went over to the car. He looking at me through his window. I motioned for him to put it down. Shipell lowered the glass with his face set like he's superior.

I returned the same stink attitude. I threw a gang of hunnits right in his face and said "Now shut the fuck up."

Shouted at a cab I saw approaching jumped in sped off. Shipell still got to my building before me. When I got out the cab he leaned over to open my side of the Benz. I knew if I didn't get in Shipell was gon go nuts in the street right in front of 210.

So I sashays over and was off again back to Manhatten. Shipell looked so mean and was speeding like a idiot.

As soon as we was up in our room at The Marquis he pushed my back up against the door knocking the breath out of me telling me don't Fuck! with him. Next muhfuckin time I throw something at him he don't care if it's a gotdam feather he gon kick my ass.

Digging his fingers in my shoulders Shipell axe "What's this money from?"

I knew he was undercover happy so I felt free to answer "A hour of my time."

Baby gripped me tighter. "Two thousand for a hour? Shit." Slammed me up against the door again. "Go get your freak ass in the shower." Ordered me to come out clean and do to him exactly what I did to get this money.

I didn't argue with Shipell. Hurried back fresh to the bed. I looked inside my head and got my mojo back out. Some new shit he never seen me do before. Nothing I did made me feel shame or think twice. Or wonder if Shipell was curious about who I learned it from.

I showed my Daddy a trick with a hole in it.

Almost a hour later Shipell almost stop breathing. He made me quit what I was doing. Raised up to look at me. He pinched my face until I had a fish mouth. His other hand squeezed my throat. Shipell said he would break my ass like glass if I ever freak another muhfucka like that.

Before he rolled over to sleep my baby motioned at the knot I donated laying on the nighttable. Told me to take back half.

While I sat on the side of the bed to count up my bills I kissed my teeth and told Shipell to make up his muhfuckin mind. But he already snoring.

New Year's Eve

Me and Shipell was together ten months before we truly fell out.

The day before New Year's Eve. I was tired of arguing about money. I fussed when he tried to cut my notes. I understand he's my boss but he got me used to certain digits.

And he know I'm never gon buy time from no man. Not even him.

That's why I'm twice not concerned that Shipell got as many wimmen as he can paying him minute to minute. I understand he got to get dough. He live for it. We need it.

I'm just the only one not paying him and the only one Shipell paying to have all for hisself. So when Shipell start up about me making money it makes me sick. I hate when he act like he don't know how we do.

And I do have a job. Knowing how to king my flawless man is my full time employment. Treat him first class all the way. But I'm the top shelf dame he got to maintain. That's what frustrate Shipell. We both feeling something new and he fighting it because he the one supporting us instead of the other way around.

He tripping because the Game say love ain't shit. Love don't get no bread. Love is the easiest way to fall.

But Shipell must want to keep me. I was ripe when we met and baby got me rotten now. Plus I'm stuck on Shipell. I been down in this town long enough to find out that even in New York there ain't many like my baby.

Until I met Shipell, it took me a minute to meet the cash really on my level. I had to juggle dumbells when I first got here. I'm saying. Before I got mainline on the cash line I had to play fools two three at a time just to meet my basic luxurys.

Men giving money and steady gifts usually can't give good fit and jockeys usually ain't good for nothing but a ride.

True true playas like Shipell gifting ice dough gold and pole usually expect and get some kind of payback. It takes a rare Big Girl like me to know how to stay on the bottom and handle a winner.

I ain't on my back and stay off my knees except with him. I'm steady paid cause I know how to treat a ruler. I am his evrything and make him feel brand new. My Game stay nice and virgin tight.

The way Shipell keep me and his juicy love is gon make it hard to find a equal replacement if he ever left me because my baby got it all. But Shipell refuse to accept that love is me and him.

We both slipped up and met The One. What's wrong with that? And that's the tender spot my man won't touch.

So it's the last night of the year and I wasn't gon celebrate with Shipell. But who was staying home? Who? I'm too Fly not to cause upset. Bad rags and big stones. Face frame and attitude. No question. My message straight up fly finessence. Splendacious and untouchable. Sho you right.

Had to flash. Wore cash. I put on amazing shit. Ehhthang custom. Dressed to catwalk past Big Girls trying to be unique like myself. Black mink mini mini. Matching short mink jacket tight in the waist zipped down low. Diamond hanging off the end of the zipper.

My ice was a light show. Dig. Dangling at the top of my titties on a thick gold link seven dazzlers hugged all around they big rock mama. Had twin monster teardrop sparklers in my ears. Bezel headlight frightening spitting lightning sitting like Buddah in heavy 24k on my long right finger. Couldn't hardly lift my left hand because of the starburst boulder on my pinky. Ice gleaming both of my wrists. I was froze and dripping.

What. Nails sixty. Black baby gator stiletto boots twelvefifty. Thigh high lacetop stockings from France cost forty. They more sexy than pantihose. My makeup so natural it look like none except for my shiny juicy Sade red lips.

And no bag. Left my blond floorsweeper in the closet. Wasn't gon be outside but a minute so wasn't no sense in getting my butter mink smoked up in a club. I didn't wear no panties no blouse no bra. Didn't feel like it. Wasn't nobody unless it's Shipell getting up under my clothes.

Girl name Jaszia over at Hair Enchantment did my hair. Wimmen always stop me in the street axe who do my weave. But my shit is real because I got East Indian blood from my Jamaican side. I told Jaszia I wanted to run my hands through it all night. Irratate all them hard fried jelled up weave witches. Frengirl hooked me up. Left out of Jaszia chair with big loose sexy curls falling all over my head thick down my back.

I quit my house early. This wasn't the night to enter late. Walked out my building about tentwunny. Stood tiptoe and hid my keys on the ledge on top of the front door.

Luck was mine. Cab turning the corner stopped on a dime when he saw me coming down the stoop. I got in and muhfucka tried to rap "Baby you solo?" He heard "Shut the fuck up and drive. You ain't got no money." I was madder than a fuck!

Took me to Paradisio in Manhatten because that's where Shipell said he was going and where I better not be. O? I considered that my personal invite. Baby was gon see me and I was gon see who. Exscuse me. What he was with.

I was so pissed I didn't count the money I snatched up off my nighttable. Tucked what I guess was close to five bucks in hunnits and fifties between my titties. I like to carry cash close to my heart. Tossed cabbie a fifty when I got out and told him to keep it. I was gon spend Shipell fucking cash.

It was close to eleven when I got to the spot. Igged the line to get in because T Rex was on the door glad to see me. Acted surprised it was just me. Axed for Shipell. Smile different his eyes changed when I said I'm alone. But whatever that bulldog was thinking was truly just his heavenly fantasy.

Paradisio was live. So much ice in there Paradisio was blizzid like Alaska. Playas and they dates out to celebrate. Ehhbody out early because this was the first stop. Dj deep in the pocket. It was packed.

Parted the crowd with my presence like I planned. Bitch or five turned from they convasations to show me they faces and axe "Where Love? Where Daddy?"

Got close to one and imitated Shipell phrasing so she know

who she talking to. "Relax sugar. Daddy coming. Enjoy yourself." Tapped my palm light against her cheek before she could react.

Folks heads jerked around watching that tramp reaching out realizing too late that I had put my hand in her face. Bum was spraying spit cussing loud "Get off me! Bitch I fuck you up!" but the crowd had already closed behind me by then.

Got the seat I wanted at the bar by standing behind it. Man got right up smiling like a goon in my face. Then at the back of my head. I was heated. Throw a match on me and I would have blew up. Whuuut the Fuck am I doing alone on New Year's sitting at this gotdamn bar?

Shipell had already told me that New Year's Eve was his favorite holiday and he never spends it by hisself. This was suppose to be our first New Year's together.

I started swallowing champagne for real. Wouldn't recanize anybody wouldn't let nobody talk to me and I don't really dance.

Admit I was waiting on that bastard and just might fight any Miss Unlucky I catch him with. New Year's Eve ain't a night for finance. If he comes in with a woman she his date and Rakim gon kick that bitch ass!

Elevenfifteen here come my spotlight. I knew he was gon be out early. Didn't see him come in but knew the minue he set foot inside the club because I heard people saying his name. Then I saw him coming my way.

Baby killing me in a quietcut black raw silk tuc. Black silk shirt and tie. Knew without looking that he had fabalus reptiles on his feet. Looked like a artist drew his hair. His face like baby skin and those laser eyes.

Black mink floorsweeper sitting on his shoulders. Diamonds headlight diamonds. Shipell flexed so much ice he should have been freezing. My baby was the North Pole. And King Tut gold.

But. See. Shipell tried to Game me.

He let some short fat weaved up fake redhead bitch walk beside him. He a comedian. Shipell come with BoBo the clown. Sloppy hips straining some cheap ass short gold sequence mini. Sleeves all boofed up. Gold fringe around the hem. Nerve to have on a matching sequence cowboy hat. Gold pleather pumps with laces tied crisscross up to her chubby knees. A monkey did her makeup.

Her jewlry was pitiful. Looked like pieces of thread and glitter around her neck. Glass in her ears and on her thick fingers. Do it yourself nails from the beauty supply. Skimpy jacket over her arm could have been a cheap white fox or a bathmat. Grinning at my man like he her dentist. Looking around like a tourist. I was furious.

How he bring a skank someplace he truly know I'ma be? Like he putting me down in front of evrybody. Embarrassing me in front of these bitches. O baby. I was froggy but my profile wouldn't let me jump.

Crowded and flashy as Paradisio was Shipell saw me in a movement because I made sure. Glanced his way flashed him with my wrist. Baby recanize his jewlry.

But cold playa passed me by. Knew he was sitting that dishrag at a table way in the back. Waving over a waitress. Knew he was saying "Give the lady whatever she wants."

My mind saw him leaning down into the ear of that cow telling her to enjoy herself "Order whatever you want babydoll." He'd be back in a moment. There was a few people at the bar he wanted to greet.

I know he said it proper. Shipell can talk like a teacher when he wants to. He say that's because he Is a teacher. "I'm a genius sweetheart. I can explain evrything you need to know."

And I know Miss Goldie didn't know that she was out with such a magnificent educator. She wide eyed and tripping. Shipell steady schooling. Getting her eager to graduate.

She don't know that the graduation ceremony is the first secretary paycheck she cash into his soft palm. Like it's her good idea.

If she ain't careful Shipell will take her into higher learning. Let her get her masters. Polish those stars in her eyes. Build air castles. Talk plans about their future together. Having something. Convince her to contribute her weekly paycheck as proof of her commitment to their tomorrow. Because it's the right keep it coming thing to do. And it's also best to let her man handle the money. Put it together with his. He gon give her what she need.

Then if he feel she qualify for her phd? That's when he gon put her on lock with the soul sex. That deep pocket nasty stroke he never gave her before. Po thang. Cause Shipell was born balling. When he cover her head to heel under his muscles and the only thing moving is his magic hips? She done. And when he show her how to enjoy herself kneeling between his thighs worshipping his? It's over. She lost. Because when she come back to herself girlfren truly be reborn.

Be a brand new dame ready to quit her chump change job. Be eager to appreciate the logic behind the science of having money dates. Ready to get frenly with strangers. Fully understand the intellect behind Shipell's wisdom. Itching to get on the track.

Soon Goldie be the one insisting that Shipell let her go out and handle her bizness. Sell her seduction for the honor of handing her man the loot for some more of his goody pole.

Agree that neither one of them should be free.

Okay. So my baby boss like that. Get money whenever money to be got. Big Girl like me can understand. Money comes first. He got the rest of the night to be with me. That's why he came out early. Get bizness out the way.

I'm thinking different now. Looked past what I could see. Mad got glad. Shipell financing. And some of that cream I'ma lick. Baby securing my rent allowance shopping hair and nails restarants taking cabs on the regular like I'm used to. Logic. She's a donation.

If Miss Woman had been a winner like me I would have worried. Might have meant going Olympic with my Game if she was a Big Girl trying to share my riches. Not this low rent broad.

Now I'm straight. The music started sounding better. I recanize and greet some people I know. Shake curls off my face. Used my sparkling left hand to rearrange my mane. Stretched my body slow for those who missed it. Let my ice zap and cool off the bar.

This is Rakim. Shipell's bottom. I'm the fly testamony to how very well my baby does his thing. I got happy about that pooch. She was resource. She gon buy me those purple suede kicks I saw on Madison.

Also something else this fool didn't know. Her New Year's was all fucked up because the second I saw Shipell he was with me. He knew it too. Goldie would just have to make up a story for the girls at work.

And I know my man. He still gon keep her even after Goldie realize that Shipell is New Year's Eve gone and she all by her New Year's Eve self. Even though she gon be mad as hell she gon stay.

Shipell gon get with her and feed her some pure bullshit that she gon swallow after she pout for a while. Whatever he tell her she gon go for. And understand. She better. We need the money.

Watched Shipell take his time prowling to me. Popular playa. Got to talk while he walk. Buy drinks for his partnas and they ladies. I turned back to facing the bar nonchalant.

Shipell come ease hisself up against my back couldn't pass through a piece of paper. His beautiful hands on the bar his mink arms caging me in. He smelling the rose oil in my hair.

Elevenfiftynine Shipell said quiet in my ear to kiss his muh-fuckin ass. He told me not to show up here. Said "That better be my money" between my tittys. It was. But not the way he meant it. So I act like Shipell talking to hisself in another language.

The stroke of midnight he reached in my titties and threw my money on the bar and told the bartender to "split this tip." Snatched me around his eyes mean mouth not smiling. Slapped my face light it didn't hurt and said he accept my apology. Ehhbody else in the club shouting and kissing.

Evrybody probably except Miss Goldie. She probably stretching her neck nervous tapping her tips on the table scanning for my man. I hope she had money to pay for her check.

A minute past twelve Shipell took me out of Paradisio strong arm pulling me down the street to the Benz and shoved me in. Both of us riding silent because when I said "Happy New Year" Shipell said "Shut up." I'm so hot to sha sha and he knew it.

Took us to The Marquis. He had the same suite he said he get evry New Year's.

Soon as we on the other side of the door I didn't have time to look around the livingroom good. Shipell walking me backwards to the bedroom. Stripping me. In the few seconds it took for the back of my legs to touch the bed I was nekked.

He just unzipped the jacket unzipped the skirt and I was standing lushcious in boots ice and thigh highs. Shipell said Shit and took off his clothes fast. Pushed me back on the bed and yanked off my boots. Ripped my thigh highs down to ankle socks. Tore them off my feet. No prelim. Shipell just wanted to ride. Acting like he so mad. Why? Wasn't we both where we wanted to be?

Baby hesitated putting it in just long enough to say nasty words about breaking me off. It's my bizness exactly what he made me say and I whispered what he told me to.

But when jockey hit the gate I showed Shipell how it really do.

I got a honeydip fit. Rakim rose got a pout so ready. The slide Shipell got was stupefying. Baby hit bottom and froze couldn't move or you know what would have happened.

Then I got up under it for real and started showing him the way to shangra la. Right before Shipell jaws turned to stone and his breathing changed he stopped my hips.

I looked right into Shipell eyes and axed my spotlight if I was gon have to do this by myself.

But you can't stop a stepper and I don't want no man I can whip. Shipell cold smile and took away my prize. Wouldn't give it back even after I beg pretty please. Finally showed me the eyes his wimmen see and the curl of his lips when he's not with me. Dog put his thickness in his hand and slow rubbed that joint all around what I wanted him to fill. Baby made me tremble.

Baby raised up on his knees and faced me. Made me get up on my knees too. Pushed me back to sit my ass on my thighs. My face was right in line with his thick. Shipell told me about my pretty mouth and filled it up. I'ma just say I couldn't talk around it. Mmm.

I put my palms on his hips and made sure my nursing lips didn't empty his bottle because we both wanted my lushcious to suck it too.

Shipell flat me on my back. Used his baby maker like a tongue to tease me again. This was his show now. And when I was quaking deep and high on the thrill of Shipell he slipped it home. Went so deep. Laid still soaking and swelling. Seemed like it took him a hour to pull up and put it back down.

He went to work. Baby got a stroke that belongs just to him. Rearranged my petals. Gave us a sweeter fit. Smoothed my velvet in different directions. Wasn't through neither.

Baby had me drunk like likka and ehhthang allowed. Shipell made it my excellent idea to worship his love one more time. Before his altar I praised him from foundation to the steeple because when it comes to Shipell my mouth was devout. Took his offering just like that and baby shuddered hisself right to sleep.

Before I cut out the light I took a look around. It was a beautiful room. I noticed the fan of hunnits on top of the dresser. I knew it was mine because baby always spread my money out like that.

Shipell woke up after me on the first day of the new year saying "Good morning sweetheart Daddy hungry." He walked past me into the bathroom. I picked up the phone and ordered two deluxe pancake breakfasts with extra sausage coffee two fruit cups and a pitcher of orange.

I went and got in the shower with Shipell. Baby was smothered in lather. Soon as I got wet he laced his fingers behind my head guiding it down. Made me kneel. Crazy brazen playa. Knew I would shout happy when I spotted the diamond and ruby plat bracelet hanging around the base of his vertical.

Shipell leaned back against the shower wall and told me I knew how to get it. I sho did.

Had Shipell pulling my head deeper by my wet hair. Swearing I ain't never gon leave him....

Later when we eating he won't speak to me and won't answer me. Didn't rest his eyes on me one time. While we dressing Shipell still acting funky don't open his mouth.

After we got downstairs and he left the room key Shipell walked through the lobby like he was by hisself. I caught up to him outside on the street and axed again what's wrong.

He started up again with "That west indian shit I must be

working" on him.

Now I'm the one not talking. Looking at him neutral. My candles baths prayers and consultations ain't Shipell bizness. Just kept admiring my new jewls sparkling on my wrists feeling the money snug between my breasts and was quiet.

On the drive to my house Shipell was glaring at me instead of looking at the traffic. Driving like he wanted to get rid of me quick. I understood. Mr. Love needed to regroup. He probably regret giving me plat.

But this is Shipell and Rakim. This is The Fit. This is the first time Shipell feeling somebody in his heart except his mama.

He didn't say a word until we got in front of my building. Kept his eyes straight ahead when I got out. Shipell said he would check me in two weeks. Pulled off before I could say anything to change that plan.

But that was still the best New Year's in my life.

Can't tell me Shipell don't love me. Can't tell me.

Use Your Keys

Baby please
On my knees
With the phone
The dial tone...

All alone
Why you roam?
Come on home

Why you be
Cruel to me?
Loving you
Hard to do
Always blue
Crying too...

Wish I knew
What to do
I'll be you

Tell me to

It's a crime
You so fine
Just divine

You want pay?
That's okay
Like they say
Stick and stay
Got your name
On my game

You so cold
Brazen bold
Brutal hold
On my soul
No control...

I would lie
Alibi
Would if I
Had to die
You so fly

Still your slave
In my grave

Don't know why
You won't try
Understand
You my man

Cheating on Shipell

I only cheated on Shipell with one man and it wasn't supposed to turn into nothing.

Fly frengirl of mine name CeeCee was rolling with this true playa name Bigman whose main man didn't have no lady.

He was fresh from lockdown but playa hadn't let that static stop his paper. So he wasn't checking for no ordinary woman. CeeCee said king wanted a unique queen. Wasn't trying to get with no whole lot of wimmen neither. So frengirl recalled my name.

Only reason I even entertained her convasation is because Shipell was on his pull back routine. Like he does evry so often. But this is the first time it's been this long. Since New Year's I haven't heard from him ain't seen Shipell in weeks and weeks.

Paged Shipell until I was sick of doing it. He either got a new number or I been cancelled or replaced. Or he was in prison.

I didn't want to go out but I didn't want to stay home. I didn't want no man except Shipell. But I wasn't about to keep being the solo provider of my rent and maintenance neither.

I didn't know what to do. I was twisted. I needed fresh funds. But I couldn't afford to be in nothing with nobody when Shipell came back. But I couldn't afford to be alone too much longer. I had to quit this crazy cycle taking me nowhere.

I had to do something else except be confused.

So about three weeks after New Year's my pride broke. Started looking for my baby. Went where I thought he would be. Couldn't see him. Week after week I went to a lot of spots more than once.

His associates smile say "Hey beautiful" and claim they hadn't seen him or he just left.

Muhfuckas looking right in my face lying about Shipell but telling the truth about wanting me to stay for a drink. Got sick of that shit. So after close to three months of steady looking and paying my own bills I was open. Spring was coming. April just around the corner. Time for a new beginning.

Definitely ready for new finance and a different taste in my mouth.

Called and asked CeeCee if that man she told me about was still looking. She said he was. He had been spending time with some chicks but Bigman told her that homeboy hadn't found the one that made him satisfied. She repeated that he was looking for a special woman beause he was ready to claim.

Worked out something with CeeCee to meet this man. And when we met we clicked. Name Teddy. Street call him Supreme. A big surprise that a brother so damn fine with a bossballer rep ain't got wimmen pregnant and praying. Losing they minds. Crying. Cussing cutting each other over him.

Better yet Supreme truly looking to hook up? With one? Right. Not long out of prison and he ready for just one pocket? Huh. You know I went in skeptical. Especially since CeeCee tipped me that Supreme was Mr. Dough Almighty.

And on top of that he was Fine. A face like a icy Eddie Murphy. Smooth deep brown skin and dimples. Sexy deep brown eyes and real long eyelashes. Pretty silky thick eyebrows. Black wavy cesar no chemical. Teddy was tall like sixtwo. Hard. Built like he worked out while he was caged up. Body tight and bulge right but he wasn't a muscleman.

Made me feel all woman. And glad I'm soft.

Teddy dressed like a obsession. Top labels and custom tailor. Walked in reptiles. Jewlry heavy. Midas plat and iceberg. Once I saw how hard he styled I knew that I was gon have to let him peep that he ain't the only one who can stop a show. I'm just what he looking to pay for.

Supreme knew what to do. After we small talk he invited me to join him for dinner the next evening. Our first date was great. In a quiet high class restaurant on the upper east side. Started to know one another. Put fact to what we thought about each other during our first impression.

End with me accepting a nice piece of money. We had a understanding. Nothing exchanged but cash but Big Girl did wear rags with my skin out so playa could feast his eyes on his new habit. Digits came right on time too.

Since Shipell been ghost I been using my reserves. Paid my own rent for the last three months. Glad it wasn't my money paying the next. I hated touching my stacks.

Me and Supreme really started going out. Went from three times the first week to almost evry night from then on. Playa hooked me good when he said there was no rush between us. Winked at me and said "Why don't we have a ball before we ball baby."

What that meant to me is that he got some side bitch to freak his ass while he getting next to me. I didn't give a fuck cause that dumb bitch don't count. Supreme at her apartment sticking evry hole she got for a two hunnit dollar pair of earrings. Hit it then zip up. Throw her a few pieces of paper evry once in a while.

Supreme took me to the movies and all the clubs. The zoo one afternoon. Bars his frens apartments. Got white frens too. Introduced me as his woman. Squeeze me to him and say "This mine." Plays concerts. Yankees night game. Opera one night but we didn't like it. Sound like a bunch of folks screaming. Sip all the best champagne. Dom Tatt Cristal and my middle name.

We ate different shit like deer steak in fabalus places. If I felt like it I ordered something just to taste it then ordered something else if I didn't like it. No matter how expensive the spot was. Supreme didn't care.

Crawled up in private afterhour holes full of notorious muhfuckas. Supreme don't leave my side. We left a spot one night not five minutes before some fools busted in and shot it up. Teddy told me later three people died.

He knew how to treat a woman like me. Teddy never parked nowhere but in front. Said fuck a ticket. He got people to handle that shit. FiveO know not to tow. Know his plates. So my feet only touched the sidewalk from the Benz door to the front door of wherever we going.

Teddy sexy sexy. Sweettalker in my ear. Complimented the prime that is Miss Divine. Raise my chin on the tip of one of his long pretty fingers and kiss me on my nose. Didn't matter where we was. He act like there ain't no other wimmen in the spot. Hug me up tight in his chest putting little kisses on my forehead and my lips. Call me Supreme pretty baby.

Always slipping cute money in my hand. Big Girl paid my next month rent in advance. Already upgrading my jewlry. A huge sapphire in plat ring. A rose gold and ruby bracelet. Took us shopping on Madison. Lex. Fifth. Madison. Fiftyseventh. Fulton. Down in the East Village where he had a good time paying because I didn't know nothing about the stores down there. Teddy couldn't care less how many kicks and rags I snag. He let me go off.

Ehhwhere we go wimmen roll they eyes or stare at me. Prance around like foolish ponies in front of Supreme if they with a man or not. They all want to kick my worthy ass cause it ain't luck that catch a playa like Teddy. I got skills. Used to being the star in jealous drama from being with Shipell. So a encore with Supreme wasn't nothing.

There was a few reasons why I figure I didn't run into Shipell. One is because him and Supreme control different kinds of independent bizness. One do a little something and the other do a little something else. Circles not the same but they both major in the Game. Both in the bullseye.

So I know they know each other. Know each other names and reputations. Greet when they meet in the street. Stand at the same bars. Got partnas in common. That mean Shipell got to know who I'm dating even if he in prison. Wherever he is he know.

I couldn't worry about it though. Shipell making it his bizness to stay out of my sight. Anyway he ain't check me in so long I must have been set free.

Another reason is maybe he left town. Rakim can understand about needing to do that too. But not if it means he left me behind.

And if he fucking with another broad it's a fling. Shit. Champion gon get tired of riding second best. If it's a bitch keeping him from me? I know I'ma walk all over her face if I ever see that ho. Tap that bitch for taking Shipell attention.

Bitch fucking with my money. Bitch might be trying to crawl

up under me for the bottom.

I didn't have too much time for my thoughts to be lonely or empty cause me and Teddy was having a blast. And it was hot. Hot hot. Anticipation between us was blazing and we enjoyed those feelings. This ain't a man Big Girl had to lay right away. But we did do ehhthang else. What.

Me and Teddy played a teasing game and we dug it. Usually on our way back from someplace. We park somewhere deserted and almost dark. We liked a little bit of streetlight because we like to see us being wicked in shadows. Supreme put the radio on slow jams. We get comfy in the big back seat. Then we sizzle.

Poppa stop sucking my tongue stop his lips grinding my lips to whisper he don't want me. Got slow deep fingers smoothing in and out of my. Thumb teasing my pearl.

I answer I'm glad cause I don't want you neither while I'm massaging his. So big and hard my hand hardly close around it. I lick my palm to make it slide better up and down black iron.

Teddy fingers explode me. Got me arching my back and wiggling. I enjoy watching Teddy put his sticky fingers in his mouth. Pull them out slow and clean. Taste his lips after each one like they covered with delicious. My gliding hand working stronger and faster on his release.

Soon Teddy groaning. His hands gripping the hair on the back of my head because he dig looking at me when I put my face in the way to catch his finish. We got wide open for each other. I let Supreme know I ain't a dame who shame.

After we been flowing steady about five weeks he let me know what was up. One night in front of my place Teddy cup my chin in his hand say "Tomorrow night. We in the bed Miss Divine." What. About time. I was more ready than he was.

So the next night Teddy took me to this real nice hotel near Kennedy airport. A grooving joint. Parking lot full. Couples going in and out wrapped around each other.

Told me to get a table in the bar while he get our room. Bar so crowded it was private. When Teddy got back he sat down beside me and we started drinking. We had I don't know how many double Remys between nasty convasation. Bold boasting promises hot words. Felt my likka. Loose. Toh up. In fact I lost control.

Let Supreme foreplay me under the table. Positive some folks knew he was giving me mine. Probably wished they had the public nerve. His fingers felt so good I would have put my heels up on my seat if the table wasn't in my way.

Supreme took my drunk ass out of there. Next thing I remember is getting deep tongue and grinding slow against the elavator wall. One a my titties out of my top inside his big squeezing palm.

Supreme drunk out of his mind too because he unzip his pants and free his. Rock and huge. Beautiful. We like the way that log pressing between us feel.

We also wasn't alone. I can damn near recall three four folks riding up with us. Looking like they can't believe what they seeing. Fuck them. I start pulling my skirt up my leg to be ready if he want to slip it in. But right then baby pull me out at our floor.

Suite number floor I don't know. I was too busy rubbing ehhthang I got all over his back feeling him up while he opened the door. Wrestled off each other's clothes soon as it closed behind us.

Too flaming to make it past the bathroom right next to the door. We Had to get us some. Supreme sat me on the edge a the sink in the half dark. I'ma say this. Poppa knew how to set it. Slid homeboy in like it live there. Rocking ride thighs wide I got drunk a whole different way.

The way I was sitting let me look down at what he was steady putting to me. Evry single slip hit tip to base. Supreme was checking out this porno scene too. Licking his lips. Stroking.

Still deep Supreme locked his arm around my back. Put the other one under my ass to lift me up off the sink. We chest to chest. My thighs hugging his waist. We looking at each other. I lean back to offer him a titty and he lick my face like a puppy. He started walking us to the bed. He had to stop every step to get me deep.

We was sweating. Supreme deep voice said "Damn! Baby damn! Let Daddy put it down sweet." I don't know why he even axed. Both of his hands was already full of my ass pulling me deeper on him. My heels bouncing against the back of his steel thighs and I'm lapping body likka off his neck.

Teddy said "Shhhit" trying to put us on the carpet. I put my palms on his chest shaking my head no. "Uh uh. Uh uh. Not on the floor. Take me to bed baby."

Tongue down each other throats Supreme stayed deep pocket while he carried me quick to slam us down on the king-size. I was on the bottom. My ankles crossed over the small of his back my heels resting on Supreme ass. He took me long and strong.

We was greedy because getting it had got so good.

I was so drunk on likka and his deep loving I said exactly what I was feeling. "Uh huh... Mmm hmm...Take it like you know me digger... Uh huh. Come on...longstroke Daddy... yeeeaaah... thaaat's it baby... looongstroke..." Voice low and needy.

Supreme growl "Uh uh. Nah. Not yet sugar...Calm down." He pulled out so slow I felt like screaming. But I did what he said and stopped acting like a trick. Like I never had a real pole touch my soul before.

Supreme straightened his muscle arms like trees on each side of me. Told me to look at it. Said "Rakim. Look at what you want."

I lowered my chin and saw a bat kissing his navel. Muscles flexing in his hard stomach. He saw my greedy Big Girl eyes.

Supreme challenge me "What baby. Come get up under Daddy for real. Show Daddy what you brought with you baby."

I told my answer when my hand gripped his concrete and dipped just the tip inside my. Just far enough for Supreme to feel my velvet trying to pull it in. Kept teasing like that while I winked at Daddy and warned him about the slide.

Supreme chuckle "You must be joking. Gimme my shit." He took it out of my hand. "You ain't whipping shit tonight baby but I'ma beat that ass jazzy like you like it."

Then Supreme turned me completely out. Used his fingers like I'm a piano and set my nerves on fire. Licked me with his tongue like a calf until I'm ready to climb something. Beg Supreme to tear me up. Trembling like a junkie. Pleading to get stuck with that fat needle.

Supreme slipped me my fix so smooth Rakim had to grunt.

O. Supreme made me ugly. He changed Shipell fit. Positioned us like acrobats.

My rose bloomed so much I made Supreme lick my lips because my throat was a hoarse desert from inventing new words out loud.

And this Big Girl likes to be fair. Lover had to get a workover too. So I switched my rhythm and broke his stroke. Kept Supreme pushed in deep when he wanted to pull up. His face changed from doing me to getting done.

My lushcious was so flamboyant Mr. Piston got nasty. Put more left and right in his up and down. I tightened my rose back to virgin. Teddy swelled to maximum. Hurt me good. I'm full up...Yeeeah there he go....

Then we was laying up. Calm and not drunk no more. Teddy getting personal. He ready to have One. I'm wrapped up in his muscles his hands stroking my hair happy it ain't a weave. Axed if I think about him like that.

I said "Like what?" Supreme said being with him. Straight up. Spending time in his crib. Him in my place. He ready to stop looking.

Supreme a smart man. About to conclude a plan gon give him the connections and the clean bank to legitimize. Get a house. "You want a big pretty house baby?" Open something. "Buy a cleaners and a few liquor stores and shit. Start a muh-fuckin family."

Talk about we would have fine kids. Call them "pretty ass babies with a lot of pretty hair." Said he wants two of each. He sound serious when he say he want to name his first boy Malcolm Jihad after Malcolm X. His first daughter gon be Billie Habiba after Billie Holiday. He spelled they middle names and taught me Jihad mean war and Habiba mean beloved in arabic. Teddy said I can name the other two.

I told him I like Wallaby for a boy and Teawanda for a girl. He laugh shake his head and called them "some fucked up names." I was laughing too because I had made them up on the spot.

Teddy four years older than me. He twunnyseven and had made it this far without no kids calling him daddy. He said "I made a few though." But talked the wimmen into the clinic. Blew they minds with Game lines. Cussed them and told them shit like they must be tricking because he couldn't make no babies. Lies.

"You got babies baby?" He pulled my head back to kiss my throat when I said no. "You want my babies baby?" I opened my lips to invite his tongue inside.

Supreme slid his hand between Rakim thighs and felt my nectar pooling up again. Said "Damn...baby, damn." Supreme got a bone just that quick. And we sho wasn't drunk now.

That prove me and Teddy got that kind of hot we got to watch. Or else we be going at it in the street. I'm saying. We got that incredible fit and we got to be careful that we ain't Got to get it. Get caught fucking in corners in stores and in restarant bathrooms and shit.

But below my instant flame my mind was whirling.

O Teddy got money. Like he plant it. And young. Fine as hell. A master with a master plan. Looking way past what he could see. Shipell ain't got nothing on Supreme and I think Shipell thirtyone.

In one way they both the same. Handle money. Both got deadly rhythm. Dress they asses off. Cold blooded and sharp minded. Live for the Game. Don't take no shit. Work they bizness. Love the finest things in life. Get up between select thighs and ruin a woman right.

They also dead opposite. Teddy want me in his apartment. Got three numbers including home to reach him. Calls me to let me know where he's at. Thinks of interesting things for us to do. With me as much as he can.

I don't know where Shipell live except somewhere in Brooklyn. Never had no number but his cell. I never know where he at unless he's with me. And we mostly in my place except when he want to flash. Shipell like to disappear.

Plus Shipell don't like affection don't like to kiss. Teddy do. Love to suck my tongue.

But Teddy wasn't my spotlight.

What is wrong with me? Here I am living the Big Girl dream. Winner crossing the finish line. Got a world class playa sitting at my feet. Falling in love wih me and want to show it. Don't care who know it. And my dumb ass trying to renig. Fighting what I'm starting to feel.

And why? Because that mindbending muhfucka who dropped my ass months ago just might come back. Yes. My crazy ass still want to get back. This love shit fucking me up.

I wasn't in love with Teddy but I appreciated more and more a brother who knows how to get with a Big Girl straight up. He's a unique man and we really get along. I like what he showing.

So our first night in bed I was ready when Supreme rolled over one more time. He put Shipell out of my mind. Supreme had so much soul and used it so deep. Supreme. That's right. Ain't no question how he got that name.

For our two month anniversary he took me gambling in Atlannic City. Rode down to celebrate with CeeCee and Bigman in Teddy Benz.

Had a boss trip. Playing custom mix music. Convasating. Laughing at all kinds of shit. Sipping my middle name in crystal stems. Had a big box of fried chicken and rolls. Sometimes Supreme and Bigman tune us out and talk bizness between theyselfs.

That's when me and CeeCee convasate about clothes jewls furs and kicks we gon get. Dream up the flyest outfits in the world. We look at each other and crack up because we know whose money we spending. We dog other wimmen we know.

Once we got there it was easy to see playas meant to impress. Got a spectacular suite with a big living room and a bar between two gorjus layed out bedrooms. Supreme had even made reservations at the best restaurant in the hotel. So we chilled until it was time to change and go downstairs.

We was so sharp iced so hard white folks stopped eating when we came in. Black folks looked like they wanted to clap. Me and CeeCee had teriyaki shrimp. Bigman had a steak and Supreme got salmon in this white sauce. It looked delicious. I tasted it because I think I can copy it. We was so full when we went to the casino.

I lost a lot of Supreme's money playing 21. But he was

laughing pulling me close axing if I'm having a good time. When Teddy started gambling my luck changed. Evry time I kiss his cards it guarantee he win. People gathered around us to watch Supreme poker skill and my ruby lips beat the odds. Nonchalant he won so much money.

Bigman didn't win shit all night. In fact he had to borrow from Supreme to keep betting. So all the time we was in the casino CeeCee had a attitude with me. I got close to telling her to kiss my ass but our men is frens and she wasn't gon ruin my evening.

Later up in our room Teddy gave me three thousand and diamond hoops. I thanked my new man by letting Supreme lock me in the kind of sex that can't be described. He signed his name inside. I know other rooms must have called the front desk to complain about the noise.

Even CeeCee had Bigman knock on our door and axe if we was gon fuck all night. CeeCee called out "Stuff something in her fucking mouth Supreme!" CeeCee a bitch. Some muhfuckas ain't got no class and can't afford to buy none.

O. I'm gon speak to that witch before we start on the ride home. Her and Bigman might be taking the muhfuckin Greyhound back to Brooklyn because Supreme didn't like that shit neither. But he put his hand over my mouth when he saw me open it to answer them rude jealous imposters.

We heard Bigman go back in they room and but he didn't close the door. Supreme said "Come on baby. Muhfuckas want to hear us" so he got up and opened ours. Then we turned it out triple x. He called to Bigman "Playa! Send your woman over here if she jealous." Like its a joke he really meant.

Supreme put them muhfuckas in check. I dug that shit.

In the morning Bigman and Supreme talk and ehhthang cool. Bigman must have told CeeCee to make up with me because she apologized.

Admitted to me on the low that she was just mad because Bigman lost all his money trying to impress me and Supreme. He didn't give her nothng neither. Nothing. Not even no sex. Told her he was too pissed off. She looked hard at the new diamond hoops in my ears then gazed at me all sorry eyed.

I looked away patted her shoulder and said "Better get your Game in check girrrl" and walked over to where Supreme was standing. I don't give no bitch money and don't forgive all that easy.

I'ma tell the truth. This trip made my spotlight dim a little. I loves me a strong man like Supreme.

The ride back home was funny. Teddy had me sit in the front next to him.

CeeCee was in the back with Bigman but she was bunched up close as she could to her door. Looking out the window all puffed up like a balloon. Mad. Bigman looked over at her and told her "Fix! your fucking face!" and yanked her over next to him.

He started feeling her up like they was alone. She pushing his hands away but didn't mean it. Supreme tapped my thigh for me to look in the rearview. They laying down humping. He got her titty out sucking nipple. We hear Bigman zipper.

Supreme slowed the Benz looked over his shoulder said "Yo!...Yo! Hold up! What you doing man? You can't lay your piece in my car and in front of my woman man!" He laughing.

CeeCee and Bigman sat up. Bigman laughing too gave Teddy dap. "Yo. I ain't ball shit last night man!" He worked one hand up between CeeCee thighs. His other hand brought her other titty out her top. Her head was down but I know she can feel me looking at her through the rearview.

Bigman said to Supreme "Now playa you not gon object to me feeling on my bitch. This mine."

Bigman looked at her titties and grabbed them. Had them in his palms like he weighing them. He started rolling them hard against her chest. Said to CeeCee "Sss...that wouldn't be right, aint that right baby?" Her head still low but I know she grinning. And hot.

Supreme sped up and just shook his head winked at me.

Me and Supreme talked about different things acting like we couldn't hear CeeCee low moans appreciating where Bigman fingers was buried and working deep. We acted like we couldn't tell when her sounds changed to sucking because the ho was bent over deep throat.

That's when I knew why she don't get money. Her ass too

easy. Like to get open too much. Who like sex more than me? But I'm saying. I really saw that bitch. CeeCee a stupid ho who flow with high rollers but don't practice Game. Fucking it up for superstars like myself.

Because a muhfucka not giving shit don't get shit. Especially in public. Bitch sucking pipe in the back seat. For free. Beause she sho did tell me that he didn't give her nothing.

Also made note to myself to keep my eye peeled on that loose piece.

She had no problem at all showing my man her big tities. Was ready to show him how deep her pocket is too if Supreme didn't stop Bigman from fucking her. But that bitch sho let my Daddy know about her long throat. I saw Supreme glancing in the rearview when she was swallowing Big Man.

Yeah. I put a mark on Miss CeeCee the free ho.

After we dropped them off midtown on Broadway in the city Supreme didn't take me to Brooklyn. Without saying a word took me to his apartment for the first time.

Baby. His place belong in a magazine. He got a duplex on West Eightythird. Off Columbus Avenue. Real clean and not cluttery. Like I like.

First thing you have to do is take off your shoes and leave them in the hallway before Teddy will let you in. The door opens on a short hallway to the big livingroom. Ehhthang black white and gold. The thick ass carpet was pure white. Two long white leather couches and a white suede recliner. They all full of fur pillows. I know fur. I saw black mink white mink brown mink grey chinchilla cocoa sable silver fox blue fox.

Coffee table was a long clear glass box with real fish inside. The pretty kind with long floaty tails like silk. I can't even describe his music system and tv and shit. Evrything black and the latest latest sitting inside this fly black wall unit that took up one whole wall. African masks and doodads on show on the shelfs too.

The only colors in the room was in the paintings on the white walls. Not people or nature or houses just shapes. Supreme said they by this new black artist who was getting large. Supreme told me his name but I don't remember.

Lights tracking the ceiling spotlighting different things.

Black marble fireplace and mantlepiece holding a whole lot of pictures of him and other people in gold frames all different.

There was a clear bar in with one of evry kind of likka in the world on the step shelfs behind it. Clear barstools with white mink cushions.

Tiny kitchen off to one side. Just big enough for the stove refrigerator cabinets a counter and a sink. They all black and look brand new. White marble floor. Black walls. Crystal glasses hanging upside down in a rack in the celing like in a bar.

There was a small bathroom near the door. In the exact same place as the one in the hotel where he first slipped in me. Evrything except the mirror the snow white towels and toilet paper was black. Even the soap.

A white spiral staircase in the livingroom takes you up to his bedrooms. One of them is really his biggest closet. I poked my head in the door and it looked like a warehouse. So much in there I couldn't see nothing.

The big bathroom was up there too. All baby blue with gold accents. Separate stall shower beside a sunken bathtub with big healthy green plants all around it. Two sinks set in a wide counter with a huge movie star mirror on the wall behind it. Gold faucets. Floor to ceiling shelfs holding all kinds of top of the line bath and grooming stuff. Stacks of baby blue towels thick as blankets. Baby blue carpet so plush it hides your feet. Magazines stacked beside a fly toilet.

Where Supreme sleep is fabalus. Huge bedroom black and red. Dark red walls and ceiling. Black carpet. Told me the heavy kingsize was made out of black walnut wood. Had it custom made in Italy and it had to be brought into the apartment piece by piece and put together. It had all these carvings in it. I never saw a bed like it. A tall chest in the same wood was on one wall. Supreme called it a word that sounded like omwar. Of course the matching dresser and nighttables with custom lamps was elegant too.

On top of the dresser was evry cologne they make for men. And more pictures of him by hisself and with different wimmen. Some of them must have been family because there was one with him hugging a old woman and one with him and three little girls. A diamond watch and some money sat in a deep gold bowl.

Skinny trees in round gold pots crowded one corner. Three big windows with sheer dark red curtains. The matching drapes was tied open. Music system and tv built into the wall opposite the bed. Gorjus gold ceiling fan had black blades.

Me and Supreme got up in that big beautiful bed between them slippery black silk sheets and baby. What. Teddy told me I'm the first woman to christen it. So I did it justice. Supreme drained me.

I slept all the way back to Brooklyn. He had to kiss my forehead over and over to wake me up.

But for some reason after that time I wouldn't go back to his apartment unless he made me. I don't know why. Supreme stop axing after a while and just pulled up to his building whenever he wanted to. But we still slept mostly in the street. And he still don't know my bed. And Teddy didn't like it.

He bitched about it damn near evry time I make him get a room. I didn't really have to make him because Teddy got a sweet side that don't like to tell me no.

It's not the money that makes him not want to hotel. His manhood is the reason. "What fucking sense does this make? I'm paying rent on two apartments and sleeping in the street. Rakim? This is the last time " That's what he says all the time. But he keeps doing it because he got to do me.

Me and Supreme rolled into three months. And he still ain't been in my place. Kept making excuses. My place dirty which is always a lie. I want to go to his place. Which was a lie most of the time. I want to go out and show off all the new things he buy me. That ain't never a lie.

But I'm happy with him for real now and mean it.

I got to make up my mind to really forget Shipell because last night Supreme told me he was coming to my apartment. Because if he kept waiting for a invitation he about to be a trick. I been his for over two months so he was inviting hisself. He gon lay down eat and watch tv in my bed where he pay the rent. But never seen.

"This bullshit is over" is what Supreme said.

He never showered a woman like he does me and not see

how she live. Said he never showered a woman like he does me period. Supreme said that if I wasn't with him damn near evry day and night he would be very suspicious about why I keep him from coming inside my house. Might have some other muhfucka living in there.

"Another muhfucka living off my money? Then both y'all dead" he joke but his face look like murder.

So last night Teddy say he's expecting dinner at my house day after tomorrow. Alright. My decision is made. I'ma blow his mind because he don't even know I can cook. I'ma use some of his money to buy him a couple of robes and some slippers and shit.

And when I make him at home in my crib Muhfucka ain't gon want to leave. For real. His cradle is flyer than mine but my nest got me in it.

I'ma marinate some beef short ribs in plenty of chopped garlic onions olive oil winevinegar tyme and country pepper. Bake them slow until they falling off the bone. Thick gravy. Stew baby red potatoes with whole string beans and baby carrots. Plain lettuce and tomato salad and scratch butter biscuits. Cold lemonade. Make a butter pound cake to serve with vanilla ice cream.

Alright. I'ma cook for my Teddy. That's how I'ma think of him from now on. My Teddy. My new king. Alright.

I'ma get some boxes and put all of Shipell stuff in it. All the fabalus things I bought with love and his money.

Yes. I'ma have to keep dimming that spotlight still beaming my mind most nights after I close my eyes. Got to make that spotlight a flashlight and then make that glow a match light so I can blow it out.

I'ma try.

Last To Know

Look like you about to cry
Baby
Must have done you wrong
Baby
Must have sung a song
Must have sold a dream to you
Must have swore he loved you too

"Why Not Me?"

Tisha was called Hum because she didn't part her lips when she laughed.

She wasn't the type to add much to a conversation but she wasn't against passing on any good story she heard. Hum didn't care whether the information was true or if it would do any damage. Good dirt was good dirt and she felt in the center of the circle when she could carry a tale to her friends.

Hum knew a lot of women but didn't have a good friend. The women in her building came closest to that distinction.

Hum was the youngest of the 210 neighbors, twenty-three, and was in the second year of her first apartment. Her neighbors thought she was enterprising, able to wear such nice clothes and jewelry, party all the time with a good job and keep her own place by herself.

She never revealed to the girls that her mother and father, who lived in Newark, usually paid her rent. Last month they threatened their only child with eviction. If she didn't act more responsibly with her money, they were going to come get her and take her home to New Jersey. She made a good paycheck, so why was she always broke?

Tisha had shouted her outraged denials when they asked if she was messing with drugs.

They were tired of paying for her independence. They reminded Tisha of the reason she'd screamed in their faces for moving out a few months shy of twenty-one. They quoted her bone-deep "need to be on my own because I'm grown!"

Besides, it didn't make any sense for them to be paying a mortgage and the rent on her apartment too when she could move back home into the furnished basement apartment. There was a new bathroom down there with a stall shower. Big bedroom and living room. A washer, dryer and a separate entrance on the side of the house.

Her parents tried to convince her that they wouldn't bother her and it would save them a lot of money every month. And, her father added when his wife wasn't listening, if she came home he'd buy her a new car. No, not a BMW, was she crazy? But don't worry, pumpkin, something nice.

Hum had a good job, although she didn't work in accounting, the field she'd gotten her associate degree in. Hum did data entry for a large insurance company. She'd been there two years and made very good money. Working at night added an additional fifteen percent pay differential to her check. She did as much overtime as she could fit around her social life.

Layaways on label clothes, once a week at the nail salon, once a week at the hair salon and outlet designer shoes ate her money. Hum wore real gold, no carat under fourteen and real, but small, diamonds.

It seemed like the bills always came around so fast, she always thought she had more time to put money aside. Next thing you knew she was calling Newark, and hating it. But not enough to change her lifestyle and she was adept at tuning out her parents admonitions.

Her phone was on one-way right now and she was going to have to pay a deposit to the light company to keep the service. Every week she told herself that "next week" she would use her entire check to start catching up. Then she'd see something she had to have.

Hum's problem was streetmoney. She'd seen how it lived and loved it. Wanted to live that way too.

She followed it with a crew from work that she went to clubs and bars with. Pat, Gina and Jenelle, women who, like her, knew players casually, but not well enough to be on the inside. They weren't the girls hustlers took out, sexed, bought clothes and jewelry for, gave money to.

But her club buddies didn't care, as long as occasional, complimentary glasses of champagne came their way, sent by a gangster who, with a nod and a wink, thought one of them was cute. They were all pretty girls.

Flirting on the rim of street life was a diversion from their workaday worlds, affirmation that they were indeed visible, young and alluring. Pat, Gina and Jenelle didn't care that their seductions didn't go past that glass of Cristal or Moet. They were satisfied with the thrill of a baller stepping up to weave a few minutes of logical confusion with dazzling words.

They listened and liked the way their hearts thumped and crotches tingled. Hum's friends didn't really have the nerve to do what the smooth men suggested, "You need to see me again," as they moved on. Hum's friends weren't really ready to truly connect with Game. Players were breathless, sexy fun.

But Hum did care.

She cared alot and couldn't figure out why she wasn't already claimed by a drug dealer, a gangster, hustler, number banker, top booster, any kind of independent moneymaker.

She was cuter than alot of the females she saw streetmoney with. She was red-brown with smooth skin and not too tall, her thick hair swung on her shoulders. Her breasts were big, her ass had weight. Her legs were a little skinny and she was a bit thick through the middle, but so? It wasn't like she had a real big gut. Plus, she didn't have no kids!

Hum went to the clubs that streetmoney went to and kept herself in its sight, but she didn't press up on anybody and make a pest of herself. She didn't allow herself to sweat on the dance floor and wasn't a liquor sponge, coke fiend or puff weed in the bathroom. She usually sat with her friends near or at the bar with a split of champagne that she paid for and acted fly, but approachable.

So what was the problem? Why didn't a man who made hills of tax-free money walk up and talk to her? It didn't matter if he wasn't good looking. She was dying to get with a man who had a lot of digits that he wanted to lavish on her.

She'd sat at bars close to "players choice," a phrase she'd invented and taught her neighbor Susan, for women who didn't work and got paid for being...what? That's the part Hum made up because she didn't really know.

And it seemed like she wasn't ever going to find out. She'd eavesdropped these lucky women's conversations about their bills being paid, jewelry surprises at three a.m., not giving up leg or lips to any man not handling and steadily breaking bread, but she still didn't understand how these women did it.

She'd sized them up. Everybody was well under thirty or lying if they weren't. Most of these females were late teens or early twenties like her. The ones gleaming the brightest were usually very pretty, mostly light or bright-skinned, or if she was real dark, had a hot body. Long hair, real or sewn in really well, was preferred. A short cut had to be kept sharp.

Streetmoney loved a big, round pair of real titties, but a big, round ass seemed more important.

These lucky women usually didn't talk much to any others but themselves and stayed put at the bars in the clubs. She'd never heard any of them talk about education, not even a GED or a training certificate.

But there had to be something more than how they looked or acted because there were so many exceptions to those rules. Hum saw plenty of ugly, loud, out of shape women being claimed, pushing fly cars, swallowed by diamonds and furs.

There was something they knew that she didn't. These females were part of an exclusive club in which she wanted membership. Hum was constantly alert for some phrase or action that would allow her entry into a world where she'd be taken care of by big money, by a man who laughed, didn't smile and knew danger.

She wanted to be kept by a man in expensive clothes, jewelry and reptile shoes that drove an expensive car and wore mink when it was cold. She wanted him to be pissed if she flirted with other men who lived just like him. She'd seen that. Streetmoney snatching his woman around at the bar, threatening harm in a deep voice, because she'd smiled too long at one of his partners.

Hum was ready for hers. He'd be from twentythree to maybe forty and could look busted, average or fine. Tall or short, big bellied or slim, a thug or debonair, she knew he owned the scintillating diamond rings that showcased the manicured hands that pulled twenties, fifties and hundreds off thick folds of bottomless money. She wanted to be a streetmoney showpiece, a milliondollar announcement of what he was worth.

What did she lack? In the clubs and bars, they passed right

by her, going up to the women who threw a signal she couldn't identify.

She'd sat right beside the showbirds and watched them effectively pretend to be highly agitated when hustlers approached, turning their faces away from sexy introductions. They sucked their teeth and rolled their eyes to the ceiling when players asked their names.

Hum wondered where they got the nerve to toss their hair and examine the diamonds they already owned, ignoring inquiries about spending their time.

She'd marveled at how they threw attitude over their shoulders, chilly, "I got a man," snatching their heads back around to continue conversations among themselves. Like they didn't give a fuck that opportunity was standing right there, chuckling in response, "Baby, speak what's really on your mind. That's what you thought until you saw me."

If streetmoney saw a crack in her armor and decided to pursue, he'd take the woman's attention. Ordering a bottle of champagne, his strong-talking lips near her perfumed ear told the nightbird to agree, "If you had a real man I couldn't do this. Don't fool yourself, school yourself, baby."

More times than not, the player would lead that petulant woman away, whispering what Hum knew were promises of incredible sex and pretty things if she'd act right.

Hum came to understand why players called these women thoroughbreds. Just like those expensive horses, these women loved to be pampered and ridden for money but were skittish and had to be led to the track and coaxed in the gate.

And like the races, hustlers that ran hard Game finished in the green. The fillies they rode mentally and physically got rewarded too, if they galloped fast enough to be winners.

A woman under a player's saddle held a defined position. She was business wise, made money for him one way or another. Or she could be trusted to give or take information, maybe she held or changed his money.

She might be business dumb, living as his personal relaxation, home most nights by herself or with the baby, or out with girlfriends, spending the money he gave her. All positions demanded obedience to his wants and needs, no questions.

Hum wanted the latter, to be kept in control through luxurious ignorance. She didn't want to know a thing about whatever her man did to get paid. Hum was ready to be recognized in public as a wife in the Life.

She ached to be a spoiled woman who only wore labels, who everyday had to select from a growing cache of thick gold and platinum links for her neck and wrists, pendants rich with diamonds, incredible earrings and more big diamond rings than she had fingers.

Hum wanted to sweep into a packed hair salon on a Saturday afternoon, kiss the owner and never have to wait. A floor length black mink with the silk lining folded out, showing her embroidered name and draped over the back of her barstool was status.

She wanted so many shoes and boots and bags that she had them in crazy colors and they all stayed looking brand new.

Hum wanted a knot of money that her man kept replenished, to spend on whatever, stuffed in her designer bag. Cabbing it wherever she went. Hooking up with the other wives for shopping sprees and then have an expensive restaurant lunch.

Heaven on earth was having a man come home before dawn to wake her up, commanding, "Get up, make me a steak, I'm hungry," before throwing knots of cash on the bed, ordering, "Put that up first."

She wanted to be closed-mouthed about where she and her man lived, because too much money and confidential information were involved.

Hum aroused her nature imagining the driving, demanding, satisfying sex he'd conduct every night. She'd be the release he came home to. She'd know how good or bad business was by the amount of thug in his love when he drove her ass down into the bed.

Tisha longed to complain to the other choices that her man was always handling business, all the time out getting money or checking on the crew under his control.

She wanted to sound deep when she bitched about her emotional needs. She wanted to tap her perfect air-brushed dragons on the bar, flip her precision weave and threaten that if she didn't get her cherry-red soft top BMW by her birthday, that would be it. She was leaving him. It wasn't like she couldn't trick wheels from one of the other muthafuckas always sweating her.

Tisha wanted to drop science and explain that it wasn't about running Game, she really wanted to stay with her man. He was her baby. But it's about moving up, right? So her reeeeally needed to hear her, for real, knowhumsayin? Plus, her period was two weeks late, so....

Hum would let her fantasy get really crazy, seeing it all bell-clear in her mind. She secretly wanted to be a hustler's baby mother, fully bonded with the street through a balling baby daddy, as ignorant as she knew that dream was.

Even if he left her or got locked up, she would definitely consider getting pregnant by streetmoney. Carrying his baby would obviously cement her rank as player's choice. Would prove that they had been together and he had taken her skin-to-skin and gave her his next of kin, so she must be worthy of his seed....

Hum would be at a club jealous as hell with any chance of having a nice time spoiled as she watched players flirt with other women and buy their drinks. She'd be ready to go home because none of the regular men, the ones with nine-to-fives, measured up, no matter how handsome or accomplished they were.

No matter how cordial they acted or how pretty they told her she looked, she only pretended to listen when they smiled and introduced themselves to begin their conversations.

Tisha never gave out her number so they gave her business cards or wrote down their numbers on bar napkins, making it clear that they hoped she'd call. They'd like to see her again. Maybe dinner? The movies? Whatever she'd like to do.

"Fuck these broke-ass fools!" she'd say, alone, when she got home, tearing up the cards and napkins. Hum never wanted to take their information, but she had to put up a front for her friends. She had to look in demand.

She never called any man she met. Her friends didn't understand. Yeah, they knew she wanted a hustler, she'd talked often enough about her desire, but girl, they advised, don't get hung up on it. Sweetie, live and have a good time, they said.

Jenelle told her, "It ain't like you meeting bums! Damn, Hum, that man trying to talk to you last Friday at Paradisio was fine! He was nice too. Single, one kid, right? Told you he was a marketing consultant and drove a Benz, right? Who's to say he can't afford to hook you up?" Jenelle's tone was reprimanding.

"Hum," she added, "you are truly out of your mind. If you really ain't interested in that good-lookin' man, give me home-boy's digits, sugar, I'll damn sure call him!"

Tisha didn't answer because she wouldn't do that, and couldn't if she wanted to. That number had long been garbage.

She didn't want a man who had to put her jewelry on layaway or credit. Who had to be at work in the morning, no matter how impressive his title. Hum wanted a joker who started his day at noon unless impressive money called for earlier negotiations.

Her 210 friends didn't know her club friends. Her neighbors didn't really party. They didn't go out often and when they did it was to a local bar like The Fantasia Lounge or a jazz club in downtown Brooklyn, out to eat, like Red Lobster, or to a friend's house to celebrate a birthday, a holiday or an anniversary.

Hum was like their little sister and they liked to hear her stories of the club life. She entertained them with descriptions of the many men she'd met, spicing up bland conversations, but didn't utter a word about the kind of man she was praying on.

Because she seldom dated, they figured Hum was picky, but they thought picky as in a fine executive, or a handsome computer programmer, a professional like herself.

Hum knew they'd be completely shocked to hear that Rakim was her ideal. Rakim Moet Divine was exactly who she wanted to be.

Then there was her secret. What had happened to Hum four months after she'd moved into the building. The incident that still humiliated her every time she recalled it. Thinking about it filled her stomach with flutters.

"Damn…damn…" she'd say over and over when it crossed her mind. She hated to think about it but usually couldn't help herself.

It was the first time she'd come to close to getting her desire. For her twenty-first birthday Hum and her club friends had gone to celebrate at The Lot in Manhattan. It was June sixth, she'd never forget.

She'd sat at the bar with her friends in a new outfit, a tight, short, deep cleavage black silk Dior knockoff with rhinestone spaghetti straps and matching strappy black silk stilettos. She'd pinned up her hair soft and sexy, wore heavy black eyeliner and glossy red lips. She knew how good she looked. Straight up doll.

A new diamond rode on her right ring finger, two square carats, set high on a platinum-like, white gold band. It was the biggest one she had, fresh out of layaway where she'd faithfully paid on it weekly for almost ten months. It looked good with her other bling.

Hum wore all her ice, a carat hung from cobra-link gold around her neck, a carat in white gold dangled from each ear and almost five more sparkling carats were divided on three more fingers. She'd tried to squeeze out the bucks to pay off her tennis bracelet with square cut stones, but she couldn't swing it.

When her friends admired her new ring, especially the size of the diamond, Hum languidly lied and told her friends in an off-hand manner that it was a gift from "Some lawyer dude trying to get with me."

Hum had used her big rock hand to wave away her girl-friends' comments of, "Alright, Miss Thing!" "Work it, Hum!" "Homeboy must be sprung!"

Her pals saluted her birthday with a bottle of Cristal. They each chased a glass of champagne with a shot of Courvoisier. Hum ordered another one, a double, finished off the Cristal, then one more cognac and got very drunk. And liquor bold. The alcohol blossomed how badly she wanted a streetmoney man.

With brazen eyes she scanned the bar until they snagged on the best looking man in world at the other end. He was standing with a group of sharp men and caught her gaze.

They all were all hustlers, she could tell. His dress and obvious smoothness verified success in his enterprise. He looked sexy, mean and exciting.

Returning her look, he lifted a snifter to his lips, sparks crackled from the ice on his fingers and wrist. He looked like a gangster movie star, everything she worshipped.

Hum drunkenly thought that maybe her birthday was the charm, tonight was her night. The liquor had her staring dreamily in his eyes longer than she should have. He licked his full lips and winked. Hum was startled and started to tingle.

Tisha turned back to her friends and pointed, "See tha' pretty thing ova' there?" Their eyes followed her arm. She bet her friends that she could get him.

Gina, Pat and Jenelle looked at the danger she'd singled out, saw him watching them watch him. They turned away and hooted, yeah, right, laughing at her.

Jenelle said, "Hum, you drunk as hell. Slow down, girl! You ain't ready for that, Miss Woman. He'd chew your ass up."

Hum was so loaded all she could do was suck her teeth and twist her hand to dismiss Jenelle. She slid off her stool and pushed through people to get to where he stood.

He was talking to someone but the liquor told her to wedge herself between him and the other man who stepped back. She found herself pressed against her dream looking up into his face slurring, "I saw you lookin' at me. Right? You like what you see?"

Her high had her weaving slightly as she tried to strike a sexy pose with her hands on her hips. "So?"

Gina had walked over and tried to lead her away but got cussed, "Hey! Wha'chu doin'?! Can'chu see I'm talkin'? Why you all up in my fuckin' bis'niss?" Hum snatched her arm from Gina's grip, stumbling.

That man and his friends stopped conversing to watch Hum carry on. She thought she was captivating them with Game personality. Gina walked away, embarrassed. People were staring.

Hum tried to press against her choice again but he wouldn't let her. He held her away with a strong arm and Hum almost fell backwards. The same arm reached to steady her upright.

"Uh-huh, You got me, don'chu? Whuus yo' naaame sweet thaaang?" Hum sang. His associates told him to bounce this drunk bitch. The ladies at that end of the bar looked over their shoulders and told him the same thing.

"I'm Love, baby. You want a drink?"

"Hell yeah! Gimme wha'chu wan' me to have, baby."

Love ordered a split of Moet and the little black bottle came stuck with a long black straw. "Drink up baby," he said, handing it to her.

Hum drank as fast as the bubbles allowed. Damn, she was drunk but showing everybody, especially Love, that she could hang. She belonged in his circle. "Hey Love! T'day's my birfday, yep, I'm twen'nyone!"

Love turned from Hum and said something to his friends. A couple of them chuckled but all picked up their drinks and walked away. He winked at Hum, "Oh yeah? So what's up after you leave here?"

Thank you, God. If you make him mine, I'll do anything to keep him. Let this one be for me, please. "Oh, I'm not doin' nothin'. Why? You wan' do somethin'?" Although she wasn't quite finished with the first, she took the second tiny bottle of champagne he offered.

"Yeah, baby. Drink up and let's go someplace quiet." Love put the straw up to her mouth.

Hum was nauseous but drank in gulps anyway. She looked up and there were Gina, Pat and Jenelle, all saying something she couldn't understand. Their mouths were moving but Hum couldn't comprehend a single word. Pat had Hum's bag, Gina was trying to pull her away and Jenelle was talking, talking.

Love stood back and looked away, Hum panicked, he might be changing his mind and she couldn't wait to get going. "Get off me! Y'all jus' go head! I'm awright! I'ma leave wit' who I wan' leave wit', okay? This My fuckin' night! Le' me haf a good time!"

She pushed Gina. "Bitch, I aweady tol' you to leaf me th' fuck alone!"

Pat threw Hum's bag on the bar, Gina told Hum to go fuck her drunk-ass self and Jenelle said, "Hum, you know, you right, you twenty-one. See ya!" Her friends turned and left.

Grinning, Hum turned to Love who asked, "You ready, baby?"

Love started walking towards the door. Hum knew she was under every woman's gaze. She took her bag off the bar and followed her desire.

Hum made sure that she held her head high and walked seductively. This was it! Miss Tisha was leaving with Love! Hooo, the room was spinning and there wasn't enough air. Hum knew she didn't need any more liquor.

She was bumping into people, stepping on their feet, apologizing, "Ooo, 'scuse me! Sorry!" trying to keep up with Love's back.

Out on the street there was a breeze, she breathed deeply, the fresh air felt good and she felt a little better. Hum patted her hair and pressed her lips together trying to revive any color left on her mouth. She hoped she still looked pretty.

Hum tried talking to this heart-stopping man, but he didn't respond or even look at her. When they got to the corner, he turned and she followed him walking along the side of the club.

He stopped at a big black Mercedes. He opened the door on her side.

"You feel all right?" was all he said to her, shutting the door after she nodded and climbed in.

Yeeesss! This is where I belong, Hum congratulated herself and sank back in tan leather, cocooned by the dark windows. The car smelled rich like the money Love obviously didn't do without. Love walked around to his side and got in.

"How long you had this car?" She tried again to start a conversation.

Love barely parted his lips, "A new one every year." He stuck the key in the ignition.

Hum was still liquor dizzy and couldn't tell if the seat was really moving. "Is the seat goin' back?"

"Yeah, I'm getting comfortable." He cut off his car.

Hum heard his zipper going down. What? What was he doing? "Love, what you doin'?" Hum tried to make her tone sound sober and casual.

"Nothing. Come here. Why you way over there, baby? Sit closer to me." He pushed up the armrests and finally looked at her. Hum couldn't help but blink, damn, he was gorgeous.

Hum hoped he was going to kiss her, she leaned forward, shut her eyes and parted her lips.

Instead, he pulled her closer by the back of her head and

began pushing her face over his lap.

The way she was sitting, Hum was uncomfortable but would never admit it. If he wanted her close, she'd be closer. Love's hand was messing up her hair. Shit, she didn't want to look ugly. Hum was drunk but too anxious to be agreeable so she didn't twist away. The movement made her stomach lurch, but she couldn't repel the weight of his palm pushing her head.

He pressed firmly until Hum couldn't believe that her mouth was in his crotch, her lips brushing against his dark silk boxers. Love slipped his other hand into the fly. His penis, released, poked her in the eye, then the thick tip pressed against her lips. Love shifted his hips on the seat.

"Sss. Yeah. Yeah, go head baby, suck my dick. Look how big and hard it's getting baby. Suck it down for Daddy. Taste why they call me Love, baby. Put your lips around my pretty head, babydoll. I'ma give you something nice if you suck it good."

"No! Uh-uh, stop. Love, stop!" Her protests let him slip steel between her lips. Hum didn't know what to do, she just let it rest heavy against her tongue and kept her mouth slack. She felt it swelling even more. Oh shit, is this what the women who sat at the bar did to get what they got? Was she supposed to act like this was nothing but an exchange for luxuries she'd receive later? Maybe so.

Hum exhaled and tightened her mouth.

He was right. It was so large and hard!...Kind of sweet, like honey was somewhere on it...He encouraged her...Coaxing...Velvet voice so wicked and deep...Sexy low moaning... Rolling his hips...Come on baby. Won't nobody but me and you know this is how you want to celebrate your birthday...Sss...Look how brick Daddy is, baby. I know you sucked dick before...You got nice big lips...You want to do it. You want to taste it baby...Get sexy, babydoll... Give in and enjoy yourself...Sss...Come on baby, suck big Daddy...This is your birthday present baby. Do it...Yeeeah, that's it...aaaah, yeah, suck it deep, baby...deep....

Hum let the liquor make her hot, be her excuse to pass her limits. She closed her eyes tight and let her mind wheel off. It only took her seconds to get into it. Became an instant pro at something she didn't even know she could do so well. Moans escaped her lips, she began throating him, licking, lapping, showing Love what she could do. Love was right, the windows were up, no one would know.

Hum paused to lick her palm and synchronize it with her noisy mouth, up and down his shaft, teeth tucked behind her lips. His soul groans rewarded her and were ecstasy to her ears.

If sucking off Love made her his, shit, what was wrong with that? She'd be doing more than that anyway, once they started seeing each other after tonight. The alcohol said she was finally on the right side of happy, she was in the club!

She got up on her knees and shamelessly bobbed her head in his crotch. This was going to be her man. She had to be better than every other woman who wanted him and there had to be many, a whole bunch of dimes at his feet and Hum refused to be nine cents.

Hum showed Love she could blow his huge piece like a vacuum cleaner, down to his base, his hair tickling her lips, demonstrating the deep throat he'd get every night if she was his.

Hum twisted her ass to help him put his hand inside her panties. She was so wet, Love's long finger slipped right inside to the last knuckle, jamming in and out. She began jerking her hips. He added another finger. And one more.

His steel started pulsing in her mouth about to release.

Love snatched his fingers out of her pocket. He pressed both palms hard on the back of her head to fully deposit his charity, thrusting his ass upwards as it left him.

Choking, tears sprang to Hum's eyes. Her arms were flailing and she felt like she was about to vomit because he came alot, thick rapid shots far down her throat. Love let go of her head and pulled his heavy, spent sex from her slack mouth.

Hum sat up coughing, retching, sucking in air, wiping tears with the backs of her hands.

"Swallow! Bitch, don't throw up in my car." He watched her struggle to keep down his seed. She passed the crisis, Love patted her head, petted her cheek for a job well done.

"Shhhit. Baby. Gotdam! You can suck dick, baby. Good girl." Love leaned over her to open the glove box and pull out a pristine handkerchief to wipe his manhood with. He carefully cleaned away their sex. He put away his snake and zipped up his pants.

"Pussy tight too," Love ran the fingers that had moved inside her under her nose and tried to bully them between her lips. Hum snatched her head away.

Love laughed and methodically wiped his fingers off on the cloth instead. He reached over her again and retrieved cologne, applied some drops to his palm and rubbed his hands together.

Hum didn't know what to say, to do, feel. Other than like something in the gutter. She remembered to pull her dress back down over her ass.

"Why you do that to me?" The back of her mouth and down her throat felt coated, thickly slick. She coughed trying to clear it. Her eyes shimmered, Hum was trying not to cry. She was still half drunk.

Love ran a hand over his immaculate hair. "Do what? Bitch, you sucked my shit like it was your lifeline. You wanted me to fuck you too. Still do. Don't get cute."

Love obviously looked at his diamond timepiece. "Fix yourself, time for you to get out."

Hum knew she was dreaming, "You not going to take me home?"

"What? Bitch, you crazy." His words were frosty, Love arranged his clothes and checked his face in his visor mirror, ignoring her completely.

"My name ain't 'bitch'!" Hum rallied, trying to regain a little identity.

"Whatever the fuck your name is, bitch, get the fuck out." Love turned the ignition key and started his car.

Funny how shocking reality can be, Hum realized he'd never asked her name. Her friends must have called it, when they were trying to talk sense through her stupor, so he must have heard it. Her name didn't mean anything to him, plain as that.

"Please take me home, please." She couldn't stop pleading tears from glittering her eyes. She was sobering quickly and wanted to die. Hum put a begging hand on his arm, the withering look Love gave it made her remove it quickly.

"Ask one of my partners to take you home. They right outside. Look." Love lowered the window on her side.

Sure enough, there stood two of the men Love had been with at the bar. It was clear they knew Love had just used her. They crouched to look in. One winked at her and unzipped his pants. The other stuck out his tongue and snaked it. Hum covered her face with her hands and tried not to cry.

"So what's up baby? Wit' yo' big titty self." The one with the unzipped pants reached in the car and grabbed her breast, squeezing it with a big palm. Hum slapped at his hand and looked a fearful appeal at Love.

The man continued to offend, kneading her breast through her dress hard and slow, finding her nipple, pulling and pinching it before he drew back his hand.

"Gotdamn, I loves a bitch wit' big titties, shit!" He held out his palm for dap from his partner. Hum tried to protect her breasts by folding her arms over them.

Love paid her no mind and chuckled to his associates, "Baby, this broad is on the ball. Man, this bitch sucked my dick like she just got out of prison. Bitch got the bone! What? Drank it all, man."

Love turned to Hum, chucked her under the chin and complimented, "So you's a natural, huh, babydoll? Ho by nature. A little gold mine." He said to his friends, "This fresh piece is full of commerce my brothers, I need to put her healthy green ass to work."

"Get paid. Shit, tell her how to choose you, Love."

"Fo' sho'. Maaan, her cat tight as a knot in a wet rope! Pussy tight as a fist even with three fingers in it."

"Don't let that fingerfuckin' fool you man. Better ride that pussy. Jus' call it man, I'll check that fit for you, pa'tna."

"Sho' you right." Love winked at Hum, "Yeah. I sho' should find out how you fit pipe. See if your pocket is delicious as it feel." Sinister eyes peered at her. "You would let my man here split that box if I tell you to, won't you baby?"

Hum was frozen. Love had to be playing with her. He wouldn't make her have sex with this nasty man. He was trying to see how far she would go. Maybe if she acted grown and a little tougher he would stop scaring her and take her home. Call his bluff like she knew he was bullshitting. "I'd rather do it with you."

Love's laugh was hard. "Do 'it'? Do what? Fuck me? You want to fuck Daddy, babydoll? Say it. Say 'yes, I want to fuck you, Mr. Love'."

"I, uh, yes, I want to fuck you, Mr. Love." Oh, Lord, she glanced at the other men who looked amused.

Love's voice was deep. "Babydoll, that's every woman's dream. Baby, platinum snake ain't free. You want to work? You want to pay me so you can buy some of my expensive dick, baby?" He winked at Hum and massaged his prize.

"Man, this bitch don't know what you talkin' about. Let me fit her, Love. My shit hard as learnin' Chinese! I bend the rules, baby. I damn sho' fuck that fat ass for free." He reached in the car for Hum again.

This time he slipped his hand inside her bra and fondled her bare breast roughly. Scared to stop him, tears slid down Hum's cheeks as the hustler squeezed her full breast.

He said, "Bitch if you jus' relax and enjoy it, you gon' want me to fuck you right here in the street."

Help me somebody, she silently implored, lips trembling because her nipple was responding. She turned her body away to stop him from trying to pull her breast out of her dress.

"Come on, baby, let me suck that big titty," his voice was commanding.

Like quicksilver Love went from relaxed to irritated. He was deadly. Playtime was over. "Come on, bitch, I said get the fuck out my car before I throw your ass out."

Love leaned over Hum and opened the door. The street-light played on his large diamond pinky solitaire and diamond crusted watch. He tossed her bag on the pavement.

Hum looked after her bag right into the crotch of her bogey-man who was fully exposed, stroking his hardness.

"Bitch, shut up all that fuckin' cryin'. What the fuck is you cryin' for? All this big pretty dick I got? I'ma give yo' silly ass a reason to cry." He bounced his penis on his palm, angry.

"Shit, Love, the bitch done made me mad. I'ma put her up

against that muhfuckin' wall an' get some pussy. I'ma fuck her like..."

The second man broke in, "Slow down, C-Born." He held out his hand to help Hum from the car. "Get out, sweetheart. Love got to go, baby. My name is Shotgun, I'll take you home..."

Hum's relief was so immediate and intense it weakened her. She put a trembling hand into Shotgun's. "I, I..."

"...But you got to turn up that ass to pay for my gas." All of them started to laugh.

Hum scrambled out of the Benz, scooped up her bag and ran.

She stumbled a few blocks, mindless, before she thought to flag a cab to take her home. When it stopped, the driver leaned from his window and asked with concern, "Miss, you alright?" Hum imagined how wild-eyed and anxious she must have looked, disheveled like she'd been assaulted.

"Yeah, yeah, I'm okay. Just take me to Brooklyn. 210 Jefferson Avenue, off Nostrand." She all but fell into the back seat.

That night she lost some of her hustler illusions. During the ride Hum reflected, admitted to herself that even after what she'd just gone through, she still wanted a player. She'd just gone about it all wrong. Picked the wrong one.

Love and his friends were fucking dogs. Used to them slack bitches that do anything. And fuck that muthafucka who was grabbing all over her.

She blamed all that damn liquor for messing her up. But nobody would ever know. Then Hum had a thought that was a knock upside her head. "Ohhh shit!" She sat up straight in the taxi.

The driver turned his head around, "What's the matter? Miss? You okay?"

"Yeah, yeah." Hum waved him away and sank back in the seat and slapped her palm on her forehead. Love was a goddamn pimp! They were all pimps! Ohhh shit! "And Love was trying to turn me out!" she whispered to herself.

Damn it to hell, why did Love have to be so rich and fine....

When she got home, it was past five in the morning and nobody saw her dash into the building.

Hum took a quick hot shower, climbed naked into bed and spent two hours staring into the dark, reliving every tortuous minute of the night she'd just spent. Her twenty-first birthday.

But the torture was laced with pleasure. She did have that rich, pretty man for a little while, a pimp, and she had made him come. She had made a pimp feel good and he had practically said she gave him the best head he ever had. A pimp. And he had to know good head. Getting good head was his business.

He told her she was sexy. Yep, she'd sucked his dick, and let him fingerfuck her, swallowed too, wasn't no getting around that.

Man, when she did get her streetmoney, she knew now that she wanted a drug dealer, she couldn't handle a pimp because of what it meant, she just couldn't be a ho, well, not a for real, for real one...No! She could Not. Ho. Sharing him, giving him the money she got from sexing any man. Naah....

Anyway, when she did get herself a drug dealer, no doubt that she'd keep him satisfied. Wouldn't no outside bitch be able take her man, at least not with her mouth.

She asked herself if she really would've had sex with Love, if he had been serious. In front of those other pimps? In his Benz? Although it was just Hum and her thoughts, embarrassed, she pushed back that tiny one that tried to chirp, damn straight.

The next afternoon she went without calling first, to Pat's apartment. Her friend opened her door, put her hand on her hip and said, "Well, well. What's up, Miss Drunk Birthday?" Hum asked Pat to call Gina and Jenelle to come over.

As soon as they were all together, Hum apologized. Pat and Jenelle said they understood because she was so drunk, "Toh' up from the flo' up!" is how Pat put it, then added, "But don't dare try it again, girlfriend."

Gina didn't say anything at all. Hum asked Pat for some aspirin because her head was splitting.

Lying on her stomach across Pat's bed, Hum let them tease her without mercy about how wasted she was and how loud and crazy she'd acted.

When they asked her what happened with that pretty-ass gangster, Hum rolled over onto her back and said, "Shit, when we got to his car that muthafucka wanted to fuck me. Y'all know your girl ain't no ho, so I told him to kiss my happy ass. I got out his Benz and took a cab home. I went back in the club to look for y'all, but y'all must have left."

Pat, Gina and Jenelle sneaked glances at each other and said, "Uh-huh."

They'd never tell her, but last night the rumor had shadowed right behind her out the door, about the drunk girl who was leaving the club to do a train of pimps in a Benz around the corner. "Look, that's her," "Drunk ho," "There she go," was repeated over and again. Fingers and chins pointed her out as she'd reeled through the crowd behind Love.

That afternoon was the last time Hum and her friends got together.

After Love debased her, Hum dropped her club friends like she never knew them. She found out that she couldn't trust those witches anymore.

At work it didn't take long for the gossip about her to reach her. Hum felt that if her homegirls were real friends they would've let her know what was being said behind her back.

Her ex-friends tried to explain that they weren't the source of the talk. Other people from work had seen her at the club. Hum's friends thought they were sparing her feelings by not telling her, she had no idea how badly she'd acted that night.

Hum didn't believe them. She'd accused them of being the ones who'd started the jealous lies in the first place.

Besides, Hum concluded that the odds gave her better chances to catch a baller if she rolled alone.

Cruising by herself, Hum tripped up on luck twice in a row and managed to inveigle herself into the affections of minor drug dealers. Chilo and Laredo, players but not masters of the Game.

Neither were bosses, but at least Chilo was a lieutenant. She suspected Laredo was only a runner, although he'd claimed lieutenant status.

Neither owned a car, they drove rentals when they didn't take cabs. Hum got in but couldn't stand riding in rentals. Even if it was a luxury ride, she still knew that the driver wasn't the owner.

In both relationships she wouldn't let the men visit or pick her up at 210, which was fine with them because she didn't know where they lived either. Keeping it on the street was not a problem.

If the 210 girls saw Hum dressed to go out on her nights off, or if she left hours before time for her to be at work, she made up lies. Hum told them that she was meeting a lawyer or young executive or hanging with females from work or from around her old neighborhood.

Both of the men expressed decreasing patience for her having to work nights. She was off Saturday and Sunday, but on weeknights Hum couldn't hang out later than eleven thirty to get to work by twelve.

Even with taking cabs to get to work faster, she'd gotten written up several times for excessive lateness and absence. She'd received her first warning. It was hard for Hum to get up and leave a spot when it was getting hot and all the fun was just coming in.

By the time both relationships were over she'd used up her vacation, personal days and all of her sick time. After that, when she took off Hum didn't get paid for those nights.

She let Chilo and Laredo take her to short-stay motels in Brooklyn and Manhattan where she gave them missionary sex with uneager sounds of encouragement.

The first time each man had laid her down, she'd made it clear that she "Don't suck nothing! I'm serious, so don't ask me." She never felt their ears brushing between her thighs either.

Chilo and Laredo couldn't, or wouldn't, give her the finances to upgrade her style, what they spent on her was, in her consideration, just change. After all, the only reason she ran with them was to reap the material benefits and the prestige of being identified as a player's girl.

With each relationship from the very beginning, she was impatient for the money to get better.

So far, there were no gems, no minks. Chilo gave her a pair of gold tube hoops that were light as hell because they were hollow.

She had to damn near twist Laredo's arm to get the one

gold chain he bought her and it was just eighteen inches and medium weight. And she bought the small diamond pendant that hung from it.

Neither bought her clothes or took care of her hair. Chilo did pay for her nails. The four or five twenties she was able to pry from each once a week was hardly a stack. At best, their money was a dribble that put a little more time between her calls to Newark.

When they took her out, she felt like snatching the rocks from the throats, wrists and ears of the women perching at the bars. She had to control herself not to reach for the big bills she peeped when they opened their designer wallets.

If a birthday was being celebrated and the bubbly was running, Hum always managed to enjoy a pour. Hers was always one of the anonymous glasses attached to an arm pushing forward from the back of the well-wishing throng.

Hum was frustrated in both relationships. If Chilo and Laredo represented as good as she was going to get in the life she desperately wanted, she was standing up nibbling at the buffet. Damn it, she wanted to sit down and feast at the banquet.

She refused to believe she couldn't do better, or at least make them do better.

Because of her intentions to improve her boyfriends both alliances were brief despite her willingness to get behind them and push them into success.

Hum thought she was doing a good thing by always making them aware that they hadn't a moment to waste. They must plan to move inward from the fringe. Become one of the boss-men who spent the big dough, lived the high life, gave the orders.

In the bars, at the clubs, she whispered intently in their ears, look at those men over there, pointing to the big ballers, that's where you supposed to be, right? Right?

She insisted that their wants match hers, to be in the bulls-eye where money talked and shined.

Chi and Laredo took her to the right places, all the sets where the high rollers held court, but they never sat in the inner groove.

It made her mad that her streetmoney seemed content to just loud talk among their cliques of other budget players. Sitting too far from the real cash. It ate her up how, before the night was over, her nickel and dimers would make sure to edge up to the elite with respectful acknowledgments.

Fading back, they'd return to bodaciously lie about how tight they were with the big ballers.

She had been mortified to learn that some of Laredo's crew still worked jobs during the day.

Chilo seemed to feel some of what she was saying, he had ambition, he wanted to be a boss. They were together for three months before he quit her, tired of "a bitch trying to tell a man how to be a muhfuckin' man."

Not long after they broke up, but before she'd met Lared? Hum heard that he did become his own boss. She was livid, t] money should by all rights be hers. She was the one who'd | up with the broke times, been his inspiration and motivation

Indignant, she'd even called him, but Chilo got funky a told her she was the last female he'd ever enhance. He went on Hum, telling her that he had another woman the whole ti] they were together because all Hum did was criticize and sc] tinize. She never appreciated anything he did for her, nothi] was ever good enough.

"And fuckin' your dead ass was like fuckin' cardboard. Chilo had broken the connection with a slam.

Close to a month later, the same night she'd met Laredo, she'd seen Chilo at the bar at a club and he'd glanced over her, didn't speak, acted like he didn't know her.

He had some babyfat teenager clinging to him flaunting a huge diamond encrusted gold cross on a heavy gold chain. Hum had scanned her replacement from head to toe. Chi and that ho were matched in custom black leather. The wiggling little bitch had rocks in her ears and serious stones on two of her fingers. 'Gator boots. That bastard made sure Hum saw him keep his palm on his new woman's fat ass.

Hum was so evil she took a stool at the other end of the bar and said a deep hello to Absolut and grapefruit.

Soon the drinks had her feeling better, but vengeful. She'd stared through the crowd at Chilo and his bitch, catching glimpses of them all hugged up.

She'd felt a tug on her arm and turned to hear a young gangster calling himself Laredo ask her to dance. Hum let him lead her to the floor where she worked her body hard to turn Chilo's head her way.

She let Laredo get behind her his hands holding her hips and hump and grind the ass she grinded on him. Hum's arms were waving high in the air and she tossed her head, whipping her hair.

When Laredo moved his hands to cup her breasts, she let him roll them for a few seconds to the music. Hum bent over to touch the floor and Laredo lifted one bent leg high as his crotch bumped her upturned ass. Hum made sure that she had the spotlight.

He quit first, leading her back to the bar with her neck hooked in the crook of his arm. Hum looked around for Chi while she let Laredo lick her cheek. She saw him and his new woman looking sex at each other heading for the door.

She turned to the bar ordered a drink on Laredo and let him feel her titties again. She let him take her to a hotel and that's how they hooked up.

Laredo was just hardheaded. He kept waiting for a promised promotion in his organization. Hum couldn't convince him to strike out on his own.

She sucked her teeth and outtalked him when he declared that he was down for life with his people, he was part of a master plan. Hum called him a master fool and said he wasn't going to ever see real money unless he ran his own enterprise. And if he was worried about a bullet, that wouldn't be his concern if he had the sense do what she said.

Laredo stepped off after four months, he could no longer stand the way she made him feel like a sucker. She'd actually said to him, "You say you know Love and his people. Some of them do what you do. Or change what you do. Why can't you be like one of them? Watch them and imitate how they get money."

He'd replied nastily, "Bitch, you want me to pimp yo' ass?"

Hum responded to the part that had made her mad, "Who you callin' 'bitch'!?"

They broke up the last time they went out, arguing in the

street after a party. Laredo shouted, "It's over, bitch!" called Hum a "Fuckin' nag!" and she'd shot back, "Because you ain't got no fuckin' backbone, punk!"

If she hadn't seen it coming and ducked, that lunge Laredo made would've caught her.

He didn't speak to her either when he saw Hum in the spots. He especially made sure she saw him the week after they broke up, cruising behind the wheel of a brand new silver Lexus, knowing she'd break her neck to check the back plate. She had. It read "LAREDO," just like he said it would.

Hum decided right then, enough of the bullshit. Fuck them wannabe chumps. She was doubly glad she never gave them what she'd given Love.

No more dealing with popcorn players. If the streetmoney she chose already had a number one she'd just have to take over that position. With her magic mouth.

So when she went out, Tisha researched, looked over the pool of jeweled sharks, decided which were largest and drew the most green. Once she took inventory, every weekend was a mission. She began to ingratiate herself with the women whose men she wanted for herself.

She'd listed it as jealousy when one chosen female feeling charitable, got Hum alone in the bathroom at a birthday party at a bar called The Good Life. She told her, "Hum, you ain't heard this from me, but you need to chill, for real. Females startin' to call you a bug. And they gettin' mad, sayin' you grimy, tryin' to slide up under they men."

Hum's flippant, "Oh girl, I ain't worried about that," turned her informant's advice into a warning.

"Oh yeah? You better be. Bitches talkin' about seriously cuttin' your ass. They will fuck your face up, you get caught scammin' a bitch for her moneyman. You better watch yourself Hum. You close to gettin' hurt."

A spy entered the bathroom, Hum's confidant clamped her mouth shut and stepped from Hum like they hadn't been talking. As the informant went into a stall, Hum's advisor had leaned into Hum, twisted her mouth to the side and whispered, "Let me leave first, you wait a few minutes before you come out. If I was you, I wouldn't stay out too long tonight."

Hum left the bathroom and went home. Quit the sets for awhile.

Love had been at that party too and it wasn't the first time she'd seen him since he used her. Hum had seen Love in the spots quite a few times, but had only spoken to him once, the third time she'd seen him standing at a bar.

That night after she'd gotten friendly with Hennessy she'd found the courage to approach him.

She'd walked up close behind him tapped his shoulder and said sexily to his back, "Hey, you. Long time. How you doin'?"

Love had turned around and louded her, "Bitch, back up. Long time? Who you? You must want to know me."

His elegant manicured hand held his drink and his icy gaze scanned her, "You trying to choose?" Love locked her eyes, "You looking in my face so what you bring? And bitch you better not insult me."

Chuckles started at the bar and Hum had turned from the laughter on swift heels. She must've caught him in a bad mood.

Wherever she saw him after that, she'd watch Love from a distance, snatching looks, quickly shifting her eyes and lowering her gaze if he looked in her general direction. As soon as his attention went elsewhere, she couldn't help but steal glances. He was so wickedly handsome her heart would race, always thinking of what they did...what she did.

When she saw him, Love was usually out alone, but always surrounded, laughing and smooth talking with different associates.

Sometimes he showcased beautiful, cold sexy thoroughbreds, barely dressed in the finest scraps, dripping jewels and posing unconcerned, until he gave them his attention then they purred against his shoulder.

Sometimes Love squired women that gaped, dumbstruck in his presence. With a pang, Hum knew which group she'd be in if ever lucky enough to be at his side.

Since she'd been warned of getting cut, Hum had stopped going out to the clubs and bars almost every night. It quickly dwindled to a couple of times a month, to not at all.

Getting it together at work, always there and on time, hanging at the building with the 210 girls, Hum convinced herself that she was taking a break, taking care of business and working it out, saving money to buy a car. She wanted something nice and then she'd get back on the set.

Wiser now, surely when she got back on the move she'd meet Mr. Make Money. And he'd want her. They'd be together. Like heart and soul.

Many mornings, after work, Hum went to bed composing the man she wanted. Alone with her thoughts she always allowed him to be like Love.

Time and the distraction of being with Chilo and Laredo had given her encounter with Love softer edges, it didn't seem so brutal. She'd decided it was a lesson. It made her grow up. Of course top streetmoney like Love had to test a woman before investing his valuable time.

Plus, she had herself to blame. She'd acted like a drunken fool, so he'd treated her like one. Love really could've treated her much worse. He could've let his friends run a train on her like the rumor said.

Or he could've driven her someplace far, fucked her and left her. Maybe even beaten her. He didn't do any of that.

Love said he liked her. Looking at it one way, he must have, because Love did put himself in a very vulnerable position. If she was a crazy bitch she could've bitten the crap out of him. But she'd done everything he said.

Hum felt she proved she was a woman who'd listen, support his every decision without question. Worthy. But what happened? She squeezed her eyes together tightly and behind them replayed his orgasm down her throat.

He'd shot so much, maybe he hadn't had sex in a while, maybe. And he let her take care of him. So, in a way, she knew a lot about Love.

Her grandmother used to say, "Nobody is never where they don't want to be." Now Hum knew what that meant. She was drunk in that Benz with Love sexing him with her mouth and letting him put his fingers inside her because that's what she wanted to do.

She couldn't really blame the liquor and he hadn't really forced her, not in the strictest sense of the word.

She made herself believe that Love had treated her roughly because that's how his women had to take it sometimes. This is when Hum's eyes got heavy and her next thoughts were part of a dream.

Hum's shame over her experience didn't stand up until Rakim moved into the building. In fact, up until then, Hum secretly thought of herself as being broken in, a real woman now, had handled a situation. Streetwise. After Love, she'd gotten Chilo and Laredo, right? That's right!

But when Rakim moved in it got hard for Tisha to think of herself as a gangster's girl.

Since Rakim's appearance, Susan and Baybay incessantly ripped her to pieces, Miss Rakim Moet Divine in 1A. "What kind of name is that?" Baybay had snorted, back when Herman answered her question about the name of the new tenant who'd moved in. Baybay and Susan took over monitoring her from that day on.

Hum always paid close attention to their conversations because they claimed that Rakim's man was a big name on the street. Her type.

Hum was quietly stunned when she first realized that Shipell was Love, her fantasy man. Her Love. Shipell was definitely Love. She knew it for a fact. Their detailed, repetitive descriptions of him might as well have been copied directly from Hum's mind.

And she'd proved herself right the first time she'd seen him from her window climbing the stoop. It was a coincidence that she'd seen him at all.

It was near midnight on a Saturday, her night off work and she'd just finished watching a movie. Hum just happened to be at her window about to close her blinds.

As they shut, Hum's eye had caught a black Benz parking in front of the building. Her heart racing, she knew it had to be him. Barely parting two slats to make sure he wouldn't see her, breathlessly, intently she watched LoveShipell get out of his car and lock it. He looked amazing.

He looked both ways down the street before walking

through the gate and up the stoop. He paused on the landing then she couldn't see him anymore as he opened the front door.

Hum jumped away from the window like she'd seen the devil. Lightheaded and nervous, she wished she had a drink, no, a bottle.

Hum didn't sleep a wink that night. She tossed and cried and gritted her teeth, devastated that Love was right downstairs in Rakim's apartment. Probably giving her new jewelry, of course money, and baby-making sex. She hated Rakim. Hated her!

From then on Hum always kept her blinds shut tight on weekend nights. She turned off her livingroom lights when she peeked.

She saw him, saw them, a lot, coming, going.

Then she'd sit on her couch with one of its pillows on her lap, pounding it, looking at the TV but seeing completely different scenarios made up of what Love and that bitch Rakim were probably doing in and out of 210.

So Rakim's arrival made Hum jumpy because she worried that somehow her neighbors would find out what she'd done with LoveShipell. Hum couldn't help but fear that there was a chance, although it was a small way-out one, that her street life of chasing hustlers would be uncloaked.

It wasn't until Rakim came to live at 210 that Hum began to envision what she did as raw and lowdown.

Humiliation stiffened the soft brush she'd used to paint pretty curlicues and pastel colors over grisly facts. She'd gotten pissy drunk and sucked off a pimp. In his car.

A damn near legendary pimp, who didn't want to know her name, had his penis pumping in her mouth with his fingers plugging inside her not a half hour after she'd met him. Came roughly way down her throat and made her swallow it.

And she would have fucked him until he'd told her she'd have to pay him to do it. Hum knew that if his sex were free, she would have let him screw her in front of the other two who probably would've sexed her too, as soon as he was through. He'd put her out of his car. He didn't give a fuck about how she got home.

When she sank her deepest, to the bottom where her recollections tangled with shame, Hum whispered about herself, "Goddamn drunk cocksucker ho." But she couldn't hide that she liked the way it sounded, a rude truth. She'd liked doing what she did with Love. It had felt so, good. Nasty. Tingling exciting. She'd do it again.

It had been over a year and she still hadn't had her mouth on any man but him.

The only part that hurt was how Love had dogged her, flexed his manipulations all over her, simply because she'd bugged him, interrupted his conversation. So he'd gotten strict with her and left his contempt down her throat. And didn't remember her after that.

At least she was a fooldog in secret and it had happened before Rakim moved in the building. Those two puny facts were her only defense against feeling like feet-wiped trash.

So far, she managed to keep her face still when the talk turned to Shipell and Miss Divine. Hum wanted to crawl into a hole whenever Susan and Baybay described Rakim's incredible clothes, abundant jewels, how often Shipell parked his Benz out front.

Hum tried to remember if Rakim was one of the chosen women she'd seen out with Love. Even if she were, Rakim would never single out Hum to remember from the staring crowd.

Felines like Rakim never noticed any woman but the one in the mirror. Thank God.

When Baybay and Susan talked about how fine, rich and cold blooded Shipell was, Hum wanted to jump up shake them by their shoulders and shout, bragging, finally revealing that she'd had LoveShipell begging, moaning with grinding hips.

But she swallowed her story and agreed completely with the girls that Rakim was a real ho. Nasty bitch. And what woman but a scheming tramp like that would go with a mean pimp like that Shipell, fine or not.

Hum also knew full well that even if she ran into him nose to nose on the stoop he wouldn't remember her. He'd already proved that.

The 210 girls called him Shipell, and the black Benz was brand new, but he was Love, her twenty-first birthday man.

Damn, why can't I be Rakim, why can't I be Miss Divine, was Hum's shameful mantra.

Hum's foolish heart, cautionless, also promised that if she could somehow be with Love one more time, fuck Rakim, she'd gladly repeat what she did the one night she had him. Only better. She'd try to get him in a bed so she could give him her whole soul.

Even in the Benz' back seat, she'd fuck him there, too. And she'd pay, whatever he said it cost.

Even if she had to call Newark and lie.

"I'm A Strong Black Woman"

Jocelyn and her kids were moving. She'd be out of this building before her rent was due again. She wasn't giving Mr. Drayton any notice either, he'd know when he saw the truck and the movers.

Her new place was on Linden Boulevard, Building A, in a new complex called Lexford Terrace, in Brooklyn but nowhere near 210. Her new apartment would be ready in about two weeks.

It was time to go. She had moved on Jefferson Avenue right after she had Lamarr and he was ten now. And she was thirty-one. Her baby girl was just over six. Been here long enough. Her kids were getting too old to share a bedroom.

Her new apartment, on the twelfth floor, was large. It had three bedrooms, a master and two smaller ones, an L-shaped combination livingroom-diningroom, an eat-in kitchen, a big bathroom and a terrace. The terrace made her feel like she was moving into a house. It would be her yard. She had plans for green outdoor carpeting, potted trees, wrought iron furniture with floral cushions and a small grill.

She had never seen a welfare-assisted apartment as nice or as big as this one in such a nice complex. Jocelyn took the fact that she got it as a blessing, she must deserve it.

This would be her first time living in a tall building with an elevator. Last week when she'd gone to the rental office to pick up a letter for her caseworker, she'd again walked the tour the super had given her when she was first approved.

There was a Key Food supermarket right downstairs. The laundry room was in the basement. It was nice. Clean and big with long counters for folding. A big screen TV sat on a shelf high on one wall across from a long bench for watching the stories. Soda and snack machines. Change-giving attendant and a quarter machine.

She'd stopped in and spoken to the few women who were washing, folding, drying and talking to each other and the TV. Jocelyn excused herself to get their attention and told them that she was Jocelyn Reynolds, a new tenant, moving with her two kids into 12C.

They'd paused, smiled, looked her over and spoke briefly, "Hey, 12C," "How you doin'?" "Hi, I'm Marie, 8D." "Hi."

Their reception had thrilled Jocelyn. She was looking forward to making new friends, ones who didn't talk about other people all the time. She wanted friends who did things, like going to plays and taking their kids to museums. There were so many things she wanted to do. She wanted to learn french. This move was her chance for a whole new way to express herself.

Besides, in a complex, her neighbors wouldn't be all up in her business like they were in 210.

She hadn't told LaKeesha-Pam and Lamarr yet because she didn't want them to tell anybody that they were moving. She knew her children were too young to keep such an exciting secret. They were already questioning her about the boxes she was stacking beside the front door.

She was closing this chapter of her existence and whether the nosy women living in 210 thought it was cold-hearted or not, they would not be a part of her new life. She would leave a phony phone number, lie about where she was moving. Whatever. Goodbye would be Good. Bye.

She was going to leave them with plenty to talk about. They'd probably talk about her for years. She made a note to herself to tell the movers that there was a nice tip in it for them if they didn't tell anybody, not a soul, where they were going.

Jocelyn had worked it out to be settled in her new home in enough time to register the kids in their new school, which was a part of the complex too. She was happy, things were looking up. She was proud of herself. Doing her thing with no help from anybody except the State.

Neither Lamarr senior nor LaKeesha-Pam's father, Derrick, had ever helped her much with their kids.

Money from Big Lamarr came spotty at best. He would send Lamarr a card and a fifty-dollar bill for his birthday and one hundred dollars for Christmas. A couple of twenties every few months.

He would call his son now and then from Richmond, Virginia, where he lived with his wife and their three sons, but never sent for his junior. Senior always sputtered a lame excuse too, every year Jocelyn suggested putting Lamarr on the Greyhound to come stay for summer vacation.

She wasn't taking no for an answer next June. Lamarr is supposed to know his brothers, be around his father and learn how to be a man. And feeding four is the same as feeding three. Lamarr and his wife both worked.

That damn Derrick was a roaming bastard who she hadn't seen or spoken to in going on four years. He never sent his daughter anything. Jocelyn didn't have a clue where he was.

It broke her heart when every once in a while LaKeesha-Pam would sniffle through tears, "How come my daddy don't call me and send me somethin' like Lamarr daddy do? Why my daddy don't love me, mommy?"

Jocelyn's smothered anger wanted to tell her little girl that he was dead. Instead, she'd hold and soothe her baby and remind "KiKi" that mommy had promised her that a new daddy was coming. Soon. Remember? Remember mommy said her new daddy would be here before she turned seven?

At the same time she'd be praying for God to hurry up and send her a good man so her daughter wouldn't make her out to be a liar.

Jocelyn was taking care of business and raising her family anyway.

Lord knows, it wasn't easy, but her kids were growing up fine. Lamarr was a little hot headed, liked to fight, and LaKeesha-Pam didn't like school much, but they were all right, good children. This move would be a chance for them to make new friends and have new experiences too.

Jocelyn couldn't wait to get out of this building. She wanted to be out of 210 before she started to really show and that would be any minute because she was almost three and a half months gone. Her belly had a little pot now and was about to bulge.

A new baby. Well. She hadn't really wanted any more children, but Jocelyn believed that if she created life she would give life.

She definitely wasn't in love with the daddy but she'd pretended emotion to keep him coming back. She didn't have a man to curl around at night and his fit was tight. This man knew how to rock and roll with serious soul. Ooo, Jocelyn remembered with a sly smile, her mind continuing the private poem she'd made up about him, that man could stroke, he ain't no joke, got technique that keeps me weak.

This baby was unplanned, but inevitable, her "passion baby" she called this one. She'd been so wide open, so greedy taking what it took to make this child. Because of bare lust that nearly drowned her, Jocelyn irrationally expected this baby, definitely her last, to look exactly like the daddy.

When she writhed with this man they stopped for nothing, the second they were alone they had to put it in, rushing. They'd been so careless, no time for condoms most times.

Locked in their deepest fit, both pushing forward hard on his release, they never yanked themselves opposite ways.

They were hardheads ignoring logic, savoring the raw explosion from a gun they both knew was loaded every time he pulled the trigger.

He made her want sex more than she'd ever had in her life. He made her focus all the time on what made her a woman. Even in her condition now, he'd continued to mate her in ways that blew her mind.

When she pulled up the erotic memories of her times with this man, Jocelyn locked her bedroom door and indulged her new pastime by reaching between her thighs.

Before the home test came back positive, she was planning to take a free six-month training class in computers that she qualified for, get ready for a job with growth potential. And she was still going to do it. She'd make it. The kids would have to help.

She would tell them about their little brother or sister after they got to Lexford Terrace. LaKeesha-Pam had said last year that she wanted a little sister to name LaTangela-Pam, or a little brother to name Lamont.

Besides, when she moved it would prove to Charles that she wasn't waiting on him to make any important decisions about her life, she was the one to decide what would be going on. She was moving and keeping their baby.

When she'd told him three months ago that she was pregnant and didn't believe in abortion, he actually didn't trip, he'd said they'd work it out.

He didn't split either, kept coming to see her like nothing was different. Although, a week after he knew, he did rub her belly after they'd exhausted each other and say "Damn, Mellow, we made a big mistake. But your honey is so sweet! I swear I can't help it."

Charles had looked at her and winked. "And you don't help none, puttin' that thang on me like you do. Be bareback in it before I know it." He'd nuzzled and kissed her neck. "Mmmm, it's my fault you feel so good, girl?"

After that callous statement delivered like a compliment, Charles hadn't said another word about discussing being an outside baby daddy because they'd started kissing. He'd gotten hard again, hissing from passion because of how urgently she was easing him back inside.

It took nothing for their flame to blaze and since she was already planted, they pounded.

She never mentioned her new apartment because she didn't want him to think that he was welcome to come by. She was starting a new life in more ways than one.

And here she was, close to two weeks from being four months. The last time they were together she'd brought up the subject of his seed again.

He'd started hemming and hawing, talking about, "Mellow, I know, give me some more time…and you're sure you want this baby, 'cause it's too late to, uh." Charles stopped talking because Jocelyn's calm gaze locked his and looked straight into his panic.

Jocelyn told him to take all the time in the world. He didn't know she was moving, so in a couple of weeks, whatever happened between Charles and his wife would be no business of hers. Baybay would never have to see her husband's new baby. Charles didn't either if he didn't want to.

Plus, Jocelyn had never asked, or even hinted, for Charles to leave home. He surely wasn't KiKi's new daddy. She didn't want a man who cheated.

But Baybay deserved to know and although she'd never believe it, Jocelyn never meant to hurt her. She'd just gotten lonely and weak. Drunk on her friend's husband's ride.

His wife would never understand that it was the best sex of her life. It was getting hard to look Baybay in the eye because she felt like a two-faced backstabber. She was.

And for some ungodly reason, she was also mad at her friend. Nosy-ass Baybay, always so damn busy checking everybody else's smoke while her own house was burning down.

Jocelyn decided that the best way to handle the situation was to just move on and not see Baybay or 210 anymore. Ever. She just didn't have the energy right now to figure out what she and Charles were going to do about child support and that kind of business. In time.

Charles had two weeks to talk to his wife. If he didn't tell Baybay about his baby by then, on the day she moved, she would. Then it would all be over and she'd be out.

She hoped for a girl.

Telephone Love

"Peace."

"So you got a new man."

"O hello. After all this time you made a mistake and called this number?"

"Rakim. What's this with you and Supreme?"

"Who?"

"Yeah. Play with me."

"Play with you about what?"

"Rakim you Supreme?"

"Why I'ma search the deck when I got the ace baby?"

"Bullshit. Bitch I'ma break your neck. You know Supreme."

"So what. If I know him I know him. You saying I can't know nobody?"

"I'm the only muhfucka you need to know."

"O yeah?"

"O yeah. Alright. Stay there. I'm coming to 1A right now."

"I don't know who you gon see. I was almost out the door when the phone rang. I got to leave now or I'ma be late. Call me later or I'ma call you."

"On what number?"

"Well if it changed just give it to me and I'ma use it later. In a couple of hours okay?"

"Is this how you showing me you miss me?"

"If you say so."

"Yeah. I got to see you so I can check that big mouth. You know better. Change your muhfuckin tone."

"No baby Rakim straight. I Did miss my baby you know I did. Don't pay me no mind. But I got to go. Give me your number baby and I'ma be calling you in a minute."

"Where you going? I'm coming."

"Come on Shipell. I'm a fren lending support to a fren about

119

a private matter. Give me the number man I got to go!"

"Rakim. Where you going?"

"Shipell."

"You can't tell me because you know I know your tricky ass is meeting Supreme."

"Whatever Shipell."

"I know Supeme white Benz. I know his people Bigman and Sincere. Yeah. My partnas say Rakim been exclusive Supreme for months. Look like you out the Game and he's your only man."

"Who? Who told you that shit?"

"Is it true?"

"I ain't say that. I axed who you heard that shit from."

"Rakim how you been paying rent?"

"In cash like I always do."

"Oho yeah. You is Supreme because you talking silly. Or else you out your gotdamn mind. Talking to Love like this."

"Says you."

"You scared to tell me what I know?"

"What do you know? Because I ain't say I was with nobody."

"What you saying?"

"Nothing!"

"Rakim how long you been fucking Supreme?"

"Hold up. I'm sick of this shit now. What kind of shit you bringing after all this time? Let me axe you. Why you acting like I done something to you? I seen you? You been in the wind what? Six months? Plus who's the one taught me that the past ain't got nothing on today? Wasn't that you? You the one who went and pulled up. Not me. What you yourself seen? Same bitches and muhfuckas reporting on me want to get with me or want to get with you. You know it."

"Rakim tell me the truth about you and Supreme. I don't want to hear all that bullshit."

"Fuck this. Shipell believe what you want to. I'ma go now. So if you not gon give me your number call me later."

"I know you miss me baby."

"You's a lie."

"Baby...baby. Is it still slippery when it's wet baby? Huh

baby?"

"What. You miss this slick road honey?"

"You the honey baby. Sss. You the honey dripper. Yeah. Daddy know you been just...sss...aching for Daddy to be all up...mmm...In it baby... Mmm. Fantasizing about me...sss...sliding in an out...All this snake you love... Creeping deep in that bush...."

"Whatever...Listen...."

"Mmm. Remember how good my hands feel on the inside of your thighs baby?... Yeah."

"Shipell..."

"Yeah babydoll. What. I hear your voice getting soft...And you getting wet...Mmm... And baby we know how wet you get...sss...All that honey stringing...making lace between your thighs. Mmm...You wish I had my hand in your panties right now. Huh baby?... Stroking my pretty kitty. Tapping that clitty....You want me there right now so you can turn it up for Daddy don't you babydoll. Yeah...So I can't miss it when I hit it...You obsessed with me...You want me sucking your big tittys...Sss yeah...Can you feel me pinching those nipples babydoll?...Sss...Mm m m...huh? What? What you say baby?"

"Stop Shipell."

"Stop what baby? You don't want to relive the best times of your life? Huh baby?"

"I remember."

"What you remember Sexy?"

"Ha. This sweet hot box recall making you hooked like dope on the Divine Rose lover. Yeah baby? Uh huh. Rakim remember rubbing...aahh... all my sticky licky in your face and that's why your skin is so nice."

"Yeah. You want Daddy babydoll. You ain't had no real di...."

"I'm talking. Listen. You made sure you kept my number huh baby? You the one been fiendin dreamin and schemin about this ho between my thighs...my magic slide...Huh baby? Who else but this masterpiece keeps your gotdam branch so muhfuckin hard you cries like a newborn at night?...Uh huh...You got your hand around it right now don't you Daddy? It's alright.

Pull on it. Go 'head baby...That's My. Big piece of meat...Get it ready. I know you...mmm...want to cream...in the back of Rakim throat...Can you feel them? You feel my lips covering that head?...Say what baby...."

"Yeah. Daddy got what you need sugar. Your king cobra babydoll. Ready to choke your nasty ass. Yeah. Wait for me. You ain't going nowhere."

"Uh uh. No Shipell I really can't. I really got to meet my fren. I promise I'ma call you. Very soon if you ever plan on giving me the number."

"Who you meeting?"

"Like. I Said. A fren."

"Her name?"

"You don't know them."

"Who's them?"

"You don't know Her!"

"You lying."

"   "

"Talk."

"What Shipell."

"You got money?"

"You give me any?"

"What I'ma give you is until ten to get your fresh ass over to 44."

"I'ma try. Give me the number."

Shipell finally recited the number and warned "Be careful. Don't go too far with me Rakim. Happy Birthday" and hung up.

That's how me and him got back together. On my birthday. Number twenty-three.

I rushed to met Teddy midtown on the east side for a quick cocktail at eight because he had to be uptown by ten. I was late getting to him. I had to tease him out of a bad mood. Had to satisfy him with a answer why I'm not on time. Told him a old fren from the past had kept me on the phone.

Teddy spoke to me like he never did before. "What the fuck. Fuck a old fren. Ain't a muhfucka more important than me Rakim." He was hunched over his drink a vein beating in his temple.

"You right honey this baby so sorry" and add it won't ever happen again. He grabbed me strong by the back a my neck and kissed me hard. Said let's go.

We left the bar in enough time for both of us to get where we had to be but me and Teddy made a mistake. We started kissing when we got in the car. And we flared right up.

My nipples was standing like cherries. The front of Teddy pants looked like a cucumber lving in there. We both know what's collecting in my panties.

Teddy desire turned his face concrete gangster. He pulled away from me started the engine and took off fast. I know he was trying hard not to get on top of me. Trying to go handle his bizness like he supposed to.

At a red light he put his hand under my mini to the top of my thighs and they opened right up. "This is your fault" Teddy said when the light turned green. Teddy screeched a U turn went down some side streets turning corners left and right and stopped the car.

I didn't know where we was. Behind some factory buildings.

We sat quiet for a few seconds then I said "What's my fault?" like I didn't know. I felt Teddy looking at me so I axed "Ain't you gon be late?" Meaning I'm gon be late meeting Shipell too.

Wherever we was was dark and deserted. I expected him to jump on me but instead Teddy said "Rakim look at me" and turned on the roof light.

"Happy birthday baby." Supreme reached and opened the glove compartment and next thing I know he was closing a plat chain with a giant ice teardrop around my neck.

"Oooo!" I closed my arms around his neck. Released him quick then got out my side. Teddy killed the light then got out his side. We opened the back doors and got in the back seat.

For once we in black dark. The tip of my tongue licking at his face seeing in my mind his mean eyes. I knew there wasn't gon be nothing gentle in what Supreme was gon do to me brutal.

He took me like a warrior. Supreme. What's his name. Supreme. Whose is it. Supreme. Who own it. Supreme. Who?

Supreme. Holding me so tight. Muscles like coconuts in his arms. Strong fingers knot my hair. Pleasurepain run across my scalp. Working deep rough talking "Take it. You mine. Stay on it." My eyelids fluttering. I'm a ragdoll drowning....

Seems like only a minute go by but soon ninethirty come and gone and both of us about to be late. Rearranging ourselfs we was still breathing heavy. I'm acting like I ain't rushing.

Axed him to drop me off crosstown in front of Club 44 because I'm late meeting a frengirl for a late dinner. Taking a chance on the lie because I know he's in a hurry too and don't have time to come in the restuarant.

We speeding and I'm joking if my frengirl see me like this she gon know why I wasn't on time. Pulled down the mirror scrambling to fix my makeup. Tried to pull a comb through my messed up hair. Teddy glancing at me but I can't help it can't see Shipell like this. Needed to get to a bathroom.

Soon as we was in front of 44 one of my feet was out the car on the sidewalk. Teddy said "Baby." I looked around at my other man.

Teddy said "Rakim I know you know Shipell back. I saw him last night drinking with Blue."

I just rolled my head to the side pulled my leg back in the car closed the door. "Teddy" came out my mouth like a sigh.

"Nuh uh. I don't want to hear no fucking 'Teddy.' What you about to go do Rakim?"

"Listen. Teddy..."

"Baby I know you was Shipell before I claimed you. I know he discovered you. I know he left you. Now you Supreme. And I ain't proving to a muhfucka that you mine...You listening to me?"

"Yeah."

"Yeah what?"

"Yeah I know what's up. You boss."

"So don't make a mistake and fuck up what we got for some bullshit you holding onto in your mind." Teddy gripped me by the arm.

"Teddy get off me!"

Teddy voice scary. "Say it again." He leaned into my face

spoke deep and low. "You running me?" I'm gazing straight ahead. "You meeting that muhfucka right now? He back so you crawling?"

He jerked my arm to make me look in his face. "That's why your ass was late meeting me. He the old fren. Fuck what we been doing for months. Right Rakim?...You better look at me...Now you Gaming. Made me drive you to meet Shipell?" Teddy motioned his chin towards 44. "Shipell inside?"

"What you want me to say Supreme?" I wasn't admitting to nothing.

Teddy grabbed my face. "You ain't got to say shit. Look down at that igloo around your fucking neck. That say it all. Ain't another muhfucka you know giving plat holding freeze like that. Bitch you ain't gon do this to me... Bitch I'll kill you."

He see my eyebrows go high. "What. Bitch I'll kill you? That's right. And I'ma tell you what bitch...You ain't got no choice to choose. Get the fuck out. Go tell that ex muhfucka of yours what's up. This shit is settled. Handle it. Hit my cell when you get home and you gon meet me later." I didn't move.

Teddy let go of my face reached over me and opened my door. "Bitch I said get the fuck out my car."

I had to pull myself together because here I go again. Didn't know if I'm being clowned or if I'm the grand prize.

H-O Yeah

Get off on that stick
I want to suck your
D-i-
See
Me lap that candy
Hand inside my panties

Got that keylock fit
Other women ain't
S-h-
I
Don't mind
Long as I'm first in line

Let's go get stuck
I know you love to
F-u-
See
Me offer wide
Juicy fruit between my thighs

Bring that concrete to me
Lay foundation in this
Puss-
See
Me wind it up on you

He Leash Me

Dashed through the door I think five past ten. Scanned the restaurant until I saw him. Went straight to him. Ignored evry "May I help you?" because they couldn't.

My mind was all wound up. Forgot to take off my new ice and plat chain. Met Shipell wearing it. That's probably the first thing he saw when I walked up. I remember him looking at my neck but he never mentioned it. And I forgot I had it on.

This is the first time I laid eyes on my spotlight in months. Shipell looked better than my dreams. Stylesetter. Navy linen collar to hem. One leg crossed casual at the knee. Foot dangling modeling a navy silk sock and a navy lace up baby gator.

Skin so smooth like he bathe in milk. Thick black curls looked arranged strand by strand. Showcase plat. Most people never saw a link like the quiet one Shipell had on. Handmade and said money at a glance. Presidential Rolex rimmed in ice. Rocks in plat on two fingers on one hand. Baby didn't have on too much.

Stood up like a gentleman before I sat down. Shipell sharp eyes hawking mine. Felt like I'm about to fall. Felt like Teddy arms still caged around my waist. This also the first time Shipell was ever at 44 before me. Wasn't sure how much I was late.

Glass of Dom was sitting on the table ready for my lips. Broiled lobster tails arrived right away. Shipell dipped a piece in liquid butter put it on my tongue. Took his time pulling his fingers out of my mouth.

Shipell said he knew I missed him so much "It's been too long sugar." Licked his pretty lips. "You alright baby? Your man home. Right before your eyes on your birthday. Your heart alright now?" Said I'm so damn fine. How I been taking care of myself?

I didn't answer and he didn't axe me no more. Crazy coincidence I worked navy linen too. Shipell chilly smile and comment that he had stopped to read my thoughts before he got dressed.

I had never known Shipell to look at me so deep. Put his soft full lips on mine so offen. He reminded me I been loving him a long time. Knew I wanted his baby. Said he was going to take me home move on me special. Said this night is our night like our anniversary.

Never said it before Shipell said he love me. Pulled my face close to his when he told me. I like to died I like to died. He said don't cry honey. Said tonight we gon make a baby. He got a surprise for me. I'm weak like a baby. Shipell paid the bill and had to hold me up going to the car.

When we got to the Benz it was full of red roses. The car was damn near packed with roses. So many you think I'm lying. Looked like more than a hunnit all long stem without the thorns. Some was full open some just buds just gorjus.

My nose snuggled his neck while he was driving. My lap hidden in roses. Shipell hit play and jazz music started seducing me too. Poking in my mind something wondered why my necessary man let me off so easy about what I been doing. Especially after that convasation we had earlier about Supreme.

But fuck it. Crazy for me to bring up a problem. Not this night.

Shipell pulled up in front of my place about five to midnight and told me to give him my keys. Told me to sit still while he came around and opened my car door.

Helped me out then lifted me up over his shoulder like I'm light. Grabbed as many roses as I could. Left a trail up the stoop. Left so many in the Benz. He got one arm holding me on his shoulder while his hands open my bag and pull out my keys.

Shipell said "Be quiet Rakim" because I'm laughing kind of loud about nothing except being happy. Shipell back. My man back. My waist was caught on his shoulder I was dangling over my spotlight like a sack. Baby opened the front door. Used the key to open the second door.

I'm on the first floor and with a few steps Shipell was standing in front of 1A. He pulled me off his shoulder by my hair. Cradled me deep in his arms. Kissed the shit out of Rakim. I lost myself in it because Shipell don't like to kiss. My baby mouth sweet like candy.

Next thing I know we on the other side of my apartment door. Shipell reached his foot back and kicked it close. Carried me through the livingroom into the bedroom and told me to throw my roses on my queensize. Put me on my feet and told me to pull off the petals because he didn't want the stems to hurt my back.

He pressed up behind me feeling me up while I destroyed most of the blooms. Soon as the bed was covered with rose petals I laid my hot trembling self down. Reaching up for him I wanted Shipell chest on mine.

Shipell leaned into me grabbed me tight by my wrists. Stretched my arms over my head. Laid all his weight down on me slow. Pulled back his head like a snake to look in my face while he grinded me.

Then pulled me up to my feet. Lead me to the shower like he reading my mind.

He didn't turn on the bathroom light. In the dark he undressed me undressed his hard sexy self. Held me tight against him with one arm while he reached the other to turn on the shower.

Lifted me in the tub and got in too. Got us wet under hot water. Shipell used the soap to lather me ehhwhere with his hands. Took his time soaping between my thighs.

We didn't say nothing but we was talking. O yeah. Ready to intercourse on evry single level. Turned me around slow rinsed me until I'm sleek. Shipell turned off the water and we got out the tub. Dried hisself quick but took his time with me.

Dried me like I'm glass. Towel gentle under my breasts. Held each one in his hands to dry all over it. Seemed like the only way to dry my nipples was to roll and pull them. Shipell dried me slow between my cheeks. Eased open where my thighs come together and patted the towel there. Petting my kitten. But right there kitty stayed wet.

I'm Shipell puppet and we love it.

Shipell scooped me up then my ass bouncing on the rosy bed. Petals flying up all around me land all over me. Shipell crawled up between my legs. Used the very tip of his tongue to taste my sugar from my navel up to the tip of my chin. Stretched his solid body out on mine his lips nasty buttaflies tingling my ears. Telling quiet threats of what he gon take made me moan.

Promised me I'm never gon forget this night.

Eased up off me so he can go down low and take his time to savor honey sips from my other wide open lips. Over and over so slow. Wickedsweet Shipell say "Ooo baby tell Daddy" when I got to shout call out. Shipell axed me who I was with earlier. I wasn't able to answer. I wasn't able to do nothing but be ready for what I was dying to get.

And I knew it was coming. Shipell raised up to come cover me. I love it when he uses his hands to set my hips. Tears running down into my ears because I never felt like this before. When the tip of his. Just barely nudged my. Evry nerve I got rushed right there. This the moment I was born for.

Shipell showed me a new bodylock. Foot and sock. Pony and jock. Tick and tock. Baby took me to the mountaintop. Then I got greedy and hammer gave me a lot.

Shipell butter. I'm butter melt.

Then he licked his lips put that growl in my ear said "Baby let's try something new...."

Shipell Play Games

I'm in a nightmare.

Spent the last hour trying to be quiet and not go crazy. Trying to loosen my wrists from my brass headboard without waking up the building. Wallowing pulling pounding my heels against the mattress. Didn't even realize at first that it was me low moaning.

Couldn't call out couldn't deal with being found like this.

Shipell had left the nighttable lamp on. I looked down at my body. Got still like a dummy. My pretty skin was burgundy all over where Shipell hardsucked and pinched bruises. Each one full of blood and tender. The back of my neck killing me from Shipell jerking jerking jerking on my plat chain before it broke. Teardrop went flying.

Yank fight and pulled until I got my left hand free and broke two of my nails freeing the other one. Sat up. Both of my wrists damn near raw. My fingers puffy and tight. Wiggled them until they circulating again.

Then tried to touch myself. Found out I couldn't hardly stand it. Just the tip of one finger on my nipple felt like a hot needle. My rose was so swollen I knew to lick my finger first before I even tried to put it there. Too electric. I took a deep breath. Then another.

Shipell had just got dirt dog nasty. While his mouth bruised me he kept his fingers moving deep inside me. And that torpedo. Evry nerve I got was over stimulated and on top of my skin. I fought against the pain being sweet. Igged the tickling ripples still running up and down inside my thighs. Like I ain't had enough.

I couldn't believe how many bruises I had. They really hurt. A couple had dent marks from his perfect teeth. And I was also hurt in my mind.

Looked around my bedroom and saw my plat chain popped and curled like a little snake on the floor. Teardrop I don't know where but I see my diamond earrings winking at the foot of the bed. Crushed petals limp all around me. Roses and naked stems scattered on the floor. Room smelled like a gotdam rose garden. I rubbed my sore wrists.

Shipell had used his silk socks to tie my arms to the head posts. It was supposed to be a love game. That's what he said when he unplugged the phone. O. But that muhfucka really got me. Treated me like a freak. Did me that hardcore shit. Manhandled me like that S and M shit. Rakim had to figure out how I let myself get in a situation like this.

Got calm put my thoughts on rewind.

After he tenderized me marked me turned me inside out Shipell stood at the foot of my bed and got dressed. Talking to me all the while. Smooth moving sliding his pants up shrugging muscles into his shirt tighten his belt slipped bare feet into navy reptile. Wouldn't let me loose neither. Dared me to speak.

Shipell called me all kinds of fucking streetho bitches. Knew about Atlannic City and a lot of the other places me and Supreme been. Shipell people seen me in a whole lot of spots hugged up being content. Sitting tall in that white Benz like I ain't had no muhfuckin man. Making him out a trick.

"I should spit in your gotdam face." Told me one of his bitches swore she seen me at a hotel near the airport drunk as a gotdam dog letting some hustler fingerfuck me in the bar. Shipell said "That bitch didn't even have to tell me it was Supreme." He knew all along who I been fucking with.

Said I can't be crazy enough to believe that Mr. Love didn't know. Came to him smelling like a man. With a muhfuckin hickey on my neck.

That part surprised me because I truly didn't know I had a hickey.

And Rakim figured that bruise was the number one reason Shipell marked me like he did. He proved a point by multiplying the stamp Supreme left. Shipell sent him a response.

Shipell called me a bumbitch. Axed if I'm fucking in the street now. Got to know that without that shower he wouldn't have touched my dirty ass.

Said I was acting like a dog. "What the fuck happened to your class? When did you lose your flow Rakim?"

Shipell told me Supreme was fucking me "Because he think I done pulled at least a hunnit grand out your foolish ass." Called me a out of pocket bitch sucking dick for gifts. He said I had to know that Supreme was planning to get his money back.

Said he wouldn't be so muhfuckin upset if I was taking that muhfucka for his paper. Shipell said he should be counting Supreme money instead of going through this bullshit with me.

"Bitch we should have been planning a vacation to the Bahamas." My shit should have been so slick couldn't nobody peep it.

"Especially muhfuckas that know me. Dumb bitch. How the fuck you gon meet me smelling like cat marked the fuck up and wearing that muhfuckin chain?"

Axed me how I'm gon let some muhfucka mark my ass when I know I'm coming to meet my man. Who I ain't seen in months.

He recalled the telephone convasation we had. Lied to him from beginning to end.

"I had to refresh your ass. You forgot. Rah we both know that soon as you seen me tonight you was wrong. Should have dropped to your knees and start begging for forgiveness." And run money across his muhfuckin hand.

"What. I step off for a minute and your fucking head fell off Rakim?" Shipell said he surprised. Axed me what happened to me. He don't want to believe it. I used to be so sharp.

"A minute? A minute? Shipell! You been gone six months! How I know you was coming back? Huh? How I'm suppose to know you was coming back!" I had to say something in my defense so he would at least untie his damn socks and let me loose.

"Who the fuck you yelling at? If I was gone six muhfuckin years you suppose to act like it was six seconds and keep your mind on me. Stay in control. Loyalty baby. And be ready to give me what's mine when your man get back."

Whatever. I had plenty of money. Wasn't none of it his so wasn't no need to mention it. "Why can't you look at it like I was taking care of myself until you got back?"

"Shut up. You trying to make me think you was playing Supreme? So give me the money. Fuck you bitch. Playing a muhfucka don't mean getting with a muhfucka. Rakim you know that." I heard that streetlaugh.

"If this muhfucka got you open like my partnas say he do that mean he claiming. Say it Rakim. Tell me it got too hard for a weak bitch like yourself to stay strong for a winner like me. I turn my head and you let another man piss on my spot. Your boosy ass just moved on to the next muhfucka without my permission or payment."

Shipell was fully dressed and pacing my bedroom.

"Letting that muhfucka drape ice around your neck like he own it." Shipell got in my face. "I thought you loved me so fucking much. But you don't have no confidence. I thought you had heart Rakim. You ain't mine. My woman stay secure that her man is coming home. My bottom know how to maintain finance by separating the physical from the mental. But what the fuck you do? Let a muhfucka run up in you centerstage. Out in the street. Letting this muhfucka give you gifts instead of cash. He your boyfren now?"

Shipell temper still rising. "Muhfuckin bums and shit telling me about you and that muhfucka Supreme. Calling y'all a love story. Your shit so wide open my gotdamn partnas telling me they wish they knew you was so easy to snatch."

But what my ears heard was a love poem.

My baby didn't realize he was declaring he crazy in love with me too. Because he's back and furious to find hisself moved over by another cat who has no problem keeping me high profile.

It would have been no problem dating Supreme if I kept it cash bizness below the waist. Shipell would have been proud to know that I finally got up off my "lazy ass" and went to work. He could have heard that I was with Supreme evry night if I was working. Stacking cash for my mack until he came back.

Shipell out of control because he said my ignorant ass was out of control. Way out of pocket. Freely snuggling in public with Supreme who's playing me like a flute. Jamming my mind as well as my.

Shipell also didn't realize that all that mighty love we just made was more absolute proof that he ain't run up in a chick that can ho him down like me.

I ain't crazy. Shipell thinking about Supreme fucking me and he can't handle it. I'm convinced that Shipell still love me.

My own true love feelings was showing in my eyes but it must have looked like something else to my spotlight because he flipped.

Shipell came menacing over to the bed and snatched back his six carats. Three out of each ear. I'm lucky they had posts or he would have split both of my ears open. Flung them.

He wrapped his hands around my neck and started squeezing. "This is what you need around your fucking neck." Said he could choke the Shit out of me right now he so mad.

"You want to go? You want this muhfucka? Let me know Rakim." Shipell squeezed tighter. "You can't play me!"

I'm scared shaking my head. Shipell don't ease up don't let go. His eyes got real narrow started gritting his teeth getting into it. Evrything quiet. I really believed he was gon choke me to death.

I tried to scream but nothing but gurgling came out. I started beating my legs against the bed with my arms still tied over my head. Tears running out my eyes.

I think that's what saved my life. My tears. Shipell pushed my throat out of his hands. He stood up breathing hard running his hands over and over his hair. I'm gasping gulping air coughing wheezing.

Shipell backed away from the bed and something came over him. He calmed right down. Now he's acting like he wasn't never mad. Like he wasn't trying to kill me a second ago. His jaws got square. Shipell licked his lips.

"You fired Miss Divine. Free from the position you had with me. You are no longer level with me baby. Baby you got to break bread to keep me now."

Shipell standing back at my dresser looking at hisself in the mirror arranging his perfection. Said to his image "Shame. My pretty woman lost her place and her mind same time."

He looked at me through the reflection "Rakim is he worth it? Can he pay me?"

Pimp talking to me now. "Let's be adults about this baby. You been moved up but we can still be together if you can keep your new adventure. You need to babydoll. Because we need the money honey. And you owe me now sugar. I'm on your payroll baby."

He told me to run Supreme. Let him sop me up. "Be gravy baby." Laughed like he joking. "Do your thing. Let's get paid."

Shipell picked up jingled his car keys. "Call him babydoll. Soon as you get loose. Tell him me and you is through. He your boss. You his new heartbeat. Make him believe he own you now. But get cash. Get money."

Shipell stood at the foot a my bed looking at ehhthing in the room except me.

I really am his fool. No matter what. I couldn't hardly get my breath because my throat was sore as hell but gotdamn it I still wanted him. My eyes only on him.

He felt it because he finally looked at me and I knew he wanted to get back in the bed too. We looked at each other for a long minute. Me and Shipell realized we don't have no limits. Right then we knew we capable of killing each other. In the name of love.

But money rule.

Shipell shook his head. "Hot ass. We gon get a million for your delicious shit."

Said he gon call me before he come by for his cash. Told me to get it together because Supreme ain't gon buy no bitch with problems.

"True? Yeah. Get my money sweetheart. Get money for the pleasure of giving it to me. That's the only way you gon see me. I'm what you want sugar. I'm forever your fantasy. I'ma let you stay baby because I know you ready to pay…But don't get stupid and get fucked up. I'ma call you in a couple of days. Have money." Shipell leaving.

I watched his back move away then heard my front door close. Shut my eyes. Heard the Benz start and pull away.

That's when I got frantic and start struggling to get loose.

After I thought about what had happened I was ready to take my bath. Easing off the bed I squatted slow low as I could before I tried to ease to the bathroom.

Got out my oils and herbs. My blue salts. Turned the faucets on full for a deep hot bath. I walked back slow to my bedroom and scooped some rose petals off the floor to put in the water. It was agony bending down.

It was too soon for my feelings to come down. I needed a few minutes to get it together before my emotions hit me.

Let me light some candles instead of this bathroom light. Wait until aromas from my potions healing me soothing me. Let me slide down in the tub until the water hugging around my tender neck. Then I can truly figure this shit out.

O. Dont worry. Shipell want pay? That's okay. I'ma pay Shipell. For real. I'ma pay that muhfucka for treating me leaving me like this.

Teddy Play Games

After my bath I went into the bedroom and turned on the nighttable lamp. Got myself to where I could handle myself. Got my mind right.

Plugged the phone back in the receiver. Filed my broken nails. Put a little makeup on. Long red chinese silk robe. Found my rocks and stuck them back in my ears.

Sat easy on the side of my bed to call Teddy at home. Low sleepy voice like a drum said "Rakim what time is it?"

I answer "Almost three."

Teddy said gotdam it I'm just now calling him back? Heard him rolling over waking up. Axed me what took me so long to call? Aggravated right away. Where the fuck I been all night? Because he know I wasn't home. He been calling since tenthirty because his meeting was canceled. The last time he tried was close to one before he went to sleep. And he came in early just to be with my late ass.

So where the fuck was I? With who doing what? Why did-n't I call him from wherever I was? What held me up?

"I'm waiting for you to tell me you wasn't with Shipell Rakim." Steady interragating. Didn't leave one space between the questions for a answer. Then came this big silence that means he waiting.

"Baby I was in a deep situation. I was home but I couldn't get to the phone." My voice soft.

"Why not?"

"I can't tell you like this over the phone. And I need you. It can't wait. Just come over here. Please Supreme. Please. Teddy please." My voice velvet.

Teddy yawned and said he ain't going nowhere. "Talk to me now or forget it." He yawned again. "In fact fuck it." He said he was going back to sleep. I could apologize and explain when he saw me for dinner.

I kept the beg in my voice "Please Supreme come here" like hypnosis until he said shut up and let him get dressed. Hung up.

I knew part of the reason he relented is because he never been inside my apartment although he's paying for the privilege of me living here. It should also hit him that I turned to him because something wrong. Who did I call to fix shit? Him.

I didn't have much time to create the set. Had to hurry.

Picked up smashed petals from my bed. Picked up stems and whole roses from all over the floor. So many still perfect. Needed to be kept to use as models because I'ma probably feel like painting after Teddy leave. Slammed the crushed petals and naked stems in the kitchen trash like I meant it.

I kept thinking of the way Shipell had hurt me. Made me twist and turn like a rolling pin on top of all those petals in my bed. Wrists tied so I couldn't go nowhere. Just crushing roses until my bedroom full of perfume.

Muhfucka Shipell gon make me a criminal if I couldn't get him back like we used to be. I'ma hate roses if I didn't get him back. Or at least get back at him.

Picked my broke plat chain off the floor and tossed it in my jewlry box. My diamond teardrop had disappeared. Or maybe Shipell took it. I balled up his navy silk handcuffsocks and tossed them in the closet.

Tied my robe around me tight. Went quiet out my front door left it cracked. Went to the foyer door and eased through it too. Tippytoed to the front door and split it just enough to peep the street. Snuck outside after I made positive I didn't see nobody.

Ran down the stoop snatching rose stems on my hurry back up. Flew. Didn't miss but one. Left the front door and the foyer door open a crack, but they looked closed. A few tippytoe giant steps and I was back in my apartment. Before I shut the door I pushed in that button on the side that took off the lock.

I stood in the middle of the floor and buried my face in my red velvet blooms one last time. Got two plastic grocery bags from under the kitchen sink and wrapped up my flowers along with the whole ones from the bedroom. Stuffed all of them in the bottom of the refrigerator.

Lit a whole lot of african incense and bunches of musk candles in every room so Teddy can have the right smelling atmosphere and soft licking light to admire the roses I paint in my spare time.

Put smoky music on low. Sister singing got that husky cigarette voice sliding through all the colors of pain. Inspired me to change the satin on my bed from royal blue to ruby red. Put a red bulb in my nighttable lamp. Stood tippytoe on the bed and put two red bulbs in the ceiling light too.

I brushed my teeth with baking soda. Made a little breath potion with a couple a drops of peppermint oil. I draped seven strands of tiny gold beads around my waist. Gold rings on five of my toes. Tiny circles of diamonds around two more. Glossed my sore thighs swollen neck wrists and swollen breasts with a sweet oil call Promise. Put a few drops of rose oil on my brush and pulled it through my hair until it hung long and smooth.

Worked a bottle of Moet deep in a crystal bucket full of cracked ice. Set it up with matching crystal stems on the nighttable by my bed. Always something delicious in the kitchen ready to heat up.

The seduction shit. Plus a little juju as extra help so things go my way. Just a little insurance for my plan. My magic was one special candle out of all the burgundy ones I lit. The only purple one. For use in a emergency just like this. Fixed for me by a sister I'm cool with name MBara Kincade.

Met her in the supermarket not long after I got to Brooklyn. Almost passed by each other pushing shopping carts in opposite directions.

MBara stopped me with her hand on my wrist and said "Hey girl. What's your name this time?"

Like she knew me. I almost cussed her ass out but something told me that she Did know me. We been girls since that day.

MBara from Nawlins. That's how she say New Orleans. From twoheaded people with three eyes and double tongues and the touch to cause problems or work them out.

Told me that her mama her daddymama some aunties uncles and cousins on both sides got talent. Seem like ehhbody in her family can do a little something. Even the ones that deny it. They like a tribe. The old ones still lived down south but most of the Kincades lived in New York mainly in Brooklyn and Queens.

They like to be around each other all the time so it's hard to know who really lived where. Until she told me different I thought MBara lived up the street from me but she be visiting her sister Leyquana who was also her teacher.

MBara said LeyLey could change herself. I never axed her into what and she never told. All the Kincades funny. Not haha. They strange. Even for conjure people. Evry single last one of them real different with they personality.

Like MBara. She kind of pretty but she don't eat but evry other day. And then it's just vegetables fruits and nuts and beans. Keep herself so skinny look like she smoking. I tried to take her out to eat evry time I go see her but she won't go. If I bring her some of my good food she say thank you and set it aside. I know she never even taste it.

MBara got some peasy no grow hair that she won't comb for nothing. I don't think her scalp ever felt no air. Her nappy head look like looking down on trees in a jungle. Like if you was up in a plane. Thick and bumpy.

She real lightskin and dyed her palms bottom lip and behind her ears with powder she crush from bricks and only wear white clothes. Got all kinds of shit hanging around her neck. MBara smell clean like cucumbers or cut grass or the green part of a watermelon rind.

But all her people uncommon. They call it specializing. Quite a few Kincades only eat what they call motherless food. One won't walk on concrete and none of them bathe in plain water. One talk to trees. Her name Deslene and she believe spirits live in trees. Another Kincade only open his eyes at night. And on and on. They funny.

Don't advertise what they do neither. A session with a Kincade take some doing if they don't know you. You can't just walk up to the door. The first time you have to be brought by somebody who's cool with the Kincade you want to see. After that they let you know if you can come back by yourself.

And you also have to bring something sweet along with some money but nobody knows how much. Because Kincade prices be different all the time. The same person can leave out a Kincade house paying half they check and the next visit get back change from a dollar.

They was definitely strange and seem like most of MBara folks made they living off of hooking people up. The Kincades was the best at working nature power. Deserved the money they took from people needing something to bury chant burn cook drink sprinkle chew wash theyself with. Something to wear around they neck. A secret to put in they pocket or shoe. To keep attract destroy hurt save whatever whoever.

MBara gave me my candle as a present soon after we met. Said something was gon happen to me that a dream told her to make a candle for. She said I'ma need it. Explained how to use it.

I remember raising my eyebrows and turning my face away then looking back at MBara from the very corners of my eyes. She eyeballed me right back licked her bottom lip rubbed behind her ears and put her hands in her pockets.

My candle came with a small piece of paper full of tiny writing that I had to fold three times and burn to ash in the flame. So my candle was only good for one time.

I lit it before Supreme came. That damn MBara. How she know?

About forty minutes from when I called Teddy he was calling me back from his Benz telling me to come open the door. My satin voice told him that all the doors between him and me was already open. Told Teddy that I was waiting in 1A.

In a few minutes I heard both building doors open and my apartment door close. Footsteps then Teddy leaning in the doorway of my bedroom. So damn fine. In jeans and a white teeshirt with new Jordans. Suede bomber. Light jewlry. It was the first time I ever saw him wear denim.

Since this was his first visit he took his time walking around the livingroom kitchen bathroom.

Came back and stood just inside in the bedroom. Eyebrows frowning eyes thinking. I saw his nostrils get wide smelling the rich air.

Teddy looked at me and axed "You paint all these roses?"

I didn't answer just looked under my eyes at Teddy letting him fill up on me. Posing sexy like a centerfold. Letting desire build.

"So what's up baby?" Teddy moved to sit on the bed.

"Wait baby just stand there a minute. I want to tell you something." I sound sorry for myself.

Teddy looked at his Rolex and leaned up against the doorway. "Best be something I want to hear at four in the morning Rakim."

Pain in my voice. "Baby I told Shipell we was through. But he said fuck that. Baby he told me he's the one to decide when we through. And you ain't got shit to do with it. Baby he said fuck Supreme because I'm still Shipell." Sound like I'm about to break down.

Teddy face had no expression. "And...."

Axed him to hit the light switch on the wall. The overhead red light made my rosy walls really start living. He could really see them now. Roses covered the walls on the floor evrywhere I could find to put some paint.

Teeny buds to big giant blooms. Some got dewdrops like they weeping. They the reddest reds you could ever see.

I started opening my robe up slow.

Teddy blinked looked around. Looked around before he looked at me. Then did a doubletake like he didn't believe what he saw.

Bruises made my body look like it was blooming full of red roses too. Rose necklace made out of welps around my throat. Rose welps around my wrists.

Teddy came and sat beside me on the bed eyes roaming over me but didn't touch me or say nothing. I closed my eyes and started breathing slow. Ready to be a baby in his sympathy bathe in his anger over my violation. I'm sure that Supreme wasn't gon let muhfuckin Shipell get away with this.

"Open your fucking eyes."

My eyes fly wide surprised. "What's wrong baby?"

"You what's wrong." Teddy jaws set like a rock.

"Supreme! What's the matter? You don't see what Shipell did to me?" Raised up on my elbow. "You mad at Me? Because Shipell crazy?" Whispering like I'm yelling because I'm so amazed.

"He must of said something you was interested in because you let him in. Made you forget what I told you to do. I told your hardheaded ass that you didn't have no decision to make. So what's up?" Teddy voice deadly.

I'm holding one of his wrists because Supreme was acting like he was about to stand up. "Nuh uh. Teddy. Relax. Listen. It wasn't like that. I told Shipell we was through and I'm Supreme now. I left him in 44. Took a cab straight home because that's what you told me to do. Plus that's what I wanted to do. Wanted to hurry here. Shower and change. Call you and catch a cab to wherever you were. I wasn't at 44 but a minute. Didn't hardly take the time to sit down. My mind was on you Supreme."

Now each of my hands holding one of his wrists. Felt like he relaxed some under my touch. I put honey in my mouth. "Baby I'm straight. Come on Supreme I'm for real. Shipell came over here about fifteen minutes after I got home."

Teddy acted like he listening. "How Shipell get in Rakim? You knew it was him. Why did you open the door? You said you told him what's up at 44. You told him you Supreme. That mean you know he ain't allowed in here no more. Right?"

"I said Shipell pushed past me."

"Because you opened the fucking door."

"Come on Supreme. I didn't see no problem with that. Ain't like he a stranger."

"Bitch you crazy."

"I hear you."

"How he make them bruises?" Supreme chin indicated my thighs stomach neck my breasts and my.

"With his mouth and his hands."

"Don't Fuck with me Rakim. I know that. What was you doing when he did it?"

"I couldn't do nothing."

"You couldn't do nothing. But let a muhfucka who you say you don't want no more suck your titties like a baby. And gave him your ass because you still his ho."

"I didn't gave him nothing. Axe me what he took."

"So he raped you."

"Now you hear me."

"Rakim. You did not want to fuck Shipell tonight."

"No Supreme I did not."

"He stripped you."

"Yes. Listen to me. Like I said. Shipell pushed in here. Locked my hands behind my back soon as I opened the door. Gorilla me in here. Tied me to the bed and..."

"Tied you with what."

"His socks. So..."

"His what?"

"Socks! Socks!" I saw Teddy eyes narrow. "Stripped me and hurt me like this. He hurt me Supreme. You don't see my wrists? Look at my neck. He choked me! Because I love you now. I had to take a bath before I called you baby. Had to wash off his abuse because I couldn't stand the thought of calling you under his smell. I axed you to come here to see what he did to your baby. Against my will honey. Why you acting like it's my fault? Why you flipping on me?" My voice full of tears.

Supreme sniffed. Got a knife in his voice. "Kill that shit. You looking in my face telling me Shipell pushed in here and tied you up. With his fucking socks. His gotdam Socks. What. Muhfucka wear two pair of socks? He must have tied your hands first. What he use to hold open your legs while he tied your hands? Rakim you couldn't kick that muhfucka in the nuts if you was really trying to make him stop?"

My eyes blinking because I'm trying to think fast.

"Molested you against your will. Same muhfucka who bought you and dropped you before I picked your skank ass up. Same muhfucka who just want to see how fast he can make you run back. So he can dog you to play me...Bitch you better look at me. I got xray vision. I see what you thinking. Muhfucka told you to call. Told you what to say. But first you takes a bath to wash off his skeet. But telling me it's because you so concerned about me. You say you was raped but waited hours later to call me. Now you a damsel in distress...How the fuck did you get free?"

"I..."

"Shut! the Fuck up. I don't want to hear no more of this

bullshit. And get the Fuck off me Rakim." Teddy ripped his wrists out of my hands. Stood up. His look said Rakim was garbage. "Ho you must think I'm some new kind of muhfuckin trick." Grabbed me by my hair.

"Stop!"

"What. You don't like it?" Used his other hand and pull up my chin until I'm looking in his eyes.

"I don't know who you think you trying to work. But this is Supreme baby." Hot ice smile. "What's the plan Rakim? You suppose to set me up so you can turn trick money for this muh-fucka? Or you mad because Shipell played your ass and don't want you no more so you decided you a victim?"

His hand was squeezing my chin. "Light candles and shit? Had time to chill the champagne but you so upset. Bitch you overdid it." Supreme other hand pulled his singing phone out his jacket pocket. He checked the number and put it back. Swept his eyes over me.

"Your nipples still sticking out like baby thumbs. You still blazing for that muhfucka but trying to convince me with some weak bullshit that Shipell violated you. Where the fuck is the forty thousand dollar piece I just put around your neck? Gave it to that muhfucka too? You paid for his dick with my diamond? You about to be a hurt bitch if you did."

Supreme a pretty muhfucka when he mad. I love the way he hold his mouth when he dangerous. His eyes get small and his jawline get real sharp. He so fine and thick that my spot started getting hot. I told him in a little voice that Shipell had broke it off my neck but it was still in the room on the floor somewhere. Supreme told me I better find it because he wanted it back.

"Ho you a mess. You look like a polkadot fool." Supreme finally let go of my face. Now he all up in my dresser mirror admiring hisself just like that other bastard.

I'm about tired of muhfuckas changing from glad to mad up in my house. Calling me out my name in my beautiful rosy rooms. O. It ain't just them mad. Rakim building rage too. Deep inside.

Teddy axed me again. "What's up Rakim? Your little plan backfired? Looking pitiful but bitch you still beautiful. But you not slick enough to clown a slick muhfucka. No baby."

Teddy laugh. "What. I'm supposed to go find Shipell now and bring beef over you?" He shook his head like he can't believe it. Started talking to his reflection. I had another Shipell flashback.

"Ain't this some shit. Bitch trying to use me for a muhfucka who don't really want to fuck with her. Bitch ready to put me back in the penitentiary because I might have to kill her ass. Got me out my bed to run this bullshit." Supreme thinking out loud.

He turned around to look at me. "He choked you because you tried to play his ass too. You think you got Game to razor two sharp muhfuckas? What bullshit you tell him to make him fuck you up like this?"

I was sitting straight up in my bed looking hard at Supreme. Vibe on my face hotstepped him to me. Flashback number three.

"What's wrong with your fucking face? Fix it. Bet I..." Raised the back of his hand changed his mind. Let out a deep breath. "Rakim Rakim. Rakim you almost had my ass. Gotdamn. I was really trying to get with you no bullshit. Gotdamn!

"But I got to say you got heart Miss Divine. You crafty. You a first for me." Teddy looked at me with a different understanding. "Weak muhfuckas better watch out for your fine snake ass. But not This muhfucka. Not me baby. Supreme can fit through a crack. Invented the con you tried to pull sweetheart. You moved too fast with a real muhfucka this time baby. Fucked it up.

"I was about to breed you. Make you the first one to bear my seed in my name. Shower you with riches. Give you what your dumb ass don't even know you want. Buy your slick ass a house..."

Supreme stood still and just looked at me. "Rakim could have had heaven. Look how you fucked us up Rakim. I'm getting ready to move another way and I thought I was gon take you with me. But you like the gutter. Dirty bitch."

Teddy said alot more about getting his feelings involved with shit like me but I was just coasting not fully listening but my mind was recording. I'ma replay what he said later after he left. Know he going. Soon.

Fixed my face to get him believing I'm scared to talk. I kind of was because this shit turned out real wrong. Wise to wait and see what kind of response he really wanted. There still might be a way to fix this.

But to be honest I couldn't take too much more of this upheaval. Had enough. Been hurt more than enough for one night.

"I know you ain't got shit to say. But you better find my fucking diamond." Seem like all Benz keys jingling sound alike. Supreme finally leaving.

"Listen. Rakim. Tell Shipell Supreme said he right. You ain't shit. A nickel bitch trying to be a dime. Matter of fact I'm gon locate Shipell. Buy him a drink. Laugh about your stupid ass. Shit. Look at you. He fucked you up!"

That was the drop that made me overflow. "Shutup! Shut the Fuck up Gotdamn it! On my Word! That's It! No More! Not tonight. You hear me? Fuck you! Get the Fuck out my gotdam house Supreme! Muhfucka Get! Out! Fuck you! And that Fucking Shipell!" I snappped like a twig. Jumped up off my bed robe flying out behind me.

I flung the phone at Supreme. Some shoes. Ran around my bedroom reaching for anything I could get my hands on. I was a crazy woman cussing and looking for more stuff to throw. I tried to get to the kitchen for the butcher knife but he wouldn't let me pass.

I threw myself at Supreme but he grabbed me around my waist. I couldn't get loose from him. Clawed his face and punched him in the eye before he grabbed my arms. That made me fight harder because I'm tired tired tired! of muhfuckas holding me down.

I started biting at Supreme like a dog.

That's when he threw me to the floor. On my back I was so furious my arms and legs was going wild. Teddy battled me straddling me between his knees until he caught my wrists with his hands and locked my legs between his thighs. "Rakim! Quit! Calm! your wild ass down. Stop! Stop Rakim! You ain't going Nowhere. Shit."

He saw my throat working my lips tighten. "Bitch you spit on me and I'ma punch you dead."

That's what he said ripping off my silk. We hot. It would have been rape if I wasn't bubbling from all the fighting.

Happened like lightning. Supreme raised up holding both of my wrists in one of his big hands unzipped his jeans and pulled out his thick.

His hands gripped my sore wrists so hard they hurting bad again. Held them over my head again. Supreme leaned back down and put his granite face inches from mine. Kissed me on my forehead. Axed me why I didn't tell him I liked thug pain. I should have told him long ago I like agony. "That's my thing baby." He would have trained me lovely.

I would have been a puppy when he was through. "That's what the fuck they got me for. A misunderstanding. A woman who liked to play my way caught a bad break. It was a accident. We was taking it to another level and...."

Supreme didn't say no more. Like he didn't mean to say so much. But what was he talking about? He went to prison because the woman dead? And what level was they on? He playing?

That vein thumping in his temple and his nostrils flared like a bull. Supreme jaws clenched tight and jumping. He ain't playing. And he looking in my face. Which didn't show no expression whatsoever. I didn't even blink. Vibe told me to relax and ride it out.

Plus I was through. Nothing left to fight with. I was tired.

He let my arms go because he knew he could. I wasn't resisting no more. Just laying on my back watching him stand up and take off his jeans and silk boxers over his Jordans. Stayed in his teeshirt.

Fell on me bit me hard on my shoulder. Exactly on one of the same places Shipell bit me. Hurt so bad and that's why Supreme did it.

Picked up his hips and sank his massive like a piece of lead straight to the bottom a my. Plowed it. He grunt then laugh nasty cause I wasn't dry.

Wet and waiting.

"Bitch you a cold freak. Baby baby. We would have been perfect together. What the fuck was I doing treating you like a lady?" Supreme drew hisself out of me. His shit was so hard it was bouncing by itself.

Supreme suprised me. Yanked me over on my stomach and

pulled me up on my knees. Entered my back door with one slow stroke. O shit. I pushed back to hurry it because going in hurt so good.

Then that roughneck roughhouse roughride me. He reached around and jacked my pearl. I went lava one more time. Couldn't help it. And Supreme delivered right with me. Released in me so deep I almost spit.

Next few minutes after that are crystal clear. Recalled exactly what he did. Supreme pulled away from me and turned me around to face him. We looked at each other still standing on our knees.

Wham! He backhand the shit out of my mouth. Bam! Did it again the other way.

I wasn't expecting it. I was reeling. Dropped my head my fingers feeling my lips. Shocked like crazy because I didn't believe he hit me. Twice.

Then he said real sweet "Rakim." I look back at him thinking he gon apologize but he clocked me. Pulled back and punched me like a brick on the side of my head. Supreme knocked me out.

I must have blacked out close to ten minutes because I don't have no images of Teddy getting dressed and leaving.

I came back to myself still laying on the floor. My body crumpled up like a piece of tissue. My silk robe tossed beside me. A dark stain showed where he wiped hisself off.

Got up legs all wobbly and cut off the music the nighttable lamp and the ceiling light. My roses melted back into shadows left me alone. Got back in the bed and sat up watching candle flames.

Enjoyed how seductive I still smelled. I was calm as a clam. Sipping champagne. Color got deeper because Supreme busted both of my lips. One of my teeth felt loose. Side of my head killing me.

Made a sick joke to myself. If I keep on sipping champagne while my lips still bleeding by the bottom of the glass I'ma be drinking red wine. But I finished the bottle.

I knew my face looked just like what happened. Got punched in my mouth. And sexed like a dog. Something else was gon have to happen. Or I'ma lose my mind.

Turned my thoughts on. Got clever with it until I hit it. Started working out all the angles and details involved in my fly revenge. Took my time to look at it from evry side. Looked in evry corner. Next time wasn't nothing gon go wrong.

Evrything gon start with two phone calls. I was gon call both of my men one last time. Say whatever I have to say to get them back here. Promise anything.

Friday. Tomorow night. One at a time. Take care of bizness with one before the other one get here. Entertain Supreme first. And after I'm done with him a couple of hours later I was gon get with Shipell.

As soon as each one is at my door I'ma start talking. I'ma work out what I'ma say in advance so I be word perfect.

I'ma open the door nekked. Nothing on at all. No jewlry. Nothing. Only thing I'ma wear is all my bruises and my bust lips. Showing how fucked up I look.

Both of them gon see me drop to my knees. I'ma say I ain't all that fine right now. But this woman is so genuine sorry I'll do anything. Baby let's go to bed.

I'ma get Supreme here by telling him that I found his chain and stone.

I'ma tell Supreme that I truly must have been out of my damn mind.

Agree right away that my ass too stupid to bullseye a Real boss who been too good to me. I'm dead wrong. Wrong as two left shoes. After all he gave me? A couple of bust lips ain't nothing sweetheart. I deserved it. Needed to have my ass knocked out. Knock some sense into me. To make our relationship better.

There ain't a damn thing Shipell can do for me and I can see that clearly now. I'ma say Supreme you right. Never been wrong. I'm so sorry. Can I apologize? Baby give me a baby so I can stay home…

I'ma do Supreme. I Promise.

Then I'ma get myself together all over again before time to play slave for Shipell.

I'ma get Shipell here by telling him I got money. I'ma tell Shipell it be my pleasure to pay long as I can stay. Got enough money right now to buy his time for the rest of the night. Robbed that muhfuckin trick Supreme with finesse like he told me to.

That's how I got these busted lips baby. He was fighting me because I was calling your name. And you right. My gotdamn head did fall off. You was so right to bruise my unruly ass.

Please let me date so I can prove how bad Rakim got to be back on the bottom. Level with the ground with you....

One on one. Me and Supreme. One on one. Me and Shipell. Take my time. One at a time. I'ma put each of my babies in a trance. I'ma make sure each one of them stay mine.

Won't be no woman in they lives after me.

Got to be tomorrow night.

I'ma use my silk voice when each one standing at my door. How can I make it up to you? Can I please show you how chastised I am? Let me prove I got regret and deserve another chance. You do evryrthing for me. Let me stay. I ain't nothing without you.

What you want? Do me anyway you want to. This your baby-bitch so rock me steady Daddy. Just don't leave me. I been tripping on the moon since you left me last night. Can't think of nothing but you baby. All my fault. Come back. Don't let me go crazy....

On an on like that? I do that? Shipell? Supreme? Shit. Easy as pie. Like a fingersnap.

Once they in my bedroom each of they heads gon be sunk in my satin pillows. Getting hot watching me play with myself while I'm begging. They asses grinding on my silk sheets. Pulling air through they teeth. Holding caressing stroking they steel like it ache because it do.

Won't hardly be able to get out "Rakim. Come here."

That's my deep plan. The core is one man at a time.

Get Supreme here first then a few hours later I'ma welcome Shipell. When I'm through with my babies they gon have memories to tell God.

Supreme and Shipell. Get them here tomorrow. One at a time. That's the key. Douche inbetween.

I kept painting roses because it helps me think. I'ma show my men a trick with a hole in it.

Got to call Mbara too before the action start.

Rosy Rosy

They call me Rosy Rosy
Say I'm so round
I can go low
But nevva level wit the ground
Rosy Rosy
Come here
Rosy Rosy
Yes my dear
They call me Rosy Rosy
Say I'm so nice
My kisses not sweet evrytime
I hot some wit my spice
Rosy Rosy
What I got
Rosy Rosy
Pepper pot
They call me Rosy Rosy
Say I take care
Mek you feel comfy like a babe in arms
But yuh mooma won't be there
Rosy Rosy
Baby love
Rose Rosy
Big it up
They call me Rosy Rosy
Say I hold tight
Ever ready
Yuh dream coming true tonight
Rosy Rosy
Who yuh love
Rosy Rosy

Dangerous
They call me Rosy Rosy
Say I'm a ball
Nooo problems
Downpress me at all
Rosy Rosy
Come now
Rosy Rosy
Fine doll
Rosy Rosy

Remember Me

Got out the bed turned my music back on low. Got my paintbox from under the dresser. Remembered my real roses and got excited. Hurried best I could to the kitchen. Got my cold red roses from the refrigerator. Planned to look at them while I worked in the bathroom.

Mixed my oils by candlelight. Used my memory and creativity. Went over and over my plan with the same concentration that I was going to give the strokes on my roses.

Watched my brush swirl color and knew that when the shade was perfect my plan would be too. Just like painting it's never good to overwork a idea.

I started feeling that lightness. A sensation I get when things are going real wrong. It's scary but I'm not scared of it because usually by the time the feeling goes away I know what to do.

My head gets light and I feel like my body is holding me down. I'm living in my mind. Clear as day all I see is a door and behind it is who I really am. No matter what I'm gon find on the other side my mind got to pull it open and go through to float and remember myself.

How I got to be where I am now. When I first started moving around. How I got from Alabama to Brooklyn by way of Jamaica and Miami. When I started changing my name. Since evryplace had a different name I did too....

When I was little my mama took me to the doctor for the way I was behaving. I looooved what I had between my legs. Like I wasn't no kid. I don't know how I knew something was supposed to go in it. Couldn't wait to try. Like I was burning up with needing it.

I was seven. I wasn't suppose to know noting about sex at seven. But I did.

I must have been born hot because I don't remember seeing nobody doing it back then. Only wimmen without men lived in my house and we wasn't on no farm. Didn't own no dogs.

Me my mama and big mama lived in a little house in back-woods Chitockwa Alabama. I was born there but big mama had come from Saint Ann Jamaica when my mama was little. They lived in Montgomery before they moved after mama got pregnant. From what I could tell from listening to big mama my daddy was a good time passing through fast.

I had been playing with myself long as I can remember but mama didn't catch on until I was seven. She was coming out the house to go around to the back garden and caught me trying to force my cousin Billy hands inside my panties.

Right in the front yard. I remember saying sssahh sssahh while I was trying to make him do it. She licked me upside my head and started shouting "What's wrong with you! Where you learn that at!" Told Billy to take his nasty ass home. He ran off crying that he didn't do nothing.

Mama called the black doctor all upset and insisted me and her come there right away. She pushed me in front her all the way to his office. We walkrun the whole way. Mama steady practicing out loud how to explain my behavior to the doctor.

When she told him what she caught me doing he crossed his arms over his chest and told her she was making too much of the situation. It was normal behavior. Playing doctor. He was sure me and my cousin was just playing little kid games. Mama couldn't convince him different so we left with her hoping he was right. Huh. She talked words I never heard while we walked slow back home.

Soon as we got there I got up on the couch and started rubbing my. Mama dropped to her knees hollering for big mama. She came in the living room to see what I'm doing and grabbed me up in her chest. Started crying saying I needed the blood of Jesus because the devil done got holt of this baby lamb.

Right then she and mama closed they eyes and started praying over me. But mama peeked to see what I was doing. She slapped my fingers away from touching myself then kept praying holding on to my hands.

Evryday for about two weeks they took me to afternoon

prayer meeting at Jerusalem Baptist. I let them think I agreed with evrything they said until one day Reverend Buckly saw me sitting in a pew with my legs wide open pulling my panties to the side. I was trying to persuade his grandson to put a candle from the altar in my. He was getting ready to do it when his grandfather walked in. That stupid boy dropped the candle and ran.

I was so damn mad at Reverend Buckly I pissed on the floor of the church. He almost had a stroke. I didn't care or understand why evrybody was screaming about me.

They kicked my mamas out of that congregation because they said they was wicked mothers. Mama slapped my face yelling telling me to "Get down off your toes! Stop walking on your damn toes and listen! Listen!" to her. That's a habit I use to have when I was little. I used to like to walk around on my toes because I wanted to be a ballerina.

After the seventh grade she stopped sending me to school because I was scandalous. I let the boys feel me up. Let them get me on the ground and hump on top of me. Let a couple of the oldest boys wiggle they fingers in me. Put they little dough in my mouth until some of them became a breadstick.

All the girls didn't want to be my frens because they said I'm so nasty. They told the teacher and they mamas what me and the boys was doing behind the school. Ehhbody parents in a uproar. Wanted me out! that school.

They made up a petition and got up a group to go shout in front of our house. What kind of people are we? Something is wrong inside our house. Must be. Those grown wimmen must be in there molesting that child. Must be. They stopped my mama in the street to cuss her and tell her that they sent they children to school to learn books not the dirt I was teaching. And must have learned inside our house. We had to move.

I was like a old roadside ho with a little girl mind. Mama couldn't teach me nothing at home neither because I wouldn't pay attention more than a minute. So my reading and writing can use some work. Always could count money though.

I did develop quick. My body started coming at ten. Started to bleed then too.

They baptized me in different churches until I got pregnant at twelve. I had a baby boy by the husband living next door to where we was living at the time. Big mama made me have him at home.

That day his wife fought him like a stranger because she didn't know he was my baby daddy until my baby coming. Beause that's when big mama said she would let me holler until I said the daddy name and I screamed it. Whole block heard it. That's when the wife started to beat her husband ass.

Then she ran across the yard to our house and fought her way past mama and got inside. Her name was Eletha and even though I was in labor she managed to spit in my face and punch me in my head before big mama grabbed the iron and chased her out the house. Mama shouted after Eletha and promised her we was moving. She had spit in mama face too.

When the baby was almost out it hurt so bad I alarmed the whole block some more. Mama was so embarrassed she ran up and down the street yelling like a crazy woman. "What y'all lissening for! Mind y'all's gotdamn bizness!"

Soon as he fell out of me big mama wiped his eyes and ran her fingers around inside his mouth. She used her mouth to suck out his nose. Used something she got from the doctor to drop in his eyes. Then she pushed and pushed on my stomach until something I know now was the baby sack came out. She put a finger on it to taste it but I didn't see what she did with it.

Big Mama cleaned up my screaming baby and took the boy outside right away and gave him to a woman who live in Opaleka. She was waiting out front all the while in a car with her husband.

I never knew her name or what name she gave my baby. But it wasn't hard for me to forget that boy. I never looked at him.

My stomach went back just as flat and I didn't have no marks or nothing. Like I never had no baby. So according to me I didn't.

We moved again. I hardly noticed because I was itching to get back to concentrating on getting men and eating peaches. Because for some reason peaches reminded me a my. I must have ate a million peaches when I was in Alabama.

I do remember mama trying evrything anything to change

me but I just got worse and worse. I hurt her and big mama reputations because I didn't care about mine.

We had to move alot but I would run away for days from wherever we landed if there wasn't no peach trees on our land or close by. I would go someplace peaches was and eat my fill. Sex the boys and men and go home.

Mama and big mama were the ones who called it running away because to me I was just looking for the only things on my mind. Ehhbody talked about me. Good and bad mostly bad things to say. Blamed my mamas. My daddy not being around. Something's not right in my head. My mind twisted. Missing some kind of connection I'm suppose to have. A lot of folks tried to figure me out. Some said I needed testing.

Wherever we lived soon as I started acting up all the wimmen neighbors and church wimmen would come to the house and try to talk sense to me. Some of them held me gentle in they laps like I'm a baby axe "Honey why you act like you do?"

I shrugged my shoulders and axed if they sonhusband wanted to feel my. They pushed me off to the floor.

Some shook me by my shoulders say in a mean voice "Don't you know you killing your poor mama?"

I axed if I they brotherfather could suck my. More than one slapped my face.

Some looked dead in my eyes "Why you want to ruin yourself so young"? I answered let me suck your uncleman. They lowered and shook they heads.

"Chile what's on your poor crooked mind?" I said "Nothing" and my face was a clear answer because that was the truth. They never believed me though. Some even took to beating my ass until they realize I dug it. Made me hot.

They finally called this roots woman name Miss May Julia to fix me. She looked like a witch to me because she was real short and real old and didn't wear nothing but raggedy black clothes. But she was always real clean. Had a high baby voice and talked real sweet.

Would axe if she can have anything she see in your hands. You could be holding a ball of dust. Miss May Julia gon axe you "Can I have that?" Her voice so light and musical like she singing a baby back to sleep.

And she smelled like I don't know what. Something nasty and nice together. Couldn't tell if I liked to smell it or if I think she stink.

Once a week she brought over all kinds of stuff to bathe me in. Most times the water looked dark. Sometimes it smelled wonderful. One time she gave me this pretty red bath. Had all these flowers floating in it.

But all that bizness she dipped up and poured over me didn't do nothing except waste both our time.

I did get something out of it though. I did have fun getting jooked by her fine grandson. Evry time she came over.

He came with her because she had to look at me first before she decided what ingredients to use. He was the one who ran back to Miss May Julia house to fetch roots and jars from her shelves and leaves from her patches in the woods. When he got back she mixed what he brought with some of the stuff she had with her to potion my different baths. The granson was suppose to leave but he didn't.

Me and him was able to jam because after granny half drown me she left me alone to dry myself off. She would go inside and talk to my mamas. That's when her grandson came out from hiding around the side of the house. Or I would listen for his whistle and go into the woods where he was. Either way I was always buck nekked when we got busy.

Miss May Julia caught us. We were at it behind the house stacked like chairs bouncing it good when she walked up on us. I begged him don't stop but he scared. I found myself getting up off the ground cause he straightened his knees so fast pleading her to forgive him. It was funny cause he running behind his grandmother with his pants and draws around his ankles and his piece swinging.

She fussed in her pretty lullaby voice and popped her grandson on his head. Her music told him to pull up his pants. Miss May Julia pointed her fingers at me funny. Went in the house to tell my mamas she wasn't coming back no more.

But he did. Two more times. Sneaked around whistling at night. Saw him downtown right after the last time I let him suck me. He acted like he didn't know me.

Evry boy or man that had me acted like they was shame soon they stopped moving in me. I was usually dozy and axing for a peach. Most of them knew to bring one because they all talk to each other about me. Didn't none a them allow they sisters daughters wimmen or wives to be my frens.

Soon big mama got mad and fed up with me. By the time I was fifteen she said wasn't nothing wrong with me except being a devil chile. I was doing satan bizness being a slutass slackass strumpet and she swear to Jesus! she don't know where I got it from. Said it must be my daddy blood.

I didn't even care when big mama told mama to put me out or we both had to go. Big mama said she too old to keep moving around.

But it worked out that mama didn't have to go nowhere because one day I just didn't come home for good. I know big mama told her not to look for me no more. I was near grown and what I turned out to be wasn't her blame.

I wound up going off with this Jamaican man who used a big knife to cut fields for people who didn't have a lawnmower or horses or cows. He fixed things too.

I think his name was Delrick or Delroy. I don't remember.

He talked way more Jamaican than mama and big mama so I didn't always understand everything he said. Big muhfucka but kind of slow in the head. He had real big muscles and a real big. He looked alright too. He was thirtynine and I was fifteen.

I met him when I happened to pass by looking for what he gave me.

He had to have heard how I was about men. But that must have been what he liked best about me because I let him slip in me ten minutes after we saw each other. Right in the field he was working in. I held on to a tree and let him mate me like a bull.

Soon as he was done he took me right home with him. Didn't even finish cutting that field. Put me on his bicycle handlebars and rode me away.

We went to this little brokedown house he had deep country. Wasn't nobody living near us. Delrickroy didn't axe me nothing about myself. Just confirmed what he heard me say was my name.

That first night he stayed in me so much that he laughed and said he don't remember my name because he can't remember his own. So even though he begged me I never told him again. I know he could have just axed somebody else but he nickname me Rosy and never called me nothing else.

Just kept his. In my. All the time except for when he was out cutting grass or being a handyman or went to town to get us food.

I didn't leave his house to go nowhere because all Delrickroy had was that old bicycle. But I wasn't no prisoner. And where was I going? I was happy. Delrickroy brought me peaches evry day. Didn't make me cook clean or nothing. He did all that. I thought I loved him because he love sex and knew how to take mine.

We didn't talk about nothing much. And he didn't have a tv only a radio. When he got home from work my main entertainment was tagging behind him feeling on him until he got hard. Then I would bend over or lay down.

He was the first one to put it in my pucker. I hollered and cried so loud the first time he try we thought he wasn't gon be able to do it. But he didn't give up and when it got in I started to like it just as much as the regular way.

We left like two thiefs in the night about a month after we start living together because the one fren he had in town told Delrickroy that the police was coming to get him.

It had gotten around that I was staying with him and folks were saying it's a shame the way he abusing me. Grown man taking control a my feeble childish mind.

Most people wouldn't hire him no more so he couldn't make much money. Soon we didn't eat evry day to stretch the few dollars he had coming in. Delrickroy told me that the people in the stores didn't want to wait on him. People was cussing him in the street.

His fren also told him my mama was telling anybody who axed that she didn't have no daughter so don't nobody call my name or tell her nothing about me. Delrickroy axed if that hurt my feelings.

He didn't have enough money to rent someplace else for us to live so it was a good thing it was summer. We just kept moving and slept and did it in the woods. He stole food from people yards so we could eat.

But somehow Delrickroy got sick. He went and met with his fren in secret. Axed him to write a letter to his sister in Kingston Jamaica and axe for two tickets. I told him that my mama and my big mama was from Jamaica and axed him if his sister was rich. He said no she probably gon have to scrape up the money. He said I needed to go home with him since that's where my blood was from.

After not too long his fren found us in the woods and told Delrickroy that his sister wrote back and said in a week two one way tickets be waiting at the airport in Birmingham.

I didn't know it until then but somehow Delrickroy had also arranged to get me somebody else's passport who was my age. Picture of the girl inside looked like me a little bit.

This was also the second time my name changed. Name on the passport was Roberta Washington. Rosy was gon be Roberta. Delrickroy said I couldn't get on the plane without it. I didn't even know what a passport was. He said he was gon show them his veeza because he wasn't a american citizen. I didn't know what a veeza was neither.

Delrickroy kept getting sicker. Something was wrong with his stomach and his bowels kept running. It took us walking day and night to get to the airport. We had to stop and rest so much. We was also hiding from the police.

I was the one stealing our food this time. I got tired of eating fruit and raw vegetables. I was stealing food people already cooked.

One time I sneaked through the back door of this house and came running out with a nice baked ham almost too hot and heavy to carry. Yams in the pan too. The people the ham belonged to was sitting right out front on the porch when I robbed they dinner. We ran off into the woods.

Me and Delrickroy had a good time stuffing ourselfs with ham and yams and laughing. Joking about what them people probably gon think when they ready to eat and discovered they ham was missing. I was laughing so hard I couldn't hardly say "They probably think a dog took it!" Delrickroy made me laugh even worse when he axed "How a dog carry the pan?"

Then me and Delrickroy looked at each other and I put some of the meat in my. Made him eat it out. He stuck me too but he was like a old man because he didn't have much strength. I was getting tired of using my mouth to get him ready.

The next few days we didn't do nothing at all because he finally admitted that he didn't have no power except for walking. I had to make do with satisfying my own self. I was so mad I couldn't even talk about it.

O. But all that changed when I saw the airport. I was so excited. I couldn't wait to get on that plane. I had never been on one before and I couldn't imagine what it was gon feel like.

But when Delrickroy went to the counter to try and pick up our tickets they wasn't gon let him have them. The airport people didn't believe we was us even though Delrickroy showed our papers. We looked so bad and stunk worse.

I caused a scene. I raised so much commotion cussing and stomping around that they gave us the tickets to shut me up. I knew they couldn't arrest me because I was too young. They hurried us on the plane even though the picture on my passport was some other girl.

I saw one of mama frens in the airport with her eyes popping out her head. I remember Delrickroy saying she probably gon call my mama and tell her she saw me. Using a fake name. How terrible I looked and I was going to Jamaica with the same nasty grown man that ruined me.

I never saw mama or big mama again but it never bothered me.

The plane wasn't nothing like I thought. I was scared out of my mind when it took off. I was screaming for the waitress and she had to calm me and calm me until I couldn't see nothing but clouds. Delrickroy told me that the right name for the lady was flight attendant.

To me the best thing about riding on the plane was my first time drinking likka. When the flight attendant was serving somebody else Delrickroy stole three little likka bottles off the cart and gave them to me. They tasted horrible but I drank them like water and got stone drunk for the first time in my life. I slept all the way there. When we landed in Kingston he had to slap me wake.

O. Jamaica wasn't nothing like what I was hoping either. Mama and big mama had said Jamaica was like paradise. I sho didn't see it. Ehhthang looked poor and put together. Ehhbody goat musty and talked worse than Delrickroy.

I didn't understand nobody and that shit made me mad so I raised sand. Cussed in American at a lot of muhfuckas while we walked through the airport.

I know I didn't look and smell no better than they did but at least I could speak english right. I was mad too cause I needed my sex. This wasting away man I was with hadn't given me none since the ham day.

When Delrickroy sister saw me she looked me up and down sucked her teeth and didn't speak to me. Her name Denise. She hugged up her brother and gave him some red and blue money.

Axed Delrickroy right in front of me if I deserved a plane ticket. I didn't understand her because if I did I would have punched her in her mouth.

What I heard was "disyah raggamuffin pickny wurt me raaahsclot dolla man?"

Delrickroy told me in english what she said. But even without him translating I ain't stupid. I knew that bitch didn't say she was glad to see me or some welcome shit like that. I saw how she was rolling her eyes looking me up and down.

So I got in her face and told her to go fuck her monkey self and that bitch slapped me! O. Me and his sister was rolling all over that gotdamn airport. Somebody grabbed his sister and Delrickroy grabbed my ass up.

He said some jibba jabba to Denise then rushed me out the airport on to this crowded little bus that took us up into some hills that seem like a mountain to me.

When we got off we still had to walk and walk through a fucking jungle to a old shack. Delrickroy said it was his house. It was worse than anyplace I ever lived in Alabama but I didn't have no choice.

Being there gave him a lot a his energy back so me and him got together right away. But I never got pregnant even though we never used nothing.

I almost lost my mind when I found out I couldn't get no peaches. I begged and begged Delrickroy to steal me some but he said no. Warned me that we can't steal like we did back in Alabama. He said people cut you if you steal they stuff.

I said fuck that shit. I told him I was going back home if he didn't get me some peaches. He dropped to the floor and grabbed me around my legs begging me don't leave don't leave a sick man.

That made me realize how slow minded this grown man was. A stupid ass. Really. How the hell I'm suppose to get back to Alabama without him? Shit. I didn't even know where the fuck I was or which direction the damn airport was in.

Plus how I'm getting down off this mountain? And how I'm suppose to get on a plane without a ticket? Who giving me money for one? Delrickroy a dumb muhfucka.

All I know is even though he didn't have no job he worked out something with somebody in town and got me two peaches a week. That didn't satisfy me but I had to deal with it.

He also got some seeds from I don't know where and we started growing vegetables. Sometimes I jerked him off and made him come on the ground around the plants so they grow better.

Since we didn't have no animals we never had no meat except for when somebody gave us some. He went fishing sometimes. Sometimes his hincty ass sister brought a chicken she killed.

Bitch ignored me like I wasn't alive so I fought her evry chance I got until Delrickroy wouldn't let me be around her no more when she came over.

We lived like that for almost a year. Delrickroy got sick again and got worse fast. Stomach blew up like he the one having a baby.

I'm the one burning up the food and suppose to clean the house. Denise wound up doing it. Came by two three times a week. So I made sure I left shit out evrywhere. But she didn't say nothing or complain. Just cooked and cleaned. Even brought us a rooster and a couple a hens so we could have meat and eggs.

Since the sex at home was gone I had started opening my legs and my mouth to this boy my age who used to walk goats near our house. Sneaking because I didn't want to hurt Delrickroy feelings. But I wouldn't have really cared if he found out.

Last time goatboy zipped up his pants and wiped sweat off his forehead I told him to bring a fren with him next time.

When my birthday came and I turned sixteen Delrickroy said "Rosy yuh haffi wurk." I got to start going to town and look for a job. I told him to kiss my ass I wasn't working nowhere.

I had got good at talking Jamaican so I started jumping around in his face and told him "Blooodclot! Suck yuh mooma bwoy! Me wurk? Nevva gwan fi wurk. Hunnastan? Nah man. Wurk yuhself!"

When he said he was too sick I said "Hoh well. Me nevva keer yuh sick."

Denise started coming around evry other day to look after him and bring him soup. As a favor to Delrickroy I left her alone.

One time I heard her whisper to him that I must be working roots behind his back because he never been one to take on sickness so. She said words sounded like "obeah oomun" and say she gon get one.

If that's somebody like Miss May Julia that wasn't what he needed. Delrickroy needed a medical school doctor.

This woman who smelled like wet dirt started coming around and made him drink all kinds of teas that looked like they made out of sticks and leafs. Used rocks and shells and bones and dust to work on him. Bathed Delrickroy in all kinds of stuff.

Didn't none of it do a bit of good.

So after a while she gave up and claimed that whatever had him had already spread deep roots. I just grunted at her because I believed she didn't know what the fuck she was doing. I peeped her. She was a faker. Crazy woman had just made shit up to get money.

Soon Delrickroy was flat on his back for real and couldn't hardly breathe. He was using the little breath he had left to croak my name.

Since this gotdam rootswoman couldn't cure him she got word to his people that a dream revealed to her that it's my spirit killing they brotherdaddyunclefrenloverson. Eyes that never once seen me started pointing my way.

I didn't even know Delrickroy had family except for that bitch Denise until he seemed ready to die.

A boy my age came to the house and said he was Delrickroy youngest son. Two almost teenage daughters. First son was older than me. Twunnytwo. Got five sisters not counting Denise. Bunch of thick brothers I got wet looking at. His mama and daddy still strong. Delrickroy had a lot of frens from the womb that came up to see him. Enough little kids related to him to start a school.

Ehhbody who climbed that hill was wailing. Reading the Bible out loud and beating tambourines. I couldn't even concentrate on a way to get the attention of the delicious new men all around me because so many people pulled up that hill to our house all times of day and night.

I saw a whole lot of crazy freaked out shit done under the light of the moon in the name of curing Delrickroy.

Things got bad for me. Five wimmen in his family snuck up on me one by one and kicked my ass tried to cut up my face and pulled out some of my hair. I got in some licks but they beat my ass evry day for a week like they wasn't trying to stop.

Those Christians fucked me up. No matter how we battled I made sure I didn't let a bitch mess up my face.

Two of his sisters jumped me together and one of them held me so the other could hit me in the head with a big piece of wood. If I didn't duck when she swung it she would have given me a concussion. A old grandma started screaming and told them not to kill me or Delrickroy would die too.

They ran me off into the woods. With just what I had on.

The sisters didn't know that for three days two of Delrickroy brothers came and sexed me and brought me a blanket and some food. Them bitch sisters realized something was up because the third day they sent the youngest one to follow her brothers.

She must have been behind some trees peeping at us. Watching from the time I made one brother take off his pants and sit wide leg on a tree on the ground so I could suck his. The other brother pants was down too getting hisself hot pulling on his. Waiting his turn.

We didn't even know little sister was there until she yelled

"Ooo!" She saw how her brother couldn't wait and had raised my ass to get to my. My mouth was still working on the other brother. Her scream made us look up in time to see her flying back to tell her sisters.

Her brothers hollered at her but didn't even pretend to stop to run and go catch her because they release was too close. I knew I wasn't gon see the brothers again so I told them to do they thing.

I also knew the sisters would know just where I was.

And I was right because Denise came straight to me the next day with the same two fat sisters who had jumped me together.

Denise screamed I killed one brother now I'm trying to kill two more. Said she a Christian so she gon get me on a plane out of Jamaica before she have somebody kill me.

Shit. I told that bitch "Fine with me." I didn't know if Delrickroy was really dead and to tell you the truth I never gave a damn. The fucking and the peaches gone? Me too. What reason did I have to stay around?

Denise was good to her word. She and her posse left and a little while later came back. Denise had my passport in her hand. They dragged my ass out of the woods and got me on a flight the very same day.

I didn't have nothing to take but my raggedy self and all them knots and bruises the bitches in his family put on me. To this day I'm not over the fact that I was stomped over and over and couldn't do nothing about it.

Denise never gave me a ticket just took me to the airport in her old car. I sat tight between the two sisters in the back.

When we got to the airport only Denise went inside with me. Not one word passed between us. She pushed me all the way to the plane. And made sure I got on.

I didn't know where I was going until I got to the gate. Which was Florida. Miami. Landed about five in the afternoon.

Ain't this a bitch. Came back from Jamaica just one damn state over from where I started out. Shit. Why couldn't I be in California or Mexico? Somewhere like that.

Anyway Rosy was dead. I went back to the name my mama gave me.

It don't matter what my name was but it wasn't what it is now. To me a name ain't nothing. I really don't understand why most people keep the same one until they die.

Miami was when I gave up peaches. Didn't even consider giving up the sex though. No sir. My country ass was still smart enough to know that's how a young woman like me get money. And don't no woman like getting up on the stick better than me. Perfect combo right?

In the airport baggage place, I let myself act my young age pretended to be scared and was picked up right away. I do remember this man's name. Mister Alvin P. Casey. Old muhfucka.

Tried to act concerned "Young lady? You alright? Somebody fight you? You need somebody to help you?" I just nodded my head stuck out my breasts trembled my lips twirling my long hair.

We took a cab to his apartment in a old folks high rise near the beach. I batted my eyes and smiled at grandpa the whole ride.

The lobby of his building was full of old muhfuckas sitting around waiting to watch a ant go by. So you know when they saw dirty raggedy young me walking in with they neighbor they stared at me like I wasn't human. Some of they teeth probably fell on the floor. We got on the elevator.

Pop Casey had a teeny one bedroom apartment on the fifth floor. Took me to the kitchen and made me watch him heat up some soup. Held a one sided convasation about how he liked to go to the airport and have coffee in the food court and talk to people.

When the soup was ready he sat me on his lap like a little girl and fed me chicken noodles. Evrytime he brought the spoon to my mouth he pressed his arm upside my titty. Humped against my ass pretending like he adjusting hisself in his seat. I acted like I didn't know what was going on but I was cracking up inside.

He was getting me hot but he was fumbling so much I got mad.

I jumped up "Like this muhfucka!" pulled my panties down grinded my ass into his crotch and played with myself until I finished. Then stuck my sticky fingers in the soup.

His eyes got wide he said "O! O!" His old dingaling jumping in his pants. Then a wet spot there. Old Time Casey ain't got off in so long he knocked his own self out.

Gramps head was hanging to the side snoring like a express train.

I took a fast shower. I went in his bedroom and took what looked like his best shirt out his closet and wore it like a minidress. Put on a pair of his grandpa boxers like shorts. Tied one of his ties around my waist like a belt. Opened the bathroom window and threw out my panties. Had to put back on my same old beat up shoes.

I rambled through his things and stole all the money I could find about a hunnitsixty.

I realized I didn't hear grandpa snoring no more. I was hoping he wasn't waiting quiet for me in the hallway or in the kitchen so he could shoot me or bust me in the head with something.

So I stuck my head out the bedroom door real easy and and pulled it back real quick. I didn't see Old Time.

With his money tight in my hand I eased out his bedroom and sneaked down the short hallway to peep around the kitchen doorway.

I saw pops slumped over the kitchen table. His whole face was down in the soup. Still as a rock.

I turned and flew back up the hallway and out the door. I didn't wait for no elevator. I ate them stairs. I melted through the lobby like running water so couldn't nobody recanize me again. Ran down streets turning corners.

I got on the first bus I saw loading and got off at the last stop. Looked like the heart of town.

First thing I did was buy some sexy clothes. Some little teeny white shorts and a white crochet halter top because it made my nipples stand out. Got red wedgy shoes too.

Evry time I looked at the scratches on my arms and legs from them witches in Jamaica I got mad.

I walked around looking for a good time. Start following behind some slick muhfuckas I saw. I was country but I knew party men when I saw them. I was ready to have some fun and spend a lot of time being wide open. I went right in the same bar they did.

The bartender tried to throw me out when I said I didn't have no I.D.

But this real pretty muhfucka dressed real fly looked late twunnys early thirties came and stood behind me put his arms around my waist. He said I was with him. Bartender said he didn't axe who I was with. He axed if I was twunnyone.

This man who got hold of me lifted one hand off my waist to take a toothpick out his mouth. He said "Wilson. If I say she with me that mean she twunnyone."

Muhfuckin bartender didn't say another muhfuckin word. Axed somebody else what they wanted to drink.

Mr. Fine sat me at his table in the back. Stroked my cheek like I was a pet or something.

First thing he did after axing my name was change it. What he called me sounded like a exotic fruit. I liked it a lot so I kept it.

Introduced hisself as Tooshay. I said I never heard that name before so he spelled it on a napkin. T o u c h e. I would have pronounced it toochee.

When he found out I was in town to stay but didn't have money or a place to live he said don't worry about it. He would take care of me and show me how to take care of myself. Which wouldn't be hard because of how I look. Touche called me a rough diamond.

He explained that after I got myself together I was gon work for him and keep a percentage. I didn't understand what he meant at first. But as time went on I got hip and didn't have a problem with it.

Touche say "A fair exchange is never a robbery." Touche say "Ain't nothing strange for the right piece of change."

He took me to a motel and rented me a room for a week. Then he said he gon take me someplace else. Touche say in six months I'ma have so much money I won't want to stay in no motel. I'ma want my own apartment.

I didn't hear Touche cause the motel was the most fabalus place I ever saw. I look back on it now and know it was a dump. But I never fault Touche because I was a investment he took a chance on.

He came by all seven days. Brought me food and a few things to wear. Told me to rest and clear my mind. He would stay awhile and talk to me. He was my teacher.

First time I heard Game was from his mouth.

After the week was up Touche took me to this she male he was tight with so I could be polished. Because I wasn't gon see a dime looking like I did.

You should have seen this she male. Name LaDonna. Fabalus. You couldn't tell she was a man. No apple in her throat and small feet and hands. Pretty pretty face. Looked like a model with long legs and big titties. Long blond hair and ice blue eyes.

But had a pole not a hole.

Incredible luxury crib right on the beach. LaDonna real high class about ehhthang she touch or do.

When Touche first brought me to her house she opened the door greeted him then focused on me. She stepped back with her hand on her chest like she can't breathe. She gave a little scream. "Now Shay you can't be serious" that's what she said.

Talked to Touche like I wasn't there and that shit burned me up. She looked me over again and told Touche it was hard to see what I had because I look like a orphan.

Touche axed her if he ever been wrong. LaDonna squinted hard at me a third time and said like she hated to admit it "She truly got body. And her face is not bad." She said "But look at all the marks all over her arms and legs!"

Waved her hand in my direction and told Touche "Sugar I'm charging you double for fixing this mess" indicating me.

I got worked up and told that faggot bitch I don't give a Fuck that she's really a man I would beat her ass. What.

LaDonna already had a blade tip in my throat a drop of blood forming. Touche never moved a muscle. I got tame like a bunny rabbit.

I lived with LaDonna for two months.

LaDonna showed me how to recanize real fashion. Taught me how to dress like class or glamour trash. Depending on who spending. Made me pay attention to my hair and nails. Taught me makeup. Gave me a special cream to clear the marks on my arms and legs. Took me to the dentist for my teeth but all he had to do was clean them good because I always had nice healthy white teeth.

We spent mornings in her kitchen. Soon I was cooking like a chef and ordering in restarants like a gourmay. LaDonna put glide in my walk. Got my walk flowing like the street was my runway. I learned how to be gracious and nonchalant when accepting money and gifts from men.

Taught me the difference between being a girlfren and a ho. Once LaDonna threw her head back laughed and said "It's basically semantics darling but the difference is all the difference in the wooorld!" I smiled at her but I didn't know what the fuck LaDonna was talking about. I just did whatever she said.

Tried to make me read a newspaper evryday. But when she realized I wasn't doing it LaDonna made me watch the news on tv at least twice a day.

She made me take up painting for what she called arts and refinement. I really got good at it. I liked painting roses the best. I could paint one that looked real.

At first she wouldn't let me talk in public too much. She did most of the speaking when I was in training to lure money men. She taught me to talk better because she said I talked like country Alabama. When I told her that's where I was from LaDonna laughed like crazy.

I did get a lot better. She was very proud of me when I start putting the endings on my words. She helped me work on pronouncing and to stop letting my tongue be lazy. She taught me a lot of new words. She did get me to stop saying fuck so much.

I wouldn't stop using muhfucka because I like the way it sound. I just stopped saying it around her.

Soon LaDonna said "Honeybunch you are ready to work with Touche."

She called him and when he came over it was the first time he saw me since he left me to get finished. Touche just stood there looking.

I was modeling in front of him and after a few minutes he said, "Get your things and let's go." He told LaDonna that he would get with her later to settle what he owe.

My mentor helped me get together what I wanted to take. She kissed me on the cheek when me and Touche left. The last thing LaDonna said to me was "Remember money is your mother."

Touche was satisfied. Right away he moved me into my own fly apartment that he found. Not too far from LaDonna. Not on her level but very cute.

As my graduation gift he paid my first month rent. By month two I had a few men paying that bill and personal maintenance. I had each one thinking he was the golden one. Finessed them all with my "come here go away" routine.

Enjoyed giving Touche his chunk of my bounty.

Touche gave me another skill. Put me with this larceny bitch name Lil Bit who schooled me how to fleece the streets and get plenty money without a man.

Touche say "Getting laid is just one way to get paid."

Lil Bit looked just like her name all tiny. Real light skin with hazel eyes and straight hair. Could pass for spanish, italian, french. Dressed like she born rich. Called herself Loretta when she working.

She made me go with her and just watch at first. I took to it like a natural and learned crime from a master who didn't fuck with no bullshit and never been caught. Lil Bit was gifted.

Lifed wallets forged peoples names on checks and money orders. Stole credit cards and used them to shop or sold them. Scammed designer clothes and showcase diamonds. We boosted only the best from anybody evrywhere. Shit. Lil Bit and me would have stole dreams if we had somebody to buy them.

Touche used to brag that Lil Bit could walk in Miami's finest jewlry store. Stop and chat with the security guards. Stroll out like a princess a little while later with some of they diamonds and plat.

Touche laughed and said the gotdamn security be smiling and holding open doors for her too. I got jealous and told Touche I wanted him to talk about me like that.

Touche hisself put the final touches on my sex game and my Game mentality. He say evry man is a potential boyfren or date.

Touche say "It don't matter if he a thriller or Godzilla he's your man if he got money in his hand. A busy ass stacks cash baby."

Touche taught me new moves until I had what he called a showcase. He made me get them down perfect.

Like the one that let me get the job done quick. Wasn't a move for newcomers. Had to know how to breathe with it because it's a advanced position hard to hold for long. But guaranteed to make any man come so strong his release feel like skipping on the edge of a knife.

Boss muhfucka Touche showed me how to satisfy any man no matter what his nature need.

Touche say "Ain't no limits when it come to getting digits." I had to be flawless because of the premium price it cost to get with me.

Touche showed me how to keep myself intact and protected from all my activity. Touche was amazing. Showed me exercises to keep my rose tight and gave me soothing stuff to put in my baths.

Schooled me on ways to position my arms to keep a log from loosening my fit. Thanks to Touche my fit stayed snug whether I was handling a pencil or a pole.

When Touche figured I was complete he gave me my first and only jewlry present. Touche gave me a gold and diamond necklace with a matching bracelet and ring. Wasn't no corny pieces neither. Heavy and top of the line.

All the other jewlry I owned men gave me or I stole. So his gift was special because it came from him. Made me cry and shit.

I still got all three pieces. I found out later he didn't spend no money. Lil Bit lifted it for him to give to me but it's the thought that mattered.

And I loved to shower him in return. He gave me a life. I was grateful for what he did. I rolled that boss in money. I wanted to give him the world all by myself.

I think about it now and know I was very happy during that part of my life because evrything was a discovery. My life was new and exciting and full of money. Even though my thoughts was cold my heart was light.

I wound up staying with Touche for five years because he brought out what I felt was my true self.

I know I gave him a million. Making bread and breaking bread. O. I was a true star getting fully paid. Any way possible. Stealing and conning along with what I got as pay for lay.

O. I was living sweet. Had the best money could buy. Renting a fly nest on the beach driving a convertible white baby Benz and ehhthang. Partying with stars. But you know how it go. Money flow. Wasn't never nothing to save.

Me and Touche wasn't never about heartlove but I loved the new life he gave me. I probably wouldn't have left Touche when I did because he made me comfortable with myself and who I was. He even gave me the honor of training two new girls he met and wanted to finish.

He was the one got rid of me! Said I had got too old! When I turned twunnyone he told me I had to go.

But wasn't no hard feelings. He was like my father and that's how I always think of Touche. Touche. My daddy and my teacher. My wall. He let me keep all my shit except the Benz.

He put my old ass on a plane that headed me up north. Kissed me on the cheek at the airport gate and told his Big Girl to take care stay smooth stay sharp. And get money. Keep living the lifestyle I had grown used to.

Touche say "Dress rest and impress."

It was Rakim Moet Divine who landed in Detroit. Stayed there a year making men my bitches accumulating more riches until I wanted to see what they talking about in New York.

New York City was the first time I didn't change my name when I got off a plane. Maybe that's why I'm all fucked up now. I must have changed my luck....

Look at this shit I called my life now. Bossbitch like me sitting in this muhfuckin tiny Brooklyn crib looking like I been hit by a muhfuckin truck.

I was starving but I added a few more buds on the wall above the toilet before I quit. Damn this painting for right now. I put my paints away and stuck the brushes in the water in a jar sitting on the floor. Clean them later.

Slowly went to the kitchen and cut a slice of cheddar to eat on a big piece of carrot cake. I was determined to eat around my busted mouth. Poured a glass of milk. Slowly took it back to bed with me. Before I climbed in to eat and think I checked my blinds to make sure they was closed tight. Damn daylight. Plus I wanted to see all the little tea roses I painted on them.

See. This one on one love shit is where I went wrong. I been major in the Game long enough to know better. You can't break the rules. That's so true. It's true that love Ain't Shit. Love is the easiest way to fall. Made me forget to concentrate on getting my money like I'm supposed to.

Hadn't been going out to the stores getting my own shit. Stopped being where the wallets was. Let all kinds of money men slip through my net. Got lazy. Let myself depend on two pretty muhfuckas to do ehhthang for me. Stopped being the independent woman I was trained to be. Forgot where I came from. Was acting like a fucking housewife and shit.

Touche would be ashamed.

My Game got so weak that I got beat. Muhfuckas pounded on me like I'm in they fan club. My steel Game in a velvet glove had turned to clay inside a punching bag.

Nuh uh. I'm not the one. Not this Big Girl. Not Miss Finessence. What. So I got my ass beat. Got fucked up.

I'm supposed to give up now? Because for the very first time Rakim blew it? I'm supposed to learn my lesson? Quit my life? Get a job? Go to school? Meet some bus riding nine to five man and get married? Yeah. Have some babies and shop on a budget. Do without. Ha. Start cooking hamburgers. Be proud of making my own curtains. Join the community choir. Right.

I'd die first. And if Shipell and Supreme peeped the deep larceny I was planning I just might die because if either one of them did I'm dead. But fuck it. I'ma Do this. Do what I got to do.

Shipell and Supreme definitely got this shit wrong. Who zooming who? Any man violate dismiss discard Miss Divine like these two? O. I got to set it straight. Make shit come back together right. It's about respect.

I don't give a Fuck who they is. Fuck a rep. They gon know ain't but one Big Girl like my fine ass. And neither one of these muhfuckas gon get away with beating it.

They call me Miss Divine. No heart. No conscience.

I see it's time to move on. A jewl like myself is one of a kind in a sea full of dopey bitches. I'm the bitch that make rich muh- fuckas go nuts.

So how did this happen?

My body bruised all over. My swollen neck burgundy and blue. Both my wrists tender. Lips raggedy. Side of my head throb- bing. Rose overworked and my ass burning. Rakim feelings hurt bad.

My money walked twice out the door saying I'm no good. Shit. Both of them muhfuckas had tried to kill me.

I ain't got no choice. I got to get them muhfuckas back here tomorrow. One more time. One at a time. Just like I planned. Watch. And when I do? O. Shipell and Supreme gon See what I mean.

Turned on the nighttable lamp so my roses could help me out.

"You's A Lie!"

Baybay, Susan and Jocelyn sat sharing three of the wide stoop steps, early afternoon sun and four different flavored pints of ice cream.

Jocelyn and Baybay, because they were responsible for kids and Baybay had a greedy husband, had dinners halfway done. Their children were running and screaming with the others up and down the block, the older ones knew better than not to look after the younger ones. Related or not.

Susan had four days left on her vacation and that morning had leaned back in one of Baybay's kitchen chairs with her legs straight out and crossed at the ankle and promised that Raymond could kiss her ass, she wasn't cooking or cleaning nothing until she went back to that damn phone company.

She was always cussing Raymond behind his back and talked about quitting him every day. Then had his dinner ready before he came through her door.

Tisha didn't have to be on the job until midnight, so she had plenty of time to sit outside with the girls for a couple of hours and still have time to clean her apartment and take a nap before getting ready for work.

She'd called from her front window, "Be down in a minute!" She was just about finished rinsing out and hanging a few undies left soaking overnight in the bathroom sink.

Again, they would discuss Miss Rakim Moet Divine.

Although she lived on the first floor with windows right next to the stoop, she was almost never home in the afternoons. But, still, the only way Rakim's neighbors could be sure of her absence were her completely shut blinds and they had to be checked very carefully.

Even when she was home, Rakim cracked her vertical slats only slightly, so it was crucial to be absolutely certain that she was out.

Once they met outside, Susan was the one to kneel on the stoop's wide concrete banister and lean over to peer closely at Rakim's windows. "Yep. She gone," she'd cattily announced that afternoon.

The women settled in.

Baybay opened. "I still wish I knew why Shipell dropped Rakim. 'Cause he sho' ain't been around. How long it been since his Benz been parked outside, Suzy? About four months, right? And she been seeing that new man about three months, 'cause when I'm up early getting Charles ready for work I see him drop her off, but he don't park. Just drop her off and go. Ho. This one got a big Benz like Shipell's except it's white. He probably a pimp too..." Baybay, paused her report, looked up, smiled at her friend and moved over so Hum, approaching, could sit on the step below her.

Hum sat, took a tablespoon from the pocket of her jeans and reached for the strawberry ice cream. She greeted her friends. "Whussup. What I miss?"

"Nothing. Girlfriend here just keeping her crown as 'Queen Don't Miss A Thing'," Jocelyn pointed her thumb at Baybay but looked up the block.

"You know something Joss? You don't have to listen to me. Or waste your time sitting here neither for that matter, am I right? You free to go do something more interesting." Baybay snatched her head and dug her spoon deep in the vanilla.

"Oh shut up. Can't nobody play with you? I'm just saying, you already told us over and over that Rakim got a new man, or new pimp, to let you tell it, with a white Benz. Ain't you got nothing new...wait a minute."

Jocelyn stood up and hollered down the block. "LaKeesha-Pam!... LaKeesha-Pam!...KiKi!...KiKi!..Yeah, over here! Take! that nasty stick out your mouth! You hear me?...Let me see you do it again! What I tell you about putting everything you see in your damn mouth? You want to go inside the house?...Do you?!... Alright then."

Jocelyn sat leaving a stern stare with her six-year-old then turned girlfriend eyes on Baybay. "Like I was saying, ain't you got nothing new on Rakim?" She switched pints with Susan.

"Ain't no new news, Shipell gone and Rakim tricking for somebody else who don't come inside her house. I knew she wouldn't be able to keep Shipell." Baybay reached into the box of mini chocolate chip cookies wedged between the side of the stoop and her thigh. She carefully perched a couple on top of the doubledip spoonful of butter pecan heading for her mouth. She offered the cookie box to her friends.

Chewing, Baybay said, "Let's see how high and mighty Miss Divine is now that she ain't shopping and lounging and entertaining Shipell or the men he sold her to. I'm telling you, right this minute, if she ain't somewhere trying on shoes she hoin'!

"She be back here about five or six this afternoon ready to hit the road again when we be going to bed. But I damn sure be awake when she be getting out of that white Benz between four-thirty and five damn near every morning. Whoever player is, fo' sho' he got her stompin' for real."

Hum took a handful of cookies and had a thought that, please, please, couldn't be true, "Maybe Lov…Shipell's locked up and that's why you ain't seen him." Anxiously, "Bay, you think?"

Baybay waved away such jabber. "Chile, please. Charles say they been trying to grab Shipell for years. He ain't going nowhere except for where he want to go. Shipell got money and money buy the best lawyers. He ain't been around here in months 'cause he ain't got no reason to come. He through with that tramp in 1A."

Baybay slanted her head towards Rakim's apartment and dug her hand in the cookies. "And she ain't going to find another man to treat her like he did. She threw a cookie in her mouth and talked as she chewed.

"Seemed like that pimp actually felt something for that ho. But the one in the white Benz sho' ain't in love, 'cause the way he drop her off say business to me. He just bringing her home from work. Yep, Mr. White Benz strictly business with Miss Divine, proving that we seen the last of Shipell." Baybay spoke with finality, expecting her words to be last.

Before she disputed her friend and took center stage for herself, Susan waited until Baybay was quiet. "Uh-uh. Rakim doing fine, and not with Mr. White Benz neither. I saw her coming in last night. I was sitting at the top of the first floor landing, lessee, about eleven thirty, waiting for Raymond. And I seen. A man. A gorgeous player. Drippin' diamonds. Carry Rakim. Up this stoop right here." Susan pointed to the step where she sat. "Right into her apartment," she wagged her head in confirmation.

"What man?! Not the one with the white Benz?"

"Who?! Carrying who? You's a lie!"

Jocelyn and Hum talked over each other with high eyebrows but Baybay didn't say a word.

"Alright then, I'm a lie." Pointing her spoon at Jocelyn's pint of ice cream Susan asked, "Joss, what flavor you got? Gimme some, whatever it is, 'cause you don't need no more, you getting fat. Ain't she, Bay?" Baybay shrugged her shoulders like who cares.

Susan feigned innocence about the bomb she'd dropped and started talking about somebody else. "Oh! And guess who me and Raymond ran into night before last at The Fantasia? Miss Taysha and her new man! Made sure I seen them too. Pushed all through people just so I could meet and greet this man. Introduced me, said his name was Bayamon or something like that. But I got to say, homeboy cute. Look black-spanish with curly hair and he shorter than her. Girlfrien' was acting like..."

"Oh," Baybay interrupted, "I got it. We suppose to beg for the Rakim information." She waved the back of her hand at Susan and said that she wasn't going to ask her nothing. "So finish what you was saying about Taysha. She still trying to be a blue-eyed blonde?"

Hum broke in, "Naah. Nuh-uh." She turned to face Baybay. "Yeah, right, Bay. You don't want to know about Rakim being carried, okay? Carried! by a baller in diamonds up this stoop and into her apartment. You rather hear about that stupid Taysha and her latest piece?"

Hum looked at BayBay and sucked her teeth. "You gon' have to get that dirt later Miss Bay, because, me, myself? I wants to know every goddamn detail about Rakim and this man...Su, tell me!"

Susan knew that Baybay was upset because she was finding out this front-page scoop along with everyone else. Usually, when she or Baybay had headline news, they shared it with each other first before they took it public. Susan looked at her best friend and knew that she was really mad.

Baybay wouldn't even look at Susan, who was calling her by the private nickname only she used. "Baytina, Baytina, you don't want to hear about what I seen last night?" Susan pushed Baybay on her shoulder. "Oh, come on, Bay!"

Baybay wanted to know so badly, she could taste it. But she had to be so indifferent, so aloof that Susan would know how thin she had stretched their bond. Girlfriend had slipped up, made her general audience.

Maybe it wasn't a slip. Uh-huh. Baybay capped her point by turning her back on Susan to look languidly up the street at a knot of children that included Jocelyn's and her own. They were singsonging over and over,

"I said three, six, nine!
The goose drank wine!
The monkey chew tabacca
On the streetcar line!
The line broke!
The monkey got choke!
And they all went to heaven
In a little row boat!"

Chanted shrilly and with much glee, the words jumped from their mouths with punch, almost like curses, especially those that rhymed.

Baybay figured she'd gotten her point and her irritation across. Satisfied, she turned her focus back to her friends, who were waiting in silent exasperation for her silly tantrum to be through.

As if on cue to begin, Susan licked the bowl, then the back of her spoon and stuck it in her waistband. From the pack beside her on the step, she shook out a Kool and lit it, her signal for wanting no more sweets that day. "Yep. Right up these steps last night. When I saw it was Rakim, you know I wasn't going nowhere. So I creeped down the stairs and peeped out the window in the front door so I could peep her business. You know I didn't want them to see me! Especially that man! But still!" Susan laughed and smoke rolled from her nostrils, "I had to see the deal!"

"You's a nosy somebody."

"Sho' you right. Like you wouldn't have been a blood-hound." Susan ignored Baybay and her gave attention to her other friends. "So, let me tell y'all what I seen..."

She narrated with large gestures and vivid expressions, how this fine, fine man with a big Mercedes had opened Rakim's door and lifted that damn woman over his shoulder. "I'm telling you, he carried her over his shoulder like she was a sack of potatoes. Her hair was swinging down his back, legs kicking like she was swimming and she's laughing!"

"Was she drunk?" Hum was leaning forward, elbows on her knees, chin in her palms.

"Sho' seem like something was helping her feel so hilarious. And check this! Girlfrien' was trying to hold on to a biiig bunch of red roses. A million!" Susan rounded her arms like she was hugging something huge. "Roses all over the ground. They was beautiful with long stems..."

Susan continued her descriptions, making pictures that enthralled Jocelyn and Hum. Baybay was engrossed, too, but she struggled to seem cool.

"He carried her up the stoop like she light. Every step he took he whispering something to her. Ooo! that man was some-thing!"

Baybay felt like Susan was taking too long with this story. She stood up and stretched, pantomiming boredom and demanded, "Get to the part when he carried her in the building. They see you?"

Not to be hurried, Susan straightened her arms and lifted her weight off the step to her palms. She shifted left and sat. She thought her friend was acting childish. "I'm getting to that. So, Bay, will you please sit down?... Thank you." She ground the butt of her second cigarette on the banister and threw it into the street. "So, there I was, steady peeping Rakim's business and they was almost..."

Baybay couldn't help but interrupt again. "What's up with all the mystery? Do you know who this man is, or what? Why won't you say his name if you do?" Sucking her teeth she concluded, "You always got to give drama. Why can't you just tell the damn story?"

"What bug buzzing up your ass?" Jocelyn knew that Baybay was jealous because she was usually the one with the new information, but she was acting crazy. "You got something else to do? No, you don't. So sit your big ass down."

"Who you talking to?" Baybay's head turned quickly to Jocelyn and began moving side to side. "You know what Jocelyn, I'm getting sick of you. You need to watch..."

"Please! Would you two pleeease let Susan finish? Damn!" Hum wanted to return to living Rakim's life.

"Thank you Hum." Susan gave her five. "Baybay, give me a break, huh?...So, I was so busy trying to see everything at once, trying to remember it all, you know? Chile, they was almost at the front door before I flew through the second door." Susan laughed, "Yo, I didn't have time to get up the stairs, I had to hide..."

"There was only one place you could go." Baybay turned to let Susan see the devil in her eyes. "You was bent down behind that high-back bench in the foyer, you was barefoot as a dog, I can guess what you had on, your eyes and ears was twice they size and Rakim should have caught you."

Tisha and Jocelyn picked up Baybay's word picture and fell out with her.

"Hoo, hoo! That's just! how she was!"

"Thinking she sexy in one of Raymond's teeshirts and some panties."

"Scarf tied around her head."

"Girl, I wish I could have been a fly on the wall if they did bust your nosy ass"

"Yo, Suzy, was you feeling stupid bent down behind that bench?"

"What you would've said if they caught you, Suzy? 'Heeey y'all'?"

"Well, since y'all know my story better than me, let me take my nosy behind back on upstairs." Feeling slighted, Susan rose and tried to excuse herself with a tight mouth.

She attempted to get past Jocelyn who blocked her and told

her to sit her sensitive self down. Everyone pretended they were sorry.

Only because she knew she would taste victory through their reactions at the end of her tale, Susan let herself be mollified.

She sat, lit a Kool, waved away its smoke and continued. "Y'all know I don't like her neither, but that bitch Rakim work her thing. For real. She work her shit. And don't say I never entertained you witches on a sunny afternoon. The beautiful man adoring Miss Divine? Kissing her? Gave her every rose in Brooklyn? Oh! Let me add this part before I tell you who.

"He never put her down. Opened both doors with her up in his arms," Susan threw her thumb over her shoulder at the front door behind her, "stood right in front of her apartment and kissed the shit out of Rakim. Bitch's feet still ain't touch the floor. That muthafucka strong 'cause Rakim ain't petite!"

Susan leaned forward into her friends that had closed around her. "I'm telling you, he kissed her like in the movies and shit. Maaan, I know she got done lovely right after he took her inside."

She chuckled and stubbed out another cigarette on the step. "Did I say I heard him tell her that he loved her? Huh? And this ain't the kind of man you would even think got 'I love you, baby' in his vocabulary."

Susan saw that Baybay, Jocelyn and Hum were about to burst. "Y'all know him. The man they say is the reason why Chiffonda in jail right now? Over cutting Barbara?...Mr. Love? Mr. Ship-pell?...Oh yes, baby, you wrong Bay, I don't know she did it, but Rakim got Shipell back slave tight."

The 210 girls lowered their heads and raised waving right arms to the blockbusting end of Susan's story with the noise she was waiting for. Susan sat content, proud mother of a story, newborn, healthy and bouncing full of speculation.

Nursed by days of figuring out, this tale would grow spoiled from over attention. Whoever told the next big story, probably Baybay, would have to include some shooting or murder, true or not, to top this juicy news.

Susan, smoking, listened silently to her praise. No matter that she knew nothing of what happened inside Rakim's apartment, she knew firsthand what had happened up until then. She and her girls could design what went on inside, later.

Now it was time to get to work, figure out all the subtle nuances of what Susan had seen in that succulent few minutes while it was still clear in her mind. Get to carving on this story and whittle plump, fresh information down to bony old news.

Through open windows in buildings that adjoined and faced 210, other at-home women heard a familiar sound and walked quickly to turn up radios and televisions that suddenly couldn't be heard due to that outside din and rising jealousy.

They weren't asked to eat ice cream on that stoop and today was certainly not the first time those loud women gathered there. Susan, Baybay and them had been sitting outside, at least two of them at a time, acting common since the maple leaves appeared, in coats if they had to.

Sounded like all of the 210 women were outside acting foolish today, so the gossip must be extra scandalous. Telling people's personal business.

Just listen to how some grown women carried on and they better be keeping my name out of their mouths, thought these indignant neighbors with narrow eyes, as certain windows were slammed shut for a few minutes to keep out all that cain.

Children dashing past 210 paused to look quizzically at the excited, yammering women. One boy started laughing, pointing, "Hey, Lamarr, Devante, what up with y'alls moms?"

The sons looked, shrugged and ran off heading the pack to finish playing its Brooklyn games.

Abruptly, Jocelyn's son stopped and faced the inquirer. "You talkin' about my mother?! Do it again and I'ma bus' yo' muthafreakin' ass!"

"Get him, Lamarr!" shouted Delqwon.

"Ooo! Lamarr cussin'! I'ma tell mommy! Lamarr figh'in'!" squealed Lakeesha-Pam. Delightedly, she stuck the end of a stick in her mouth.

The 210 clique was busy. They were systematically prodding Susan to precisely recall revealing clues. Exactly what did Rakim have on? Shipell too. He actually said, 'I love you, baby'? Those exact words? What did she say? Please describe one more time what the kiss looked like. You wished it was you didn't you?

Did Rakim drop any roses in the vestibule? Did you take one?

Each tidbit was milked, Susan closed her eyes to aid recalling the full picture....

Every Sister

When every Sister in the world lived in Africa
Different examples of every beauty
Flaunting sun-licked skin or abundant robes
Adorning their limbs and wearing treasure in their hair
Painting their gums
Palms and breasts
Or hiding it all except telling eyes
Submissive, dismissive
Seductive or wise
When every Sister in the world lived in Africa
The original essence
By the grace of God, goddess and the ancestors
As deliverers of kings, warriors, artists and believers
Prophets and deceivers
Fools, cowards and queens
Living herstory and making it history
To be recited 'til the stars exhale
When every Sister in the world lived in Africa
There was a new word everyday
Working magic they called it music
Creating sounds with no letters
Calling on the elders
To bless their chorus of peace
Loving themselves and
Loving each other and
Entering their men up under their skin
When every Sister in the world lived in Africa
Ringing with laughter, clapping hands in stubborn dispute
Soothing their souls with cooling baths and perfect songs
Getting along
Deciphering the heavens

Educating
Debating
Ideas invented or understood
Weaving, wandering
Or rooted like trees, in jealous forests or greedy deserts
When every Sister in the world lived in Africa
Making everything, the homes of their husbands and lovers
Cooking fires and games for spoiled children
Finding and hiding
Keeping secrets, lying
Revealing the truth
Mixing cures, planting, growing
Gathering, killing, making food savory
Going crazy
Causing war and scandal
Spinning evil, stirring calamity
Defying gravity
When every Sister in the world lived in Africa
Dancing, chanting together with long necks
And bold behinds in straight lines
And shifting circles since they were small girls
Slapping their palms on the ground before the drummers in
respect
When every Sister in the world lived in Africa
Scarred or petted
Free or tethered
Beaten, admired
Shunned, desired
Worshipped, forgotten
Heir or misbegotten
When every Sister in the world lived in Africa…
When every Sister in the world lived in Africa…
…They grouped to talk eagerly with bite about some wayward
woman.

Just like the captured heirs holding court about Miss Divine on
the 210 stoop, their way-back greatgrandmothers had made time
to gather and thoroughly discuss some wanton she-villager who
was the cause of too much ado.

Midnight

Rakim hung up the phone.

She quietly carried a chair out into the foyer to hold her on her toes as she unscrewed the bulbs in the high fixtures on two of the walls. In the dark she came back inside and turned off all the lights in her apartment.

She'd stood waiting at her door opened a crack. She heard the front door ease open and close. Then the door leading from the vestibule did the same.

When a piece of the blackness moving silently through the foyer reached her door she reached out and led him by the hand through her dark apartment back to her dark kitchen.

On the way he'd whispered, "How you know my phone number?"

"411, baby," she drawled.

Stopping at the edge of the kitchen counter she pressed her hush finger against his lips. "Don't say another word," her voice was liquid. Rakim placed his hand low on her stomach so he'd know she stood naked.

Silently, she pushed him down into a kitchen chair, kneeled to undo his pants, patted his hip so he would lift his ass and pulled his pants off by the hems. He hurried to pull down and kick off his briefs.

She stood and climbed backwards on his lap.

They went at it hard until the edge was off, but she kept him caught on the waves of her rhythms, her voice smoky and sexy, convincing him about how she finally had to give in to wanting him deep inside her.

"I wanted this more than you did, Daddy. I play with myself dreaming about you," Rakim moved quicker up and down on his lap.

Her back was to him, her palms were braced on his knees and

she did all the work. Her soft ass bounced against his stomach, her syrup softened his hairs, he couldn't help but bend forward and lick her spine.

One of his hands held her waist, the other played up and down her torso, kneading her firm smooth stomach, cupping and squeezing her heavy swaying breasts, rolling her erect nipples.

It was so much more erotic to him because he couldn't really see her. Just a moving shadow. He couldn't get enough. Just the way a fantasy is supposed to be. His current was building, he didn't and he did want to let it go.

She growled at him, "Would you help me out? If I ever needed you? Now that we know each other so well?"

Abruptly Rakim stood, turned and dropped on her knees between his thighs and clasped his wet erection between her breasts. So swift her movement, he thrust wildly a few hungry times before it reached his brain to savor this special tunnel. Soft as cashmere.

Her honeyed voice came from deep in her throat, "I know you watch me ev'rytime you see me...but you can't see me now. So what you like better, baby, seeing me or feeling me?" Slowly, she eased her breasts from around his manhood and then he couldn't feel her at all.

Throbbing, he bent forward reaching in the darkness, but Rakim was leaning far back, she whispered, "Wait. Let me put something in your hand."

She slid his willing hand to the top of her spread thighs urging it to rub her secret. Rakim's coaxing voice whispered past his ears like floating ribbons, "Show me how you pet a kitty. Preeetty kitty, preeetty preeetty cat."

She showed him a few things to do with three fingers. When his palm was slick, Rakim put his coated digits in her mouth. He shut his lids so his mind could imagine what his eyes couldn't see. He listened to his own grunts mixing with the sounds of Rakim sucking his lollipop fingers.

Rakim gave him back a clean hand. She shifted on her knees and moaned, "I know how long you been dreaming about what I'm getting ready to do now." He was unprepared when Rakim circled her hand around his hard passion and held it like a microphone. She flat tongued it once slowly from base to tip. His breathing sounded like a heart attack.

Her lips breathed her words against his man. "Now I'ma give you what you really want. Just how you want it poppa...And I know you not gon' fool me, so I'ma trust you. I know you gon' help me. We got something going now. We got to make sure this ain't our first and last time."

Rakim spit on the head of his lust. She softly clamped all he had inside her generous mouth and swirled her tongue around it. When her throat urged him to no return, his release was never better.

Rakim took him to the end of the world and pushed him off.

After she finished him Rakim stood up leaned over and caught him roughly by the back of his neck. She stopped his panting by tonguing him deeply, until he pushed her away, realizing why her mouth was so slick.

She pulled him up from the chair, helped him dress quickly and led him back through the dark to her door. There she grabbed his palms and rubbed them all over her breasts, quietly repeating that all he had to do was go home and be there for her. He still couldn't really see her but her low, sexy voice was everywhere.

She made him promise again that if she ever needed him, he'd do whatever she told him to do, just the way she told him to do it. Straight like that. Not one step left, not one step right. She pressed her warm nakedness hard against him, wrapped one leg high around his thigh and slapped her own ass, "Alright sweet lover, go on now, leave before I want you deep in me again."

He said, "Call me, I'll help you...honey. Whatever you need me to do."

"That's my man. Sometimes what a woman needs is right in front of her eyes. I'm not so scared any more. That's what I'm talking about, baby, you understand me, make me strong. Let your woman go get in the shower now, baby. You wrecked me Daddy." Rakim kissed his lips as her hand pushed his back gently into the foyer. Rakim shut her door easy. She didn't have to tell him to sneak.

One-thirty a.m.

"Hey baby. I'm so glad you came. Come in."

"What the fuck you want Rakim? Why you calling me at one in the morning?"

"You Daddy. I want you. I want you to come on in sugar."

"I know you do. But bitch it's Me dont want You. Didn't I make that clear last night? I can't trust you. But yeah. I know what you want. You liked that throwdown last night. Want a rerun. Your mouth hurt? How your ass feel?"

"This freak straight sugar. Supreme baby I love anything you do to me. I love you. That's why I just won't give up until we get back together. I'ma die I'm so wide open baby."

"Shut up Rakim. That shit don't work. What little game you really playing now?"

"Will you please come inside and let me be nice to you? You know you want to forgive me baby because you here. Let your baby do I'm sorry. Baby? Come in. You know Rakim is miserable. I'ma go crazy I love you so much Supreme."

"Quit acting. I been gone a day."

"Sho seem like the rest of my life Daddy."

"That's why you nekked? What you want me to do?"

"Fuck me until you forgive me."

"Just like I said. Want a rerun. And you know what I want."

"Me inside out."

"And…?"

"I'ma make you happy pappy. We gon rumble. I'ma fight you like Tyson. I'ma try to punch you dead in your muhfuckin mouth. All you get you gon take. I'ma get you drunk. I already got the Moet open."

"I don't get drunk …."

"So come on inside slaya."

"You got my necklace?"

"Yes."

Con

Right now I call a pimp my man
Just as much as a square girl can
A whole lot more than a good girl should
I'm knocking hard on wood
Can't resist what drives me mad
That tasty pimpish way he has
Wines me dines me stays inside me
So persuading devastating
Heartbreaker anticipating
The mack stack
Of fast G cash
Just waiting in my pretty ass
If I would just cooperate
It's a lie one woman one mate
Start believing get paid straight
Remind me how I love the pole
How I love to take it whole
And since I love up under the stroke
No sense in two stars being broke
Time for me to change my mind
About what I'll put my mouth behind
I'm too rare to be on stroll
I'm a private number call
Don't I want to live the best
Put my power to the test
Dating ain't nothing but a job
Not like the work is really hard
Honey like mine not suppose to be free
Money's the way to get next to me

But he's about to stop coming around
A woman not ready to truly get down
So right now I call a pimp my man
And I'm finally starting to understand
Grip the logic behind the science
Can't decide until I try it
Working today for our together tomorrow
White picket fence
Daisies in a wheelbarrow
That's what my Daddy said
Because I'm pure thoroughbred

Three-fifteen a.m.

"Baby! Baby baby. Hi my perfect baby."

"How much you got?"

"Two thousand."

"From Supreme?"

"Yes."

"For what?"

"I told him I want to go shopping."

"Just two grand? That's all? Baby that's wrong. We can't do nothing with that change unless he gon break bread like that evry day. I want my money Rakim."

"It's your game darling. Let me know what you need because that's Supreme's bill to pay. Rakim just the one gon hand you your cash. Come on in honey and let me give you this tiny money I got. What number you looking to see before your baby Rakim be rock bottom again? Honey what you need?"

"What I need? Baby I need it all. Show me how fast you can hand me Supreme money then I'ma see. I didn't say I forgive you. Up under Mr. Love again? Baby you disappointed me. I'm a heavy muhfucka baby. Rakim you showed me you can't carry the responsibility."

"Don't say that honey. We had a misunderstanding. You can squat all your weight on me sugar. You got to forgive me lover…That's right baby sit down on the couch and relax. Let me take off your shoes. Now that's better right?"

"What happened to your face? Supreme hit you?"

"Two times. Look at how he busted my pretty mouth baby. He did it. And it's killing me. Look."

"I see. Better watch yourself baby. You can't get what we need if you make your new man upset. Why the fuck he hit you?"

"He said because he can. So you understand. I'm out of your reach now. That's why."

"No. That muhfucka ain't say that. You lying."

"What I'ma lie for? I ain't crazy. But I'ma get your money baby. I'ma do whatever it takes for us to be in love like we was. Don't worry honey."

"Babydoll this pretty muhfucka don't know how to worry. I'm too amazing baby. Do you hear me baby? Daddy get more astronomical every day. Sho you right. Be careful around Supreme. His hands too quick. Don't let him mess you up."

"Let me worry about that trick. Get up. Come with me to the bedroom. Your back tired? You want a massage?"

"That would be nice."

"I roasted a chicken made a salad and cornbread. Let's go in the bedroom baby and I'ma bring you a plate. Pour you some Moet okay?"

"Don't pull on me Rakim."

"Baby stop being so evil. Please be nice."

"Get the fuck off me Rakim."

"Alright. Shipell will you please come with me to the bed-room so I may give you some money? Please?"

"And?"

"And I'ma get you something to eat before I rub your back."

"And?"

"And I hope the cash is enough to let me fuck you I'm sorry. Please come in the bedroom."

"I don't move until I count my money. Then you can suck your candy."

"That's right."

"So go get my money."

Pulse

Night blue pitch black
An echo looked for Jimmy...Jimmy...
Bad Luck sat nervous
Rubbing herself with oil
Night's air a madman
Panted uneasy...

Women saving curls
Under scarves tied Jemima
Kneeled at dark windows
But didn't look out
Hands clapped over their mouths
Holding back the anger
In their voices...

Children dreaming under moving brows
Raised fretful chins to breathe
Some peed the sheets
Their dogs didn't sleep
Men alone smoked naked in bed
One arm bent behind their heads...

Curled like spoons
Somebody's man and nobody's wife
Pretended devotion
Faked happy faces
Peeping the time
Both of them lying
Making vows
Meant to fool til cool dawn...

"What Happened?"

Baybay struggled up, leaning over Charles, pressing her weight on him until she grabbed the receiver off the phone on the nighttable.

Squinting at the clock radio's glow, she read 5:19. Baybay stretched the cord taut across Charles' stomach until she was lying on her back. "Hello?" she said, softly, warily. Lord, she prayed, I hope nobody in the family dead.

On the other end, Susan's loud voice was shrill. "Girl! Get up! The police is here! Ambulance too! Street full of police! Seem like everybody on the block is outside! You hear me, Bay?!"

Baybay, fully awake, reached over Charles again to turn on the nighttable lamp. She sat straight up in the bed and nudged her husband awake. "Charles! Charles! Get up! The police downstairs! Hold on Susan."

Baybay laid the receiver on the bed, grabbed her robe from the bench at its foot and wrapped it around her as she tore to the living room windows. Sho' was! Look at all them cop cars!

She ran back to the phone, ignoring Charles who sat on his side of the bed rubbing sleep from his face with slow hands. He was giving himself a few moments to fully dissolve his dream of sexing Jocelyn. His erection was softening.

"Susan! What the hell is going on?!" Shit, Susan had beat her to the punch again.

That was the question Susan was waiting for. She'd already been outside, been an early part of finding out what was going on from the beginning.

She'd been dozing on her couch waiting in the dark for Raymond to come over after work. The pulsing reflections of lights chasing along her living room walls had jolted her awake. She was drawn to run to and yank up her window and stick out her head.

She gaped at the number of police cars gathering. She noticed lights in other buildings coming on.

Susan had quickly looked each way down the street, ignoring the tail lights of light-colored car making a left at one corner, concentrating on the silent stream of police cars, some of them unmarked, racing from the opposite direction. She watched them swarm before the building, their flashing strobes causing windows to open in apartments all over the block. Heads began to appear.

When Susan saw the black Benz parked across the street, she shouted, "Ohhh nooo!" knowing right away that this had to be some serious business and it had to do with 1A. Rakim and Shipell. She set her imagination free.

Excited, she reached for her jeans slung over the sofa back. Susan ran to her bedroom, snatched the scarf from her head and pulled three strokes of a comb through her hair and hurriedly tied a fast ponytail.

All the while she ran scenarios through her head and wondered why the police hadn't used their sirens. Where the hell were her Kools!

By the time Susan's house slippers clattered down the stoop, two uniformed officers were already talking to Mr. Drayton who stood alert in the little concrete yard in his robe, light brown pants, an undershirt and wine wingtip shoes. Susan came up and stood right beside him, offering a curiosity-filled "Good morning."

Pulling herself tall, she addressed the officers with a stern, "I live in this building, what's happening?" Susan was cooperative. Yes, she knew Rakim Moet Divine. No, she didn't know her by any other name. No, she didn't know anybody in her family and no, they were not friends.

When the officers told Susan that two people had been murdered in Rakim's apartment she began to barrage them with questions. They answered none and with curt authority, stifled her salvo, ordered her to go back to her apartment and wait there until an officer arrived to question her more.

Susan had elbowed her way back into the building, shoving past all the police activity going in and out. Astounded by what she heard, she'd rushed home to call Bay....

"Susan! What's going on?! You right, street full of police cars!" Baybay was talking loud too.

"Police say two bodies dead inside Rakim's apartment! Killed tonight!"

"No!" Baybay was remembering where her company house-coat hung in the closet. "Hold the phone a sec'. Charles!" commanding, "put some clothes on will you? Two people been killed downstairs in Rakim's place...Yeeess! I said killed!...Susan's telling me now...I don't know who dead, that's what I want you to find out, if you stop sitting there like a stump and hurry get your clothes on!...Devante? What y'all doing up? Ain't nobody called y'all...You and Delqwon get! back in your damn room and close the door...No, you don't need to know where daddy going...I said, go get back in the bed and stay! there! You hear me?...Shutup, Delqwon...Y'all go 'head on!...No! Y'all don't need no soda...Goodnight!...I'm sorry Susan."

She cupped her hand around the receiver, "Chile! I can't believe it! Miss Divine dead?"

Susan informed Baybay that the police wouldn't tell her who the victims were, but she assumed one of them had to be Rakim because it was her apartment. She had tried to peek in Rakim's on her way back to her place, but an officer had hustled her along, said she was trespassing on a crime scene.

Susan could feel how hard Baybay was listening. She dropped her last gem. "And I know you checked out the black Benz parked right across the street in front of the building."

"No there ain't!" Baybay just wanted to hear it again. She also chided herself for missing it when she'd looked out the window.

"Girl, please! You know that's Shipell's car, especially after what I seen last night? You know the other body got to be his." Susan began thinking up possibilities.

"Lord have mercy! Susy, what you think happen? Shipell kill her, kill himself? Rakim kill him, kill herself? But why they want to kill each other, period? They just got back together. If anything, she kill him, because that man ain't killing himself over nothing and you know it! I told you, that Rakim a mess! Girrrl! Miss

Divine dead!"

Baybay talked non-stop wondering aloud why they didn't hear any fighting or arguing. "Well, whoever dead down there must have been stabbed, because I sho' ain't heard no gun go off." Then she lied, "Because you know I sleep light."

"Who? What you talking about, Bay? You sleep like you dead, too. But if you was wide awake with your ear to her door you still wouldn't have heard no gunshots if whoever pulled the trigger didn't want you to. That's what I think, I think they was shot. I don't know why, I just feel it."

Susan said she was going back downstairs, she didn't care what the police told her about staying home.

Baybay replied, "Come up and get me in five minutes," hung up and turned to get on Charles for being so goddamn slow!

Baybay's phone rang again right away, it was Jocelyn. She was nervous, "What's happening, Bay?" Jocelyn said that all the flashing lights woke her and when she'd looked outside and saw all the police cars out front, she'd put her kids in the bed with her.

Baybay related what Susan said about a double murder in Rakim's apartment. "No!" Jocelyn exclaimed. "Oh my God!"

Baybay said Charles was about to go outside to see what was going on. She said she'd send him over to her place later to check on her and the kids.

Baybay didn't notice Charles' ear turned in her direction. She told Jocelyn she'd call her back when she got more information.

Baybay hung up quickly, glanced around and saw that Charles had finally dressed and left the apartment.

She didn't know that instead of going down the stairs he went up.

Slipping on her quilted robe along with her good house slippers Baybay hurried to meet Susan. She called to her sons' closed bedroom door, "I'll kill both of y'all stone dead if y'all even think! about coming out that room!" She locked the front door, put her keys in her pocket and headed quickly for the stairs.

Awakened by the lights and commotion, the block leaned from their windows or milled curiously before 210 in the near-to-dawn morning. They asked questions to the police and each other then made up and speculated over what they didn't know but figured.

Susan and Baybay were already on the heels of the official investigation, holding hands, pretending to be invisible. As soon as they stepped over the threshold of Rakim's apartment, Baybay jumped and Susan swallowed shouts at what they saw.

Everywhere they looked, on everything, the entire apartment was bathed in red light and seductive with painted red roses.

It was beautiful and bizarre. The painted blooms were almost as real as the mass of true roses sitting tightly in, spilled wide around a large crystal vase in the middle of the rosy painted livingroom floor.

Susan whispered that they had to be the same roses she'd seen tumbling from Rakim's arms the night before.

Full blown and arching they weren't romantic anymore. Tawdry and gaudy, offensive, they were too ripe with florid splendor.

Their smell in the hot apartment was stifling, overwhelming and shifted with other, more metallic odors, each fighting to float on top. The room was so cloying with deep scents the women took shallow breaths.

Her throat working up and down, Susan held down nausea. She wanted to leave but Baybay jerked her friend's arm into a tight grip with her own, whispering fiercely, "No! Come on Su! I got to see this!"

Two owl necks and four magnifying eyes edged slowly along the livingroom wall out of the way of the hubbub, joined at crooked elbows, almost making it to the bedroom full of suits, plainclothes and uniforms talking and busy doing.

Susan and Baybay moved closer, they had a couple of eternity seconds to peer into the bedroom and gape at the large form laying on the bed under an emerald satin sheet. A dead body.

A detective who'd seen them sneak in the apartment stepped up to block their view and barked an order for the intruding women to leave, immediately, or be arrested. Who were they anyway?

Susan and Baybay gave their names and apartment numbers with turkey necks peering behind him. He turned them around by their shoulders and nudged them forward.

They were instructed to go home and wait there, a detective would be up shortly. The building had been cordoned off as a homicide scene, they would not be allowed to leave the premises, nor would anyone not living here be allowed access until checked for identification.

Susan mentioned that her boyfriend, Raymond, although he didn't actually live here, should be allowed inside. She didn't want to be alone and she knew her rights.

The detective, Grady was his name, put up his palms and said, "Okay, okay, we'll see," as he ushered them out of Rakim's apartment.

Baybay craned her neck, snatching a look in the kitchen as they passed it, then stopped mulishly in her tracks. She'd glimpsed another form humped beneath a jade satin sheet.

On the floor, the body was pressed against the base of the counter with its covered head towards them.

She elbowed Susan and pointedly looked in the kitchen again, knowing Susan would do the same. "Oh my God," Susan wailed, before Grady hurried them along and pushed them out into the vestibule.

Still locked together, they began to climb the stairs. Shock and disbelief turned their ascent into slow motion, their faces into pantomime. Susan was first to break the weird silence. "Daaamn! Did you see that apartment? Whoa! That bitch was crazy! No wonder she didn't let nobody inside. What was wrong with Rakim? What she paint all them roses for? Shit! Roses everywhere! On the floor, the walls, on the furniture, Bay, she painted roses on leather furniture, daaamn!" Breathless, she blinked close in Baybay's face.

Baybay drew back her head with something else pushing her mind. "Which body you think was Rakim, Susan? I think the one in the kitchen. I think I saw the foot of the one in the bedroom. A man's foot."

Her thumb found her mouth, she chewed the nail. "They couldn't have been dead too long."

Baybay had another baffling thought that stopped her mid-step, "Who knew they was dead and reported it? Who called the police? And so fast? We live here and we didn't know people was killed downstairs. Hum ain't home from work yet and Jocelyn called me right after you did, scared, asking what was going on. So you think Mr. Drayton called? But how he know? That old man go to bed before it get late. So who called the police so fast, Susan?"

"You so right!" Susan pulled her arm out of Baybay's and fell back on the banister fully absorbing what her best friend said. She repeated in agreement, "Who called the police and told them two people dead in 1A? I don't think it was Mr. Drayton, because when I was outside the police was questioning him the same way they was questioning me. They wasn't treating him like he knew anything about what happened. Damn, we got a double mystery on our hands, Bay. Who's dead in 1A and who reported it."

"It had to be whoever killed them." Baybay was sure, because that's the only thing that made sense. Susan nodded slowly.

Susan hugged herself then motioned for Baybay to keep walking with her up the stairs. She went on, "Hey, listen, I hope it wasn't no burglary. What if somebody broke in knowing Shipell was there and robbed them then killed them so Rakim and Shipell not alive to tell? Then called 911 because he's one sick bastard."

That revelation made her nervous, when Susan looked at Baybay she saw her own distress.

"Susy, you might be right. Somebody wanted them bodies found right away." Baybay shook her head as if to clear it. "Yep. This is some sick shit."

"Well, I'm home," Susan said, pausing at her door. Baybay, head down and lost in thought, didn't stop or say goodbye. She absently threw up a hand to her friend and started the flight that led to her landing.

"I'ma call you," Susan said to Baybay's back.

Once inside, the first thing Susan did was dig in her back pocket for her pack and lighter and sparked a Kool. Then she turned on a lamp. Susan fell on her couch and smoked.

She pulled a long ash as she yanked the rubberband from her hair, releasing the ponytail and scratching her scalp. She wiggled down her jeans and left them bunched on the living room floor.

She felt rather important to be sequestered. She wondered where Raymond was. Probably outside and the police wouldn't let him in the building.

She still couldn't decide whether to let him move in like he'd been hinting, talking about how they could both cut their bills in half, not to mention all the good sex.

She also made a note to herself to insist whenever she was questioned that the police put a patrol on this block until the murderer was caught. What if the murderer came back? She worked, paid taxes, she was entitled to police protection.

She would mention that to Baybay too. Baybay didn't work right now, because she and Charles both wanted her home while their boys were small. But when she did have a nine-to-five she'd paid her share of taxes as a bookkeeper, so Bay had the right to demand protection also.

She remembered that a detective was coming to question her. Susan toyed with the idea of opening her door in her underwear. The thought made her warm.

Susan yawned widely and looked at the clock and saw it was close to six. Definitely, Baybay was still up. She put flame to another Kool, picked up the cordless on the accent table and pushed Baybay's number who answered her kitchen phone on the first ring.

Baybay was standing at the table about to pour Charles a glass of orange juice while he told her what he'd heard on the street.

Distracted by her own recollections, she half listened to Susan rehashing what they'd seen in 1A. Her mind kept flashing back to Rakim's painted garden, imagining her mixing paint the color of blood and fire and using it to make the petals stroked on the walls.

Her mind recalled the pungent smell of doom and perfume wafting from death and the overbearing aroma of dying roses.

Her hands were shaking. Charles took the juice carton and the phone from his wife and gently guided her down into a chair. He put the receiver to his mouth and told Susan to hang up.

Charles stood in front of Baybay and took her hands in his.

She looked up into his face and for the first time in their eight years, didn't comprehend what she saw there. That scared her. Worse than the madness she'd just left.

Whatever was coming from Charles was bad. She hoped it had nothing to do with the mess in 1A.

She shook her head to chase the bloody, gruesome images of death and fixed her mind to race over what could possibly be going on with her husband. Concentrating on his eyes, looking deep for the man she loved and thought she knew, Baybay sat forward on the edge of her chair.

With a hitch in her voice, she said, "Baby, what is it?"

Without warning and for no reason because Charles hadn't yet said a word, tears swam then fell unchecked down her cheeks. Suddenly, she couldn't talk, her throat was closed and full.

Oh, Lord, help me. Don't let my husband be mixed up in that business downstairs because he's fucking Rakim.

Her mind said it first, Don't leave me, Charles! Ohhh God! Baybay pulled her hands from his to cover her face and began to sob.

Charles blew out a deep breath and began, "Aww, no, baby...come on, don't cry, baby...Um...Give me your hand, Bay...Come on, give me your hand, baby...Thank you...You know I love you...You hear me, Bay?... Baby? Baby, take your other hand off your eyes and look at me. You and the boys...Look at me, baby...Y'all my world...Don't Nothing! come before my family...You know that, right?...I take good care of y'all, you got to give me that...Huh, Bay? You know I love you, right?...We been together for a long time, huh, baby?...And...and...I would never leave you. Never, okay?... And...I don't want you to leave me neither, but Bay... Arbayelle, baby, we, um, got to talk...."

Herman

The police discovered a sensational crime.

They searched hard in an apartment that had been obviously cleaned after a double murder. They were counting on forensics to pull up better clues.

Recording all the evidence they found, the best piece was a delicate crystal champagne flute found in the sink. The cloudy fingerprints on it were obvious.

There was a giant spill of long-stemmed thornless roses crowding cut crystal in the middle of the living room floor and two naked men were dead with their throats cut ear to ear. Each was shrouded with a satin sheet.

Because there were no signs of a struggle, a veteran suggested that they'd probably been drugged before their lives were taken.

The detectives figured that the woman who lived here, the so-called Rakim Moet Divine, did it.

One officer had found a knife, left to be discovered and clean as a whistle, wedged between two sofa cushions.

The huddled form slumped in the kitchen had been dragged there. The sharp smell of bleach was strong. Obviously a lot was used to carefully clean up the blood.

A clean, wrung-out mop and two clean damp sponges sat in a clean bucket beside the refrigerator.

The corpse was pushed up against the base of the kitchen counter. His head rested sideways at an odd angle from the fatal wound, his life thickened darkly on the floor.

The other dead man was on Rakim's bed. His slit throat made his head tilt awkwardly, too.

Both wore frozen expressions of terrified surprise.

One hardboiled detective made a bet that Rakim had given the men something that made them paralyzed. "I seen something like this back in '81. Wife gave her husband a drug that froze him up like fuckin' concrete but kept him conscious.

"She took five minutes to stick a twelve-inch knife in his gut because he was fuckin' the babysitter. And all he could do was blink his eyes while she gutted him like a fuckin' fish. Like these two unlucky fucks. This shit happens, man. Wasn't a fuckin' thing these sorry bastards could do. I'm tellin' you, they was paralyzed when she did this.

"This fuckin' woman cuts their throats and all they could do was witness their own death. What a fuckin' way to die."

No identification was located for either man, but both wore hundreds of thousands of dollars worth of platinum and diamond jewelry.

The dead man in the kitchen wasn't wearing a watch, but the smooth sweep of the second hand confirmed the authentic diamond-bathed Rolex on the wrist of the other dead man on the bed. So she didn't want to rob them. The law deduced that Rakim had murdered over deeper concerns.

Shaking his head to emphasize his disparaging remarks about the nature of the crime, one young officer looked closely at the fabulous timepiece on the lifeless wrist on the bed.

Due to his youth spent running low to the ground, the cop coveted that watch. He still wanted one. Maybe not with a full diamond face like this one, that was too much. But he could sell it for a bundle.

Backsliding, he slid his eyes around at his colleagues in the room but no one returned his attention.....

He smiled, catching the vibe immediately, so it was going to be a mind-your-business-just-do-your-thing-quick kind of situation.

He looked and didn't see a detective pull a mink off its hanger and drape it over his arm. He also never saw that same man hurry back from going outside to his car…

Looking at the Rolex he reached out and did his thing. What watch?…

Tucked on the floor in the back corner of her bedroom closet two detectives discovered the men's clothes, two carefully folded piles of expensive suits, silk shirts, silk underwear and socks, reptile belts and reptile shoes.

The subtle hint of rich cologne made one man pick up and smell one of the shirts. He came away nodding his head. He whistled softly in admiration as he used his fingertips to lift one finely made black crocodile lace-up. Looking inside, it was his size...

Picking up a pair of pants the other detective felt a bulge in a front pocket. Turning his back, he eased out a dense fold of money. With his hand close to his side, he used his thumb to slide down a few of the top bills, they were all the same, hundreds. He held what had to be thousands.

He closed his palm and used that loaded hand to check his inside jacket pocket. The empty hand that drew back urged his luck.

He picked up the second pair of slacks, slid his fingers in the front pocket and was rewarded again with another Benjamin stack.

He bent and used that green mitt to adjust the fit of his sock. His palm was clean when he stood back up...

She had so much, they couldn't tell what Rakim had taken with her. There were three closets in the apartment, one in the bedroom, one in the livingroom and one near the front door. They all brimmed with label and custom clothes that none of them could afford to buy their mates.

Stuffed overhead on the closet shelves and stacked along their walls, they counted Louis Vuitton, Fendi, Prada and Gucci bags and luggage.

In the bedroom closet against the entire back wall behind her clothes, stacked two rows deep, floor to ceiling, were shoes and boots in clear plastic boxes. There were nine empty boxes, the shoes she took.

Rakim left seven magnificent furs. Hats. Reptile belts and bags. The oversized dresser in her bedroom was tight with more clothes in excess. But there was nothing at all on the dresser top.

There were transparent plastic boxes of gossamer designer lingerie under the bed.

She must have just taken her jewelry, with abundance like this, Rakim Moet Divine had to have heavy jewelry and they'd found none.

An investigator searching on hands and knees found a huge diamond teardrop glittering in the dark up against the wall beneath the dresser. As his hand closed around it, he forgot all about it...

There were no photos, mail or any papers at all to be found. She evidently didn't read books or magazines. Or had thrown them away.

Inside the refrigerator half of a roasted chicken and its savory side dishes were all photographed. Rose petals were scattered on the bottom shelf. There was nothing in the trash container.

They found an old spattered wooden paint box under the rose decorated dresser. In the bathroom, not dry oil paint roses almost covered the mirror.

A tall, narrow cabinet held quite an array of antique bottles and jars, all filled with liquids and things they couldn't identify.

Going for a joke to release the tension, one agent called for Officer DeVille, born in Martinique. He entered the bathroom looked at Rakim's collection and raised his brow, declaring that this woman was messing with the seven powers. He was glad he hadn't eaten any of her food. She probably left it with a purpose.

His colleagues roared. One pretended to choke, another asked if Rakim had made herself disappear.

The head badge walked in, quit the hilarity and ordered his men back to work.

By the time Susan had joined the commotion on the street, Herman Drayton had already been in Rakim's apartment with the police and looked at the scene through their eyes....

Earlier, because of "Super" beside his bell in the foyer, the law had filled his basement doorway with importance.

They'd come to his apartment to gain admittance to 1A. Pounding, they'd said, "Police! Open the door!"

Called to answer the summons at his door he'd grabbed his robe and tied it around him. Herman peered through his narrowly parted door at the badges they showed. Pushing their way to come inside the three white men introduced themselves by name, apologized for the hour, but they'd gotten a tip about a double homicide in this building, 210 Jefferson Avenue, 1A.

They needed Herman to open the apartment.

Before the law showed up Herman hadn't been back home a good half-hour. Sitting on the side of his bed he was bone tired. He was bone tired and overwhelmed.

Going with the police was the third time he'd been to Rakim's apartment that night.

Joining them, Herman followed behind, climbing three steps to the yard, up the wide steps of the stoop, through the front door into the small vestibule. He listened to what they expected to find. The detectives paused.

Herman moved through them to the second door, key ready in hand. As soon as he turned it, they entered the foyer before him and went straight to 1A.

He joined the cops crowded at Rakim's door. He hoped they didn't notice his hand shaking as he used the shiny new key on his ring to open her apartment.

The police and detectives entered immediately. Herman stood near the door and let the men find what they came looking for.

One investigator asked questions that Herman was composed enough to answer to satisfaction, because the officer said "Thank you, you can go. Somebody will be by to talk to you again."

Herman went directly to the basement and straight to his bedroom. He didn't turn on a light. He had to sit down on the bed for a minute. Think, think.

He felt like he was in a dream and there was no liquor in the house.

When his phone rang, it startled him, he wasn't expecting it to ring, not so soon. He looked at the clock on the dresser but didn't see its glowing numbers. Herman's eyes saw nothing, but his mind's eye was bombarded with fresh recollections. It had to be Rakim calling, again.

Why was she calling him again so soon? What now? Where was she?

With police swarming all over his building, Herman was just now starting to feel the electric shock of just how abruptly and thoroughly his life had changed.

He would not have been more amazed if he discovered that he'd been plucked up and dashed to the ground on another planet, one where a different Herman, but him nonetheless, had willingly and thoroughly cleaned up dead men's blood because the woman who'd killed them told him to.

Lord have mercy, what had he done.

Herman tried to remember, exactly...

It was a little before four in the morning, he was deeply asleep, drained from sexing Rakim. The phone had jarred him, snatched him from his dream-on-repeat, reliving the miracle of having Rakim, her sucking him in the dark in a kitchen chair in her apartment.

His disjointed voice croaked, "Huh? Hel, Hello?"

"Hey. Daddy, wake up. Wake up. Herman? Baby, you wake?"

"Huh? Rakim? Rakim?"

"Shhh, yes it's me, Poppa. You woke now?"

"Uh, yeah, I'm woke. What time is it? What's wrong?"

Rakim burst into tears. "Oh, Herman! I almost got killed after you left me tonight!" Her sobs flooded his ear.

"What! What did you say?!" Herman was shocked alert. He couldn't believe what he'd heard.

"You almost got killed?! By who? Who want to kill you?" Herman sat up and pressed the receiver harder against his ear as if the pressure would make him understand better. He looked at the time on his clock.

"When I see you, you'll understand. You promised to help me, and I need you right now, honey." Rakim's plea was shaky and weak.

"Don't cry sweetheart. What you need me to do? Calm down and tell me Rakim." For her, Herman had to be strong and make wrong things right.

"You gon' help me whatever it is? I'm so scared" Her voice quavered from fear.

"Now, now, baby, I'ma help you, you don't have no reason to be scared. You ain't dead, right? And I'm right here. I'll do anything for you Rakim." Herman hoped his voice sounded as solid and reassuring as he meant. "What is it?"

"I need you to help me clean something up, okay, baby?" She

sounded stronger.

"Clean something? Something like what?"

"Oh honey, I got to explain it to your face. So you coming now? I'm scared, baby, you got to come right away and help me. I'ma leave the door unlocked, just come on in." Rakim's voice was back to velvet. They hung up.

When Herman let himself in and closed her door behind him he was knocked back a step by the rose painted livingroom bathing in candle flames.

His first thoughts were, Lawd, look at what this girl done did to my walls! Could burn my place down with all these candles!

But those complaints were fleeting because then he saw her, naked, stretching on the sofa, beckoning him into her arms.

He started for her, stopping abruptly to look down to see what he'd stepped on. There were roses all over the floor. He tried not to step on too many more as he approached. When he got close he saw her bruises.

"They beat me, Daddy," was all Rakim said before she urged Herman to hurry and undress, "Love me again, daddy, love my pain away," she said, about to cry.

He was near tears himself because for the second time in one night, he was hard.

Herman damned himself as he pulled out of his clothes and rushed to slide in. Rakim gripped the sofa and grunted on every thrust, like he was using a cannon.

Soon, he groaned all the way through his finish.

She didn't let him rest but a minute before she jumped up tugging him, urging, "Come on, get up baby, it's time to help me now."

Rakim led both of them naked into her bedroom lighted by candles too. Herman peered, recognized what he saw humped on her bed and dropped hard to his knees, hanging his shaking head. Moaning, "Naw, Rakim. What did you do, girl?!"

"Get up, Herman. Come on!" Rakim roughly yanked on his arm until he stood. She pulled him into the kitchen and hit the light switch.

Herman called for God again, he couldn't believe it, there was another one.

"I pulled his heavy ass in here by myself," Herman thought she sounded a little proud.

"Help me, Jesus!" he cried, collapsing to his knees again.

"Nooo, He ain't here, but I am, so I'm your savior. Don't renig on me now. Would you please get up off the floor."

Rakim pushed the handle of a bucket holding two large sponges, a mop and a gallon bottle of bleach into his hand. "Believe me, it was self-defense," she turned him toward the sink telling him to fill the bucket and use lots of bleach. She handed him a mop.

Herman couldn't help but ask, "They came to kill you together?" He turned on the water and dutifully made the solution strong.

"No, baby, they came one at a time with the same reason, to have me or kill me." Rakim pointed at the blood trail leading to the kitchen that she wanted Herman to clean. "Clean it good," she cautioned. "I don't want to see how I dragged him."

Watching him get to work, Rakim thought about how Shipell never noticed Supreme's blood on the living room floor. She shrugged, he probably couldn't see it because it really blended so well with the painted roses on the floor. That, and the shadowy, wavy candlelight helped hide the blood.

"In fact, I could actually say that I had to kill them, because of you. I wasn't gon' say nothing because I didn't want you to feel bad, but you got a right to know. They beat me because I told them it was over. I said Rakim had finally fallen in love. And you know they was taking care of me, so they beat me."

She went over to Herman so she could stroke his cheek, "But you my man now, we in this together, fighting for our love."

Her new lover didn't know whether to feel terrified or elated, but he cleaned vigorously, changing the water often, getting on his knees to scour the track that led from the bedroom through the living room into the kitchen.

Herman understood. She was just a young thing out here alone trying to survive. Didn't have nobody but herself.

Shuh. Them snakes got what they deserved. It had to be self-defense. Why else would a sweet, pretty young thing like her hurt them street men unless they was trying to hurt her first?

Herman's pressed lips showed how aggressively he went after his task. The painted roses under the blood he cleaned were ruined.

Herman commiserated, the poor thing had revealed the truth and suffered the consequences. He knew now that he was the root of it all.

She wouldn't have had to fight for her life if it wasn't for loving him. Look at how they beat her, all them bruises! Bastards! Yassuh, he might not be a young man, but gotdamn it, he bet he still had two cans of whup-ass left to open! I wish I'd had the chance to lay my hands on them snakes! Shuh!

Switching to the mop Herman scrubbed and recalled all the times he'd seen them no good dogs from his window. Big cars, sharp suits, furs, flashy jewels, he knew they enjoyed using his woman. But she was smart enough to finally recognize her abuse and put a stop to it, in the name of love. If he had a daughter her age, he would hope that she would have the same sense to recognize and choose real heart feelings over money.

Rakim had said, "We need to get out a here, baby. Me and you together. Start our new life together, me and you."

Rakim had gone into the bedroom and dressed quickly in jeans and a shirt. She pulled three large Vuitton suitcases from the overhead shelf. She culled pieces from her dresser drawers then methodically went through all the closets with keen precision, pulling from each a scant number of ensembles and shoes. She stroked her furs as she decided to leave them.

As she packed and Herman cleaned, she kept instructing, detailing his role in making sure that they could be together in pure love. "How much money you got in the bank, lover?"

Herman didn't see any reason to lie, she was his new horizon. "Close to twenty-nine thousand."

He continued to do what he was told, frowning with anger, still fuming over how those demons had battered his woman. Shuh. "Won't nothing ever happen to you again," he'd declared impulsively, possessively. Herman was still strong, a man, he wrung out the mop extra tight, arms trembling with effort.

Rakim responded, "Uh-huh. Take out twenty-eight tomorrow morning." She resumed mapping his orders.

When she carried her bags to sit near the door, Herman had just about finished rinsing out the bucket for the final time.

Rakim joined him in the kitchen and reached into a cabinet for champagne stems, she asked Herman to get the bottle of Dom from the refrigerator. "Oh, and before I forget. Honey, would you put my roses in the vase in that cabinet over there?" Rakim pointed. "Put some water in it and sit them in the middle of the living room floor as our elegant goodbye."

Herman hurried to gather and fix the roses and place them where she wanted them.

Rakim told him to do the honors and watched him pop the cork on the champagne and pour both glasses. Herman lifted his stem to clink the rim with hers then drank quickly like she did. She had him pour them some more.

"Celebrate life!" she laughed. When his glass was bottom up, Rakim told him to put it in the sink so she wouldn't forget to wash it.

She reminded him of the busy day that faced them on the road to their new life. In just a few hours! He should get some rest, she consoled, after all, he'd come and taken care of her just like she knew he would. That's why she was so proud to be his woman.

Rakim gave Herman a deep tongue kiss as she encouraged him to squeeze her breasts. She pulled away and led him to her door.

"Go get some rest now, sugar. It's time for me to leave. You know where to meet me tomorrow." She ushered him out of her apartment, into the foyer, patting him on the back before she shut her door.

After he left Rakim blew out the candles and went back into the kitchen. She turned on the light.

She used a paper towel to lift Herman's glass out of the sink and sat it on the counter. She washed hers and dried it with the same piece, keeping it between her fingers and the glass as she put it back in the cabinet.

Rakim picked up the bottle and poured the rest of the champagne down the drain. She shoved the bottle and paper towel into the trash. She tied the plastic bag, lifted it from the container and walked to sit it by her suitcases.

Back in the kitchen she washed her hands and used paper towels to dry the basin. One more piece was between her fingers and Herman's unwashed flute as she placed it back in the sink.

Scolding herself for tying up the garbage bag so tightly, Rakim tore up the paper towels and flushed the pieces down the toilet.

She went through her apartment with a thick washcloth, wiping every surface. Rakim used the towel to open her front door a crack so she wouldn't have to touch the knob when she left.

Once everything was straight, she used the cloth to lift the phone in the kitchen. With the tip of her nail she dialed the operator to get the number for the police and quickly told the male voice that answered, "Two people dead in 210 Jefferson Avenue. 1A," and hung up.

She stuffed the cloth in the carryall that she was taking. Supreme's car keys were ready in her pocket, her luggage already by the door.

The bags were heavy but she managed to struggle them and the bag of trash out of her apartment and down the stoop in one hurried trip.

She retrieved Supreme's keys and rapidly unlocked the driver's door of his Benz. Rakim flung her luggage and the garbage in the back seat.

She jumped behind the wheel, jabbed in the ignition key and pulled off.

After she started turning the corner Rakim glanced in the rearview and saw flashing roof lights coming from the other end of the block.

Rakim laughed out loud, "'Bye, now!"….

As she made her escape, Herman sat at home brooding, reeling from overload. Everything had exploded around him. Calamity right outside.

Herman didn't know what to think about first. But he had already thanked God because the police didn't consider him a suspect. After they'd questioned him and told him to go home.

Herman didn't need to hear it twice.

But they were coming back.

Herman hadn't moved from the side of his bed, still shaken by the reality of what he'd done and the immediate investigation. How did the police get here so fast? He tried in vain to steady himself, come back to himself.

He still couldn't really believe what he'd done, the mess he stood in chin-deep.

The persistently ringing phone caught his attention. It gave him déjà vu. Didn't he already answer the phone tonight, twice before? Wasn't it Rakim both times?

The first time he'd gone to sex her. The second time she called for him to protect her. What could it be now?

He didn't care. He was willing, again. Rubbing his fingers slowly back and forth against his mouth, this really was his only opportunity. The ringing stopped.

All he had to do was be at the bank first thing when it opened and jump in a cab with his valise, go meet her and be on his way to the best thing that was ever going to happen to him in his life.

His actions had already made his decision irreversible. "Just, just…." Herman didn't know the word "reckless."

The phone rang again for a short time. He stood up in a way that showed his age and went into the kitchen where it sat on the table.

Herman switched on the light, hunted the junk drawer under the counter and found an old notebook and a pen. Herman carefully tore out a few curled pages, dragged a chair and sat hunched over the table after moving the phone out of his way. He started a letter to his sister, Mary, who lived not too far away.

He'd ask her to ask her husband Luther to collect the rents and look after his building for a little while. Like the Acting Super. He'd offer Luther a weekly piece of change in exchange for doing his brother-in-law this big favor.

It was very important that he write Mary a letter explaining what he needed to be done while he was gone, who lived in each apartment. He would spell out their names, how much rent to get from each on the first of the month, when to go to the bank, what day the garbage men and the oil truck came, that kind of thing.

He'd keep unwritten that he had to go to blazes with his angel. Just for a time. Just until he got back.

And he would be back because he knew this thing would soon be through. It was too good to last too long.

Rakim claimed she loved him, said that she'd lost her heart after he screwed her so good that first time in the dark. That's what she'd said.

But Herman wasn't stupid. Shuh. She was too young and pretty not to change her mind the fist time a young moneyman caught her eye.

He knew he was in this prime position because she didn't have anyone else to call. But there must be some truth in her declaration of love, because something had to be the reason for the violence done to her. He believed that her confession to those men that he was her man was the spark that made them beat her.

Accepting that he was the cause of her extreme actions, Herman felt this chance to be with her was the prize he'd earned. He deserved his turn with a woman every man wanted.

Herman knew too, how long he had. She was his until she was snatched by a younger man or until all his money was spent.

It was important to his welfare that he take precautions to make sure that he had 210 and its rents to come home to.

Rakim had guaranteed that if he did what she said, no one would ever figure out that they were together. Herman put all his hope in her confidence.

He convinced himself that he'd be able to resume his life after Rakim moved on and he brought his old behind back to 210.

Herman's phone called and called and fell silent.

He'd inform Mary that he'd decided just like that, to take some time to go visit a woman he'd met through a friend. She was from Philly but he'd met her up here at the funeral of a friend they had in common.

Since then they'd been talking back and forth on the phone. She'd invited him more than once to come see her, but he'd never gone.

His letter would explain that this time when she asked, she wouldn't let him say no because there was no good reason why he couldn't get on the bus.

Herman figured that this letter would seem like a coincidence, misdirected proof that he'd already decided to vacation before all hell broke loose in his building. It would seem like he decided to keep his plans.

He'd date the letter two or three days ago. So when it was discovered that he was gone, he'd have an alibi. An innocent letter left on his kitchen table that kind of explained his whereabouts. It would seem like he'd absentmindedly forgotten to mail it to Mary.

His phone began ringing again.

Herman tapped his pen against the table and jiggled his leg while he thought of what else to say. He'd write that Mary knew he never went nowhere to have a nice time. Especially with a lady friend. Just kept overseeing his building all the time.

He'd put one truth in this letter, that his lady friend made him feel young. He was still a man. Mary was deep in the church so he would be delicate and not say more than that. He would write that she couldn't blame him for wanting some female company.

He'd write her, not call, because the peace in Mary's voice would tangle his explanations, knot them tighter with his every word.

The phone started again, Herman watched it until the ringing stopped.

Herman stood suddenly, shoved his hand into his front pocket and yanked out a ball of money.

He looked down at the three hundred dollars he clutched. All that was left from the three thousand he kept secreted in the house. She'd taken all but what he held to feel secure until she was "safe under his love when we meet later on this morning."

His phone refused to quit. Herman sat, threw the crumpled bills on the floor. He'd pick them up later.

Like a dry sponge reaching for water, Herman licked his lips and lifted the receiver. Must be something Rakim forgot to tell him.

He would agree, whatever it was, because he was alone.

And tired of it.

"God, Please!"

At a quarter past six in the morning, Hum turned the corner of Jefferson Avenue.

A few steps into the block she stopped abruptly as if she'd hit a brick wall. Tisha's heart nearly quit as well. The street milled with people. There was a crowd in front of her building. There were police cars, a van that read Coroner. Stunned, she whispered, "This is it."

This was the reason why she'd abruptly stood, picked up her bag, shut off her computer and without a word, left work way before it was time to get off.

And now, whatever was happening on her block had to be the answer. And she was supposed to see it.

A stretcher was being brought down the front steps of her building.

She moaned, "Oh. My. God," running home.

Pushing through the gang of people before 210 she was halted suddenly, barred by a policeman's outstretched arms as the stretcher reached the sidewalk, heading for the coroner's van.

Like an eel, Hum slipped under the cop's restraints and dashed to the covered body, reaching it just before it was hoisted into the back.

In early morning light, before she could be stopped, Hum yanked the zipper down on the body bag pulled it open and fell back stumbling hard as if shoved.

The crowd that had pushed in behind her gasped along with her. It was that pimp Shipell! His throat was cut! All voices began to talk.

Now that they'd gotten to see the face of one of the two dead, speculation increased about the identity of the covered corpse that had been hoisted into the van about ten minutes before this one.

Some swore it was too big to be a woman, others insisted it was Miss Divine.

Hum's eyes were tunneled on Love's dead face. She never noticed the other body. An officer walked up and gently moved Hum out of the way as the coroner's assistant zipped the bag back over Shipell's face.

Tisha crumpled, sinking to the curb, moaning, holding her shaking hands over her streaming eyes. Everybody watched, curious about her deep sorrow.

Immediately, strangers helped Hum to her feet and she shook them off angrily as soon as she stood.

She began yelling hoarsely, staggering backwards, still shuttering her eyes groaning, "What haaappened? Ohhh, no. Ohhh, Lord! What did Rakim do to my baaaby! Y'all got her? Y'all got that biiitch?! Where she at!? Ohhh not my Love!"

Again Hum collapsed pathetically on the street.

The spectators enjoyed this scene just as much as seeing the bodies brought out. It added a juicy new piece of mystery to the drama. Why was this woman tripping?

Tisha thought she heard Susan's voice filtering through the others exclaiming, "Ohhh, shit! Shipell was fuckin' Hum too? Hum was ho'in'? Daaamn!"

Hum shook off helping hands a second time, insisting to be left alone, screaming, "I live here! I want to go inside and go home!"

She couldn't be stopped from plunging back through the loudly curious crowd, heading for 210's stoop, focusing on getting to her apartment right away.

Hum faltered, then ran up the steps, crying "Looooove… Ohhh, Love, Love…."

At the top, before she entered the building, Hum turned to look back at the van pulling away. She quit her noise like a tape being stopped, pressed her palm against her grieving mouth. But she couldn't hold back shocked tears.

Hum never noticed that Susan was right beside her, watching, perched still and drop-mouthed on the wide banister.

Hum felt like killing Rakim. She trembled with it. Abruptly, she ran into the building. Susan jumped to her feet and went after her.

Future History

Hot ice
So cold
Scald you and
Drown you dry
My water so deep
Your feet not wet
Noon moon
I'm high low
Dizzy you steady
Starve you full
My wise so simple
Your mind grows dumb
Wild cherry I'm
So fast
Slow motion
Hurry and wait
You long to hold me
Regret every embrace
Sweet pain
I'm your straight circle
Over
And never
Again

A Trick With A Hole In It

How long did it take for her to go to the bathroom?

Their connecting flight to Las Vegas was leaving a littlemore than a half-hour from now. He'd just heard their flight announced, leaving on time. It was about to board too.

Herman sat in the waiting area for Gate 8.

He looked at his new diamond watch and saw nearly a quarter hour had already passed since Rakim, no, Soseksi, had rubbed his head, then kissed it saying, "Daddy Brogan, let your kitty hurry to the litter box."

He was getting a little nervous without her. She'd said so many encouraging things as they fled.

He was sorry couldn't lose his fingers inside her long, thick hair, but she looked good with short blond hair. Must be a wig, and green eyes. Had on them contacts. He didn't know nothing about makeup, but she was young and pretty enough to wear it heavy like she did. Looked real light skin.

Little red dress on, hardly covering all her goodies and the click-click of her tall red heels made him feel young. He liked that she was taller than he was. His young woman looked hot to handle. She was a firecracker.

So what did that say about the man she was with? Shuh. That made him a pistol too. And age ain't nothin' but a number. All right. Herman felt like he was supposed to pray.

When she'd walked off to the bathroom he'd looked around, proud of how many men openly watched her stroll. It was Herman Drayton's woman with that mesmerizing sway. Herman reveled in the excitement of his new situation and felt like a king.

But what was keeping her? He looked in the direction she'd headed.

Daddy Brogan tried to seem unconcerned. He stretched his arms across the backs of the seats either side of his, crossed his short legs straight out and tried to relax. He thought about how he'd been turned around....

He almost didn't know her back in New York at LaGuardia airport, he would have never spotted her, she had to tap him on the shoulder. He'd turned and her beauty punched him between the eyes.

He didn't know what else to do, right away he'd given her his money. Smiling, she'd cooed loving words as she took it from his hand. She stuck it deep between her breasts and told Herman that his ticket was paid for, asked for his photo ID and told him to stay right there.

She'd picked up his bag and walked over to check him in.

Thinking aloud, "She's a sweet thing," Herman stood tall when he saw his woman pointing at him, saw the ticket agent nodding, not knowing Rakim was telling the woman that she was the old man's granddaughter and he'd asked her to check him in.

Rakim waved at Herman and he waved back.

They were early with plenty of time to sit in a lounge near their gate for morning coffee until departure.

From her bag Rakim pulled a pint of vodka and held each of their cups under the table to pour with a heavy hand, in Herman's brew anyway.

Sipping the hot liquor-coffee, Herman had agreed to her idea of holding his ticket with hers for safekeeping. He didn't know he'd sat getting drunk in the morning with a woman with false identification that secured her plane ticket in the name of LaDonna Delroy.

Herman closed his eyes. Damn, she'd been all over him in that lounge, she'd put his hand inside her dress on her breasts. She'd fondled his crotch, saying, Mmm. People had been looking and he'd loved it.

When they heard their flight to Alanta announced they were among the first on the plane.

She'd sat him by a window. All around them seats were mostly empty. She'd chosen one of the smaller airlines when she made their reservations by phone earlier that morning. She'd requested the earliest off peak flight, explaining to the male ticket agent in a sweet, apologetic voice, that it made her nervous to fly when a plane was full.

As soon as the wings caught air, she'd taken a blanket from the overhead compartment and covered their laps. She turned herself towards Herman until she sat on one hip to hide her actions. Her hands slipped beneath the cover.

She whispered between licks on his ear that life was meant to be started over and over. Life was short, he knew better than she did, how fast time flew.

Between rolling kisses she told him that she wasn't Rakim Moet Divine anymore. Soseksi Mango was her new name. Sounded like "so sexy" and she'd breathed its spelling, S-o-s-e-k-s-i, in his ear. She wouldn't answer to anything else, honey-bunch, and she was going to call him Daddy Brogan from now on, too.

Soseksi had slid down his zipper so smoothly, reached in and eased him out so quickly, the delicious wicked shock of being exposed against her sliding soft palm made him seed the blanket right away.

"Ha," she'd growled satisfied. Whispered like a promise, "Oh yeah, Daddy Brogan, we got time for me to enjoy giving you another good, long one of those."

Chanted low like a mystic, "For the rest of your life you gon' remember this trip."

He'd missed when Soseksi waved away the flight attendant wheeling drinks and snacks. Herman spent his trip to Atlanta with his eyelids fluttering, lips slack or pressed together, the back of his spinning head pushed against his seat. The second time he came, Herman saw stars, he was scared that his heart was beating too fast.

In the terminal, she'd hooked her arm through his, both pretending that she wasn't helping his shaky legs get to their gate for their connecting flight to Las Vegas, so he could sit down....

Herman looked in the direction of the bathroom again. Most of the people at his gate had gathered, offering tickets to board, already getting on.

Now they had thirty minutes exactly before the plane flew to

Vegas. He said the name to himself again. Vegas. Until she had to pee she'd stayed glued to his side talking about how much fun they were going to have in Vegas.

So where was she? Herman thought about what his woman said before she'd walked off. Lessee, he pondered, Rak...Soseksi said she was going to the kitty box or something like that. Whatever she said, it meant that she was going to the bathroom.

Then? Then she'd kissed him on his head, picked up her shoulder bag and carryon, hiked the straps of both over her shoulder and walked off.

Herman couldn't remember seeing her face anymore after that. Just the moving away of her inviting behind.

Herman got up and hurried over to the women's bathroom. He asked all the women that came out if there was a young lady inside with short blond hair and a short red dress, she had on red high heel shoes. The ones bothering to respond said no.

He poked his head inside to call out her name for himself. No one answered his "Soseksi? Sosekski, baby? You in here? Baby?"

Maybe she was already back at the gate wondering where he was. She could have used another bathroom. Sure! He'd just missed her, that's all, Daddy Brogan decided to look for another ladies room on his way back to the gate.

Striding with renewed confidence, Daddy Brogan checked his sparkling watch again. He'd never seen anything like it. He turned his wrist so the diamonds could gleam. Soseksi was so sweet. Paying for his ticket and giving him an expensive gift like this watch because she said she wanted to prove her love. It had to be worth more than the money that he gave her. It went good with his tan suit.

But it was time for them to get on the plane. He stopped a custodian and asked him if there was another women's bathroom close by.

"There's one right on the other side of that newsstand down there," the young man with a garbage bag tucked in the back pocket of his coveralls used the pole he carried to pinpoint where he was talking about.

Why would Soseksi go way down there? But Daddy Brogan

got moving that way just in case. If she didn't come on now, they'd surely miss their flight. To Vegas.

He smiled and brisked his stride, once they got their room in one of those fancy tall Las Vegas hotels, he saw now that he'd have to get into the bathroom before Miss Soseksi did in the mornings.

He couldn't wait to watch her bathe. And then after he dried her off he'd lotion her, smooth lotion all over her beautiful body....

Soseksi Mango

Herman didn't see her when she left the bathroom.

She'd walked right past him. In fact, he'd asked her if she'd seen herself. She didn't have time to laugh about it now, but she would. What a joke.

And the way he'd kept swallowing when he'd handed her that knot of cash in New York, she knew he'd been holding on to it all his life. He'd started coughing when she'd pulled it from between his tight fingers.

Soseksi Mango stood patiently at the ticket counter passively pulling fifties from the stack in her hand until she paid her passage to Port-of-Spain, Trinidad.

In the bathroom she'd quietly washed off the thick, light-colored foundation and heavy eye makeup, drawing no attention. Looking in the mirror she was caramel again. She left her face natural.

Quickly removing the short blond wig, she combed down her long dark hair and fixed it simply. Mango changed her hazel contacts for a different color before going into a stall to change her clothes.

Inside she repacked her carryon neatly, with the wig, tiny dress and stilettos on the bottom.

The young woman that left the bathroom was modestly dressed. Even behind her glasses it was clear that she was a natural beauty. She decided to board with just her bag, check her carryon, just in case anything went wrong, she didn't want it with her.

At the ticket counter when the agent asked, "Just this one bag, Miss Washington?" she answered easily, "Yes, I've always wanted to travel light. Shop for what I need when I get where I'm going. I know it sounds crazy."

Her slow smile was for him alone. "Not at all," he chuckled.

As he sat the carryon on the scale, Soseksi politely asked the agent if it was possible to give her the seat next to her sister, Miss LaDonna Delroy. Who was connecting from a flight just in from LaGuardia. They'd be traveling together from here in Altanta, she softly informed.

He checked his screen and confirmed, "Yes, Miss LaDonna Delroy. Seat 17A. Not a problem, I'll give you the seat right beside her, 17B." He appreciated her pretty, "Thank you."

The agent further proved his efficiency by expertly attaching the destination tag to her bag. Mango just smiled. She watched him place it on the moving conveyor behind him.

Soseksi exhaled, the seat next to her would be empty unless taken by a standby. Soseksi appreciated herself for being so clever. She said a silent thank you to Touche for showing her how to get getaway identification with a whole lot of money and a phone call. Her thoughts retraced her steps....

After escaping 210, Rakim checked into a hotel near LaGuardia Airport. She made the travel arrangements from her room. Two tickets to Altanta for her and grandpa. One had a connection from Atlanta to Trinidad.

LaDonna Delroy and Herman Drayton would travel to Atlanta. LaDonna Delroy would transfer there to continue to the Caribbean. Roberta Washington would buy her ticket in Atlanta and get on the plane from there.

Mango thought with glee, I'm every woman! Sitting on the bed, Mango had clapped her hands and laughed out loud for being so damn clever!

Last night she'd never packed so fast in her life and she'd just taken a little bit, stuffed only her three biggest Louies. Plus her Gucci carryon and her favorite Gucci shoulder bag. That was it. That's all the luggage she'd put in Supreme's Benz.

Standing at the ticket counter a thought reminded her, once you get where you going, dig out that long-term parking stub hidden in the carryon. Rip it to shreds and throw it away. She'd left the garbage bag in the back seat.

She tried to console herself with the truth that she didn't need furs where it was always hot. But she couldn't help missing all the ensembles she'd left behind. Damn. She wanted to cry when she thought about her shoes. Soseksi shook her head. Oh well, she'd just have to start collecting again. That thought cheered her considerably.

Soseksi made sure that she had every single piece of her jewelry, though. And except for Supreme's watch that she took and gave to the old man, she didn't touch any of Shipell and Supreme's jewelry or money. It was covered with bad vibes. But she had all of her jewelry, yes. All but her big diamond teardrop. Forget it, no time for tears anyway.

Soseksi didn't think about the forty-six thousand dollars that she carried in hundreds folded and tucked places on her body. She hated to touch her money.

She'd made it her plan to regroup with the twenty-eight grand tucked in her shoulder bag that Daddy Brogan gave her. American money was strong in the Islands. She'd live like a queen. A villa with servants. Plus, who said she had to stay in Trinidad? What a world there is to see!

"I beg your pardon, do you need this anymore?" She murmured, pointing to the passport on the ticket counter.

"No, you can take that back...Here you are, Miss Roberta Washington, along with your change and your one-way ticket to Port-of-Spain. Flight 1-6-1-7 at Gate 15. It's boarding now...It was a pleasure to serve you."

He threw a line, "No offense, Miss Washington, but if your sister is half as fine as you are, my Trinny brothers are in trouble... well, have a safe trip. I really hope to see you again."

Miss Roberta Washington ducked her head before looking up through her long lashes and modestly returned his full smile before she lowered her gaze and walked away.

Still watching that pretty woman from the corners of his eyes, Bobby Ford made himself greet the next customer to walk up. Damn, she was sexy.

He saw what moved up under her long, loose denim dress, he'd put money on it, a lavish body that was seldom handled. Bobby's imagination saw his hand pulling all her long, thick dark hair free from that flowered ponytail bow-thing.

By rote he did his job, "...And may I see your passport, please, sir?"

Her wavy hair probably felt like silk. He'd pull those glasses off her face, man, she had some sexy hazel eyes. Not a stroke of makeup covered her pretty honey color.

"Thank you, how will you be paying, sir?" Take those cheap sneakers off her feet, he knew she had pretty toes to fondle.

He'd cheat on his wife Roxanne today, to be the man who unwound all that woman. She was full and ripe for picking, he knew it.

There were alot of unnoticed young beauties like her, those pretty, steady working, quiet church-going women that had a whole lot of love stored and waiting.

If a woman's man like himself had a shot this exceptional one, unwind Miss Roberta, he'd bet his check, he'd find a freak begging at her core.

Bobby turned his head around, to see her fully one more time, this Roberta Washington, Miss-one-way-out-of-Atlanta. He told his customer, "...One moment, please."

His memory snapped a final photo just before she turned a corner.

Roxy would never know who to thank for the session she and Bobby had that night, or know whose face he saw stamped over hers when he was pounding like a piston.

Soseksi Mango went to the first row of pay phones she saw. From the pocket of her dress she pulled out the calling card she'd bought in New York waiting for Brogan. She activated it then pushed the same number she'd called from her apartment last night, when she'd started the ball rolling.

She chose the phone at the end because it was next to a wall. Faced tightly in the corner, she cupped her hand around the mouthpiece to help keep out the airport noise around her. Soseksi knew she should talk quickly.

After the second ring she heard an officer state the number of the precinct. Speaking quickly, she barely disguised her voice. "Hello? This is about the murders at 210 Jefferson Avenue...My name? I don't have one. Listen, I saw Mr. Drayton...Mr. Drayton, the man who owns 210. I live on that block... Listen!...I work at LaGuardia Airport and I saw him this morning...Yeah, I'm sure...He had on a tan suit...No, I can't hold on."

The metal cord dangled the receiver at its length.

If she didn't run, Mango would have missed her flight.

Herman missed his. He missed his plane to Las Vegas because he didn't have a ticket. Herman didn't have any money.

Talking to himself, he'd paced at Gate 8 for nearly an hour before the police walked up.

Daddy Brogan was in a mess all by himself.

Dear Brother

Herman Lester Drayton #34D7424
GMCF
P.O.Box 61
Comstock, NY 12821

Dear Herman,

I hope this letter find you in good health and in a peaceable mind. I'm sending greetings and prayers from the congregation of the First Ebenezer A.M.E. Zion Tabernacle.

Founder Pastor Earl Scott send his continuing blessings. Everyday we pray for you to return home safe in the name of Jesus Christ our soon arriving Saviour. I hope that you have accept the salvation of the blood of the gentle loving lamb.

Dear brother, I do not understand what has happen to put your life in such a shambles at your age.

Luther is taking good care of your building, but two of the tenants have move out. Miss Tisha Frasier parents came to get her soon as we realize that girl was alone in that apartment grieving her heart out, starving herself.

Come to find out she was in love with one of the two men who was killed. I felt so sorry for the poor soul. That child had been locked up like that for almost a week, until Luther knocked on her door for the rent.

It was the Holy Spirit told me to make my husband take all the tenant spare keys with him whenever he go to the building.

I'm glad Luther walking with the Lord because who else but our Maker made him check on that young girl when she didn't come to the door?

Luther said he could hear her in there crying her poor heart out so he opened the door. Lord, when Luther call me and told me what he saw, I made him come get me and we went straight back to her apartment.

I made that baby call her mother in New Jersey. She needed

to go home.

The police still got 1A locked up.

Miss Jocelyn Reynolds left the day after everything happened. She say to use her deposit to cover her last month rent. Seems like she and Mrs. Jacobs almost had a fist fight but I don't know why.

Mrs. Arbayelle Jacobs have also inform me that she and her husband have split up and he have moved out. Mrs. Jacobs ask for extra time on her rent because she going down to the Human Resource because she is going to have to get on.

Luther want to know what you want to do about that situation and the two empty apartments. He know somebody who want one.

He also want you to know that Miss Susan Henson have moved a man into her place. She also have not paid her September rent and is running Luther around.

Baby brother, I know in my heart that you are innocent and do not belong where you are. Our beloved parents, God rest their souls, could not have raised a man that murder. My brother could not have kill two people. I hope you did not know them men.

From what little the police will tell me, they was in shady business. I have never known you to truck with people like that.

Thank God for Luther, he been sticking right by me during all this. Those detectives came to my home talking like killing was your lifestyle. They ask me when was the last time I spoke to you and if I ever known you to use dope. They ask me who are your friends.

The detective say they found a letter to me in your apartment in your writing. They say it's not a confession but it is a lie because they can't find no evidence on your phone record of you calling no number in Philadelphia and no number from there calling you. They say you fully involve in the crime. They ask me questions until Luther say they have to stop.

Is it true you was messing with the young woman that live in that apartment? They say they think she only about 22 or 23 years old. Herman she young enough to be your grandbaby.

Brother, if you left with her how she get away from you in Atlanta? Was you drinking? I'm not trying to upset you Herman, but you need to understand what kind of serious trouble you are in.

I want you to know that I believe you when you say she comit the sin and make it seem like it was you. I know she the demon who got you caught up in the devil hands. If she the one who did this deed, God will help them find her.

The police think she made up a plan and put you in it to take the blame alone. She set you up and trick you into prison. Devils always lie.

There is no such a person as Rakim Moet Divine or that other nasty name you say she call herself. She a made up woman and they have not found out who she really is. Seem like she don't have no trail at all, no family, job or anything.

Because of what you said when they caught you, the police was waiting for her in Las Vegas, but no woman who look like how you describe this devil got off that plane.

I don't believe they are really trying to find her because they got you. They say you took all your money out the bank before you escape. That mean to me that you must really believe she love you. I know how you can hold a dollar (smile). Hold on to your faith the same way brother because Jesus is the answer. Bars can not confine a repented heart. I hope you are reading the Bible I gave you so you can know the King.

Lord knows I do not understand how you got mix up in this mess. When the police came to my house they say your fin-gerprints is the only ones they found in that woman apartment.

They say you had on one of the dead mens diamond watch when they caught you. Brother, you let this young woman put a dark mark on your heart and turn your eyes from the shining path.

They call you a old fool. But I put the Word in my mouth and they stop that scandal talk.

Herman, you have got to open your mouth and talk the truth. Was you the one who clean up her apartment? Tell them what you know about this woman, brother. Help my brother, Lord.

Don't worry about what the newspapers say. Keep your trust in the head reporter almighty God.

Luther say don't talk to nobody but the lawyer.

Luther say you are going to have to sell or remorgage your building because we can't put up no more money for the lawyer. Luther refuse to touch our retirement. You know that little nest egg is all we have. He say to tell the lawyer to draw up some papers.

I have also been talking to the lawyer about your trial date. He say that he won't know the date until the end of the month and he will call you and come see you.

Your sisters and your brothers and all their families are praying for you. Me, Luther, Sharon and Nonnie are planning to come visit you Friday after next. Sharon is going to drive her new car. She decide to get the Lincoln after all. It is dark blue and very nice.

We hope we can all see you together. Call me collect before then if there is anything special you want us to bring. We all love you very much and stand behind you always. I pray that they are treating you well. Keep your hand in Jesus hand and the truth shall be reveal.

Here is a picture for you of Geraldine new baby William Mathis Baker Jr. They call him Little Bill. Don't he look just like his daddy? He eight months old. Geraldine say he a big old boy who eat like his daddy too.

She make me laugh when she say the baby always pulling on her cause she still breast feeding him along with the baby food.

Geraldine say when she nurse the baby Bill be looking at her cross eyes. She going to be carrying again soon. She laugh when I tell her that. But she is 20 now and married so her babies will be create in blessed union.

I put some stamps along with kisses in this letter so you can write me whenever you want.

We will see each other soon, God spare life.

Your loving sister in Christ,

Mrs. (Mary) Luther M. Simms

The End

Thank you for reading

THEY CALL ME MISS DIVINE
No Heart. No Conscience.

Now that you've entered and enjoyed the
"Big Girl World" of Rakim Moet Divine...

Get ready for your key at

THE BRISTOL HO-TEL

Wicked...Twisted...Sex
by Tri Smith
"The Queen of supersexy fiction"

Erotic short stories for "Grown Folks"

Here's a sneak peek. Meet "DANCE"
one of the residents in the HOTTEST new book
of contemporary urban erotica

COMING SOON TO A BOOKSTORE NEAR YOU!

Log on www.millersmithpublishers.com to leave your
comments and sign up for your FREE Newsletter!

THE BRISTOL HO-TEL Wicked...Twisted...Sex is a Velvet
Touch Production published by MillerSmith Publishers

A Message from The Management of The Bristol Hotel

Dear Guest,

Looking for a place to stay in New York City? You're welcome to a room at The Bristol Hotel right in Times Square. Almost. On Forty-eighth Street between Eighth and Ninth Avenues to be precise. Before you check in our discreet establishment, we want you know a few things first…

We don't accept children. Adults only, this is a grown folks residence.

We at The Bristol Hotel pride ourselves in assuring the anonymity of our guests. Our motto is, "You Pay, We Look The Other Way." Whatever you do in your room is your business and we don't involve ourselves in any situations, ever. Stay for a few hours or make us your permanent address, we can accommodate you with a space to do your thing. Cleaning, fresh towels and sheets are an additional charge and are provided only at the guest's request.

Warning! If graphic sex however it happens in rooms all around you is not your thing, pick up your suitcase, move on, The Bristol Hotel is not where you want a key.

But if you're ready for wickedly sexy scenarios that explore the twisted side of contemporary erotica, with pleasure, we invite you inside.

…Ready for your key? We hoped so. Welcome. Enjoy your stay at The Bristol Ho-tel.

Thank you for your patronage,
THE BRISTOL HOTEL

DANCE

Excerpt from *The Bristol Ho-tel*.
Wicked...Twisted..Sex.
By Tri Smtih © 2004

Dance decided to forget it all for tonight and go to sleep. His shoulders slumped after he sat on his bed. Just home from a date, he was a little bit drunk. The alcohol opened the door on his simmering frustration and he felt his desperation bubble up into his thoughts.

Unlucky, that's what he was, not like any other man. What he had between his thighs would never get a woman. And that wasn't self-pity, it was a fact. Size did matter and he was living proof. He'd never in his life had a girlfriend that he'd had sex with. They were never interested once they saw how he was built. Then they left him. As quickly as they could and hung up on him if he called. He knew why. There was no chance of a relationship so why should they entertain his conversation?

So a room in the Bristol was enough. He didn't need space for a family or even only a girlfriend. After switching several rooms that didn't suit him, he'd chosen 928, the smallest the hotel offered. It was best because it shrank his loneliness. His solitude would be wall-to-wall whatever size the room was, so a tiny one kept it manageable.

Those other rooms had let his despair swell and flex to a size that had gotten quite unbearable. He never brought a woman to those big rooms because he knew she'd feel like crying and not at all like fucking. He remembered opening up his pocketknife quite a few times in those big rooms, the gleaming six-inch blade with a razor's edge, carried to better his chances if he was ever in violent trouble. He'd look at his wrists, then the blade, look at the blade, then at his dick. Later for his arms, this disgusting piece between his legs had the vein he'd considered cutting.

Hope always changed his mind. Even when it showed up almost too late, after he'd drawn the knife lightly across his offending prick leaving a thin red line. Hope always made him close his knife and convince himself, logically, there had to be a woman who'd want him. He couldn't find her if he was dead. God bless hope.

Even so, Dance had a lot of thin keloided scars on the base of his dick.

Living in room 928 solved that knife problem. He hadn't turned to it since he'd moved in three years ago. He felt okay about having company here.

The few dates he'd persuaded to have a drink in his "suite" laughed when they saw the box he called home. One had cracked that his "suite" had probably started out as a utility closet. "You're living where they used to keep the mops and brooms!" she'd laughed. But they all always said, "It's nice though."

Not that Dance had to do a lot to upgrade his room. When he took it, a miserable single bed and its dingy linens, a scratched narrow dresser and an uneven stingy chair were all. Right away, he'd replaced them. When management found out they didn't mind, he was a good renter. They were especially lenient when Dance assured that he'd leave everything whenever he moved and he signed something to that effect. Dance took pride in speaking correctly and handling business properly.

Room 928 was luxurious. He'd painted the walls and ceiling lavender because he thought women would like it. The wrought-iron bed had a tempting thick mattress covered with Egyptian cotton sheets, lots of pillows and a silk-covered down comforter, all purple because he'd read it was a classy shade. The chair was an intricately carved antique, heavy dark wood with broad arms and a high back. Dance had the wide seat covered with zebra skin. His dresser was a long contemporary maple box. Painted glossy black, the top was crowded in the center with fine toiletries. Two rows of three deep drawers held his beautiful clothes. Torch lamps sat in opposite corners and a real oriental rug softened the floor. His minuscule bathroom with no tub or shower was painted dark blue including the sink, toilet and floor. On the rod behind the door was one plush snow-white towel.

A flat-screen TV and DVD player sat on one end of the dresser but he never watched network or cable. Seeing men and women loving each other, sharing lives together made him want to do something crazy. And he didn't need any help feeling that way, feeling like bringing out the knife. If he wasn't working or with a date, when Dance was at home alone he used his TV to view a selection from his large collection of hardcore porn DVDs. They all featured men with big, big dicks slamming nasty take-it-all women.

Dance fantasized that he was every man he watched. He didn't use his hands to masturbate when he watched his porn. He'd trained his hard cock to come by squeezing it between his muscled gym-thighs. He needed strong thighs to press what he had. That was Dance's sex life. Dance didn't like touching his thing. He barely held it when he had to pee.

He was virgin to any woman he didn't pay. Hos took his money, gladly, but once they saw what he was working with, pro pussy would tell him, "Shit. It makes more sense for me to suck that rather than fuck it, baby. That'll feel better to both of us."

One slut remarked, "It sure is a shame, because you are so damn *fine*! I can't do nothing with that piece except suck it, lover. But you gonna get that nut, baby, I'm gonna work it over." Because she could eat her words, Dance paid that particular ho a lot.

He'd managed to find a few hookers who would fuck him but he was never satisfied. They tried, but there were no movements they could do to make him load enough to shoot. They had to finally use their throats to give Dance his money's worth.

Streetwalkers talked about his cock, the trick named Dance was a favorite on the stroll. When his BMW crawled the strip, tramps quickly tip-tip-tipped their clear platform stilettos to his car. Here was easy, easy money at premium rate. With the meat Dance was bringing, all a girl had to do was work his sensitive head. Dance gladly paid two Benjamins for mouths that swallowed every other man for fifty, sometimes forty.

"Hey, Dance Daddy! We dating tonight sweetie?"

"Heeey, boo! Here I am, lover. I know you looking for me!"

"Dance, Dance, heeey, Daaancie."

With the hos, Dance was in demand, jostled over, cooed to, but it was just the opposite when it came to real dating. When he tried to have a girlfriend, get friendly with a woman then asking her out, Dance was a constant loser. Because of his damn dick. His biggest challenge on a date was making sure that she didn't stimulate him enough to make his cock hard and reveal its unappealing size. He was a master at mind control and misdirection. When he was with a woman, no matter how much physical attraction he felt he made his piece stay soft and her touch never felt it.

He dressed his six-two cut physique in fine attire with an ensemble for every occasion. His jewelry was subtle and expensive. Dance saw his barber and manicurist weekly. He saw women's heads turn after him everywhere. He caught many smiles definitely aimed at him. Dance smiled invitingly in return, although he knew what would happen if he tried to make one of those admirers his woman. But he had to keep trying because he had hope.

Educated Dance had an advanced degree in communications that he didn't use. Too many firings from good jobs in his field because he stayed distracted, convinced Dance that he wouldn't be able to concentrate and really use his professional skills until he found her. Introduced himself to the one special woman who would eventually see his repelling cock and love him in spite of it, regardless of it, especially for it. His lady.

He gave up his condo in Brooklyn and moved into The Bristol, a hotel he'd been to with a ho. It seemed like the right move, no reason to pay all that rent for a one bedroom when he could get himself a cheaper room just as a squat until Mrs. Dance Mooreman came along. Then he'd buy her a house. In the suburbs. With a pool and cabanas. A lot of bedrooms for their eight or nine children. Birthed or adopted. She'd love fucking her man.

Dance had a laptop. He'd used it to search for a specialty maker of men's underwear and found one that promised a product to satisfy any and every man, with a money-back guarantee. He ordered a catalogue and when it came, he read it like the Bible, believing everything written about the many types of underwear pictured. There were styles to make the most of any man's package. He'd ordered online and was elated when the briefs arrived. Destroying the package opening it, Dance tried them on right away and was elated, he shouted, when they made him appear like every other man in a pair of drawers. Looking in the long mirror nailed to the inside of his front door, Dance turned his body this way and that, amazed that he couldn't tell what size dick he had. So if he couldn't tell, a woman couldn't either. He'd rushed back to his computer and ordered a dozen pair in assorted colors.

So absorbed in hiding his manhood and seeking his mate, Dance deduced that he'd meet the most women as a freelance bartender. Plus, freelance kept him on the move and ahead of potential humiliation. He'd worked it all out in his mind. He reasoned, if he had a stationary job like tending bar at a restaurant or club, his dating opportunities would be dead right after any woman he'd met at work saw his dick. If they started dating and it got to the level of physical intimacy, of course she'd rush back to that spot the very next night to report on his size. To everybody. So Dance never took a steady job. His way, he made great money because he was always available, requested, well tipped. He mixed drinks and clever conversation at jobs from corporate functions to hustlers' birthday parties. He was right, he met a lot of women and dated many. Women ready for a good time. And still undiscovered, that extraordinary one, hopefully ready for more than that. With him.

Race and age never mattered. Who cared if she was smart or charismatic? Strong as steel or weak as spaghetti, she could talk all the time or hardly part her lips. Shooting dope or living for God, she could be as pretty as flowers or an ugly dullard, all his lady needed was a pussy that wanted his dick.

Dance was so far unfortunate, what always started as her anticipation for good sex ended when his specialty briefs came off. Whether he got it over with quickly by trying to fuck a woman on the first date, or taking his time to build her trust, so she could get to know and adore him first, spending much money, every single female was always aghast. And it was always the same.

In his room or in their spaces, the first time Dance and his date attempted to get together it usually started after a sexy dinner and lots of deep kissing. Letting her watch him take off his shirt, he'd invite her to run her hands over his hard chest. Still in his pants, he'd seduce her out of her clothes with the sexiest words between passion kisses and erotic caresses. While they foreplayed, he'd never let her feel his crotch, although he'd handle her breasts and fondle her box. He needed her to be as hot as possible before she found out. Dance ate pussy like that's what he was put on Earth to do. Still wearing his pants.

But it never went the way he wanted it to. Even if she was spread on the bed, wet, panting, come-flushed and purring, pulling at his briefs needing to feel that thickness…the moment she spied his dick, her eyes widened, her legs snapped shut and she'd spring up. Jump up off the bed like it was hot coals and hurry into her clothes if she was in 928. If she was home, wrap whatever she could grab around herself and order him to leave right away. Eyeing him warily, hoping he wouldn't flip because she'd put on brakes, she'd talk…Every single one…Like the sight of his dick compelled her to make her rejection clear why sex couldn't, wouldn't happen between them…

"Listen, Dance, you're a great guy, really, handsome, too. But, I've got to be honest with you. Even though we've been out a few times, don't get me wrong, I always had a great time, but I can honestly say that I'm not the woman for you. Look, let's face it. Wow. You're not built like most guys. I mean, I know men come in all different sizes, but I need a man that can fit *me* without a problem. And I know myself. I know I wouldn't be happy having sex with you if we started a relationship. And honestly Dance? I'm not trying to hurt your feelings, but I *can't* be the first woman to tell you that she would have to be in real, *lifelong* love to commit to a sex life with you. I mean, look at what you've got!"….

"Boy! If I knew *that's* what you were bringing, I would've told you not to waste your time or mine! Come on now, you *know* you should have told me about this before now! You think I was gonna be *happy* seeing that? That, that…ugh! Get out of my house, Dance."….

"G-e-e-et the fuck outta here! Look at *that*. Sorry, hon, but

I cain't work witcha bruh. Ain't never seen a man wit' nothin' like that. You *cain't* be fuckin' wit' *nobody*, right? Damn, let me look at it. Yo, you got to get you a doll or somethin'."....

"Whoa! Ooo! You've *got* to be kidding! You might as well not have a dick, who's gonna want that damn thing? Not me. Hell no."....

"*Whaaat*?! That's your *dick*?! No way. I can't believe it! That's you? What were you planning on doing with *that*?! Shiiiit! Goddamit! That's why you stay so sharp and act so loving, trying to get a bitch to ignore that damn cock of yours. Living in this little-ass room in this ho hotel! Oh, you think I don't know where we at? This is a *ho*-tel, baby. Short stay, long stay with nothing in the middle. Ain't no vacationers in here! No! I don't want to hear it Dance! I don't want to hear *nothing* you got to say. Let me get outta this fuckin' crackerbox room... Don't you call me no more...freak."....

Those scathing comments and many more like them from women whose names he couldn't remember were swirling constants taking up most of the room in Dance's head. Only when he was slinging liquor at work, keeping his eye out for that select lady did Dance find some space in his brain for his own thoughts. Still seated on the side of his bed, wearily, he began to undress. He took off his suit jacket.

He really liked the girl he took out tonight. This was their second date. Dinner and a hot loft party in The Village. Her name was Yolanda and she was a secretary he'd met last week at a company awards dinner he'd worked. She was fat and pretty and Korean. She'd made it clear that she wanted to see him again. The night they'd met, before she left they'd exchanged numbers, and she'd turned his I-like-you-too kiss on her lips into lust, thrusting her tongue to twist inside his mouth. Dance returned it eagerly, grabbing the back of her head to kiss her good. His dick got excited but never stirred. Control.

Tonight, at the party she'd given him her vodka-flavored mouth again and let him feel her huge ass on the dance floor. She'd snuggled close to him on the drive to take her home. Yolanda had trailed soft kisses and sweet pleas against his neck to change his mind about coming inside her place for "coffee."

Dance knew what she wanted to do but he stood firm and repeated his gentle no, promising, soon, sweetheart, next time, because he really liked this girl. He could keep her as long as he didn't try to fuck her. Dance took off his tie and shirt. He liked Yolanda Ngyuen. Yolanda Ngyuen-Mooreman. Maybe? Maybe if he hoped to God....

Dance stood unbuckled his pants and let them fall to the floor. He pulled down his magic briefs. His hefty dick tumbled like a sleepy python past his knees. No one was there to see a grown man cry.

Order Form

MillerSmith Publishers

511 AVENUE OF THE AMERICAS , New York, NY 10011
www.millersmithpublishers.com

___ **They Call Me Miss Divine.**
No Heart. No Conscience $14.99

___ **The Bristol Ho-tel** $14.99

Shipping /Handling $1.00 each additional book
(Via U.S. Priority Mail) $3.75

TOTAL   (for one book) $18.74
(for both books) $34.73

PURCHASER INFORMATION – Please Print

Name: _____
      First   Last

Reg. #: _____
   (Applies if incarcerated)

Address: _____

    _____

City: _____ State: _____ Zip Code: _____

Email: _____

TOTAL NUMBER OF BOOKS: _____

Discount for Bulk Orders
WE ACCEPT MONEY ORDERS ONLY for all mail orders.
Credit cards can be used for orders made online.

Allow two to three weeks for delivery.
MillerSmith Publishers cannot be held responsible for any
undelivered books by any state or federal institution.

Books can also be purchased online at www.millersmithpublishers.com,
Amazon.com and Culture Plus Distributors.